DYING BREATH

ISBN-13: 9781636960395
ISBN-10: 1636960391

Cover design by: Damonza.com
Printed in the United States of America

BLAKE BANNER

A HARRY BAUER THRILLER

DYING BREATH

R

RIGHT HOUSE

ONE

I hadn't eaten for thirty-six hours. It's one of the conditions I impose on myself if I go hunting. I eat what I kill, and if I don't kill I don't eat. Some people might think that's a hollow gesture, or a pretentious one. I can't say I care much, but I get mad at hunters who talk about being in nature, a predator pitched against his prey in a primal wilderness, when they're carrying a camouflage tent, thermal sleeping bags, propane camping stoves and sniper's rifles with telescopic sights.

I sleep in the open with a couple of woolen blankets, I cook—if I cook—over an open fire, and I hunt with a sixty-five-pound Osage orange bow from James Easter up in Iowa. I also hunt with my six senses, and I listen: I listen to the hundreds of sounds that are woven into the breeze.

If you use a telescopic sight, you stop listening. The mountains and the forests are full of sounds that talk to you about the constant cycle of life and death in the woodlands: the animals that come and go on silent feet, that hunt in the shadows, that drink and fish in the creeks, streams and rivers which wind through the land. They tell you everything, from the twig that snaps under a deer's hoof, to the murderous flapping of the falcon's wing.

I listen and I look, not through a telescope, but

with my eyes; and I look not for prey, but for movement. A bull elk at fifty yards, standing among trees, five feet inside the shade of a woodland, might be all but invisible to a man with a sniper's rifle and a telescopic sight. Because that man will be looking for a bull elk, and at that distance, among tree trunks, a bull elk looks like part of the forest. So if you want to see it, you don't look for it; you relax your gaze and you wait for movement.

You use all your senses. You listen, you smell the air, you taste the air, and you sense how the forest feels. You can't do that if you insulate yourself in a tent, with your TV and your propane cooker. You can only do it if you're in the forest, part of the forest. If you hide from the cold, moist night air, cushion yourself from the hard ground and the stones when you sleep, shut out the snuffling, howling and crying of the night, and rise only after the sun has burned away the chill dew of dawn, then you will be deaf to the whispering of the forest. Better stay at home and get your meat from the butcher.

So, I hadn't eaten for thirty-six hours, and that kind of hunger sharpens your senses. I was lying beside a spruce at the edge of the sparse woodlands to the south of Big Red Hill and to the west of Greenhorn Mountain, in Eagle County, Colorado. I was watching the large clearing spread out before me. It was about half a mile to the nearest trees, over on my right. But a hundred yards away a bull elk stood alone, smelling the morning air.

I'm a good archer, but a hundred yards was a hell of a shot, and would depend as much on luck as on any skill I had. That's OK in target practice, but when you are hunting a living, breathing animal, a bad shot can cause a lot of pain and unnecessary suffering. The animal can get away and it can take days to die. That is something you don't want to happen.

So I waited, chose my moment, and moved forward on my belly, a yard at a time.

After ten minutes he had turned his back on me, grazing at the late summer grass and shrubs, and was moving a step at a time, toward the sparse woods that covered the foothills of the Greenhorn. I was downwind, and though I could hear and smell him, he could not hear or smell me. So I closed the gap with a couple of short, silent runs.

I had closed the distance to fifty yards and dropped to my belly beside a young cypress. He still had his rump to me, but I had moved slightly to my left, hoping to get an angle on his heart. Luck, as luck so often does, played into my hand, and then robbed me.

The bull grazed slowly toward his left, one slow step at a time while his mouth worked, gradually turning his left flank to me. With a sixty-five-pound bow I could make a fifty-yard shot with a fair degree of accuracy, but an arrow travels much slower than a bullet, and there is no guarantee your target will still be there by the time your arrow arrives where it's going. If your target moves, instead of piercing its heart, your razor-sharp broadhead might slice clean through its belly, causing a slow, painful death. I needed to get at least twenty paces closer to take the shot.

I had a tall spruce maybe twenty yards to my left and, keeping flat on the ground, I crawled yard by yard, over the shrubs and stones, toward the cover of that tree. It took a long minute, but the burning hollow in my gut made it seem like an agonizing half hour.

The great beast had started moving slowly to its right now. I still had a shot, but if I was going to take it, it had to be now, because within seconds he would have turned his left side away from me.

I nocked the heavy, wooden broadhead, stepped out from behind the tree, leaned into the bow and drew till my thumb touched the angle of my jaw. I sensed, rather than saw, the trajectory of the arrow, and in that moment a rifle exploded into the still morning and the roar of the shot echoed across the valley, bouncing off the sides of the hills.

The elk looked up, its body tense as a spring. Next thing it had bounded and was racing across the plateau toward the cover of the trees, north and east. I didn't hesitate. I sprinted after it, covered twenty paces until I could see where it was headed, and settled into a steady run.

A scared deer, gazelle or elk is fast, but they will rarely run for long periods of time. Instinctively they know that predators operate with explosive bursts of speed, which burn themselves out pretty fast. So when the elk's run started to slow, after thirty seconds or a little more, he had covered over three hundred yards, but I was catching on him, staying downwind and out of sight. Man is one of the very few predators who will stay on a single prey relentlessly, sometimes for days on end, until he takes him down.

The bull elk had reached a gentle, wooded slope that rose to higher ground above. In the trees there was an opening that led to a kind of passage that wound up to the higher ground. There he stopped and sniffed the air, then started to graze again. I didn't stop. I kept going at a gentle jog. At forty paces I slowed to a walk, but, as he was looking away from me, I didn't seek cover. I kept walking. I still had the arrow nocked and drew it nine inches. After twelve paces I stopped, drew to my ear, sensed the trajectory and loosed the arrow.

A second shot rang out across the valley. I swore violently under my breath and broke into a sprint as the arrow struck home inches behind the heart. The bull sprang and kicked and bounded up the passage through the trees, with the barb buried deep in its side.

It took me fifteen or twenty seconds to cover the distance. A third shot rang out and I scrambled up the passage through the woodland.

When I got to the top, there was another plateau, smaller than the one below, and there, three paces from where I stood panting, was the bull, lying on its side, dead. Approaching down the slight hill at a slow, heavy run were two men dressed in camouflage. They carried high-powered rifles with telescopic sights. When they saw me, the only change to their demeanor was a complacent smile.

The one in the lead was in his fifties, well groomed, with permed gray hair and a slight paunch. He had a ranger's camouflage hat and a sleeveless camouflage jacket that had probably cost him three hundred bucks. He was wearing jeans and cowboy boots, and touched the brim of his hat with two fingers as he approached.

"Howdy? Good morning to you!"

His pal, lagging slightly behind, was darker, more muscular. His haircut had cost him about five bucks, maybe less, about the same as his peaked camouflage cap. He was smiling, but the smile was for himself, and his eyes watched me with care. The guy with the perm came right up with his hand extended.

"Rex Trent, Trent Enterprises. That was a bold shot, shame it just missed the mark." I shook the proffered hand with little enthusiasm.

"It was on target," I said. "Your shot scared him and he bolted."

His mouth smiled but his eyes leered. "Shoulda used a rifle. That's the problem with a bow. Slow delivery. With this bad boy," he held up his Seekins Pro Hunter, "I never miss a shot." He pointed at my elk. "Got this baby clean between the eyes."

I let my eyes travel over him and his pal, then looked past them at where they had come from. I let my eyebrows shrug.

"By my reckoning you should have two more elk lying somewhere." He frowned at me, not catching my meaning. "I heard three shots," I explained. "One of them hit my elk. Where did the other two go?"

He didn't think that was funny and his face told me so. After a second he gave a laugh that was on the dry side of humorless.

"You call it your elk, but I'm afraid I'm gonna have to disabuse you, son. See, it was my shot that killed the animal, therefore my claim is good."

I didn't bother pretending to smile. I gave him the deadeye instead. "You said it was a bold shot, Mr. Trent, which means you were watching. And that means you fired deliberately to scare my prey. In spite of that," I pointed at the feathers protruding from the animal's chest, "the wound was fatal and the animal would have died within seconds. Your shot may even have been post-mortem. The bull is mine."

"You're new to Sulfur Springs, ain't ya, son?"

"I'm not your son, Mr. Trent. I've been here a few times, but I stay away from people."

"Well folks round here know me, see? They know me because, well..." He turned to his pal and they both laughed. "Because I own the town, huh, Jacob?" He turned back to me. "Just about everything you see in and around Sulfur Springs is either mine or it's a national park. So I guess you could say I'm like some kind of old-fashioned feudal lord. In the sense, like, that whatever I say goes."

I gave a single nod and gazed around, wondering if I was going to have to hit them.

"So," he smiled amiably, "I don't want to get into a disagreement with you. We'll just say that the damned elk is mine and leave it at that." He cocked his rifle and turned to his pal. "Earl, go get the truck so we can load this bull in the back."

I let my eyes rest on his and held them a moment. I spoke quietly. "The bull is mine."

The smile faded and he jerked his chin at me. "You look like a city boy to me. Things ain't changed around here for two hundred years. Still cowboy territory, and we don't worry so much about the law as we do about what we say… And what *I* say, *is* the law."

I went very still and held his eye for a long moment. "That bullshit might have worked back when Clint Eastwood still had hair. But things have changed since then. Different rules apply. So let me get something clear in my mind. Are you threatening to kill me?"

Jacob pulled back the bolt on his rifle with a loud clunk, put it to his shoulder and trained it on my gut. Trent laughed out loud.

"Hell, no!" he said. "Why, that would be illegal, right, Jacob? And what the hell would we do with the body in this wilderness?" All the laughter drained out of his face, like it had suddenly been punctured. "Walk away, boy, before this gets ugly."

I nodded. "Sure." I pointed at the bull. "But the bull

is mine. That arrow is mine." I pointed at him. "And you owe me for that bull."

He laughed, low and soft. "Yeah, city boy? Well you have your lawyer call my lawyer and we'll see what we can work out."

They both laughed loud at that, like he'd said something original and funny. But by that time I was already walking back the way I'd come. I thought about turning and skewering them both, but you can't just kill people because they annoy you. You can't even kill them because they threaten to kill you. Because if we all did that, society would fall apart, and it would be a world of anarchy ruled over by people like Rex Trent. Sometimes you just had to walk away and either forget, or choose your own time and place to visit them again on your own terms.

I got back to my camp a couple of hours later, and as I scrambled up the hill to where I had left my blanket and my rucksack, my cell buzzed in my pocket. I pulled it out and knew it was the brigadier, Alex "Buddy" Byrd, head of operations at Cobra.

"Yeah."

"Good morning. We need you back in New York. How soon can you be there?"

"Couple of days."

"Good. Don't dillydally. We're in a hurry."

"I'm on my way."

I hoisted my rucksack on my shoulder and started down the far side of the hill. It was a half mile as the crow flies to where I'd left my truck, but over that terrain, along the weaving path, it took me over an hour to get there. I slung my stuff in the back of the truck and after that it was a four mile drive down a dirt track, following the course of the canyon, to the intersection with the I-70, and then another half mile along Route 6 to Sulfur Springs.

Once there I paid up at the motel, loaded my stuff in my truck and drove back toward the intersection. As I passed the Roast Buck Eatery, at the exit to the town, I saw a white Ford pickup in the parking lot. It had a bull elk in the back with a feathered barb sticking out of its ribcage. I glanced at it and slowed, wondering about going in to settle matters, but dismissed the thought and accelerated away from the town.

At the intersection I turned right and east and hit the gas. I had two thousand miles to cover, and twenty-nine hours of driving to get through. With four hours' sleep, make that thirty-three. And I still hadn't eaten.

TWO

I got to New York the following evening and went straight to my small, blue, clapboard cottage on Shore Drive, on the Eastchester Bay in the Bronx. I parked my truck down the side of the house and lugged my bags inside. With the door open, I paused a few seconds in the small entrance porch, to smell the air and listen. It was a habit. But the house felt and smelt as it had when I'd left it a couple of weeks earlier. I hung up my jacket, kicked the door closed, carried my bags into my living room and dumped them on the floor.

In the open plan kitchen, separated from the living room by a breakfast bar, I leaned on the sink and spent a moment gazing across my neglected lawn at the dark bay. In the distance, a couple of ghostly, narrow sails bobbed and leaned, white on the black water.

I opened the freezer, pulled out a couple of burgers and threw them in a hot pan. While they fried I cracked a cold beer and thought about nothing in particular, except for wondering what was wrong with me, that even in my spare time I needed to kill. I had come from hunting animals to relax, to hunting people for work.

I dropped my burgers into a couple of buns with some tomato sauce and carried them upstairs with my beer and my bags. I opened the window onto the dusk and set about eating the burgers while I unpacked my bags.

By the time I'd finished, dusk had turned to evening, and small lights were glimmering over the dark water. I went to drain my bottle but it was empty.

Then the doorbell rang.

I took the plate and the bottle and descended the stairs. As I came down into the living room I could see the silhouette of a man against the glass in the door, backlit by the orange streetlights outside. I pulled my P226 from the drawer in the dresser and slipped it into my waistband behind my back. Before letting go of it I called out.

"Who is it?"

"Special delivery from Brigadier Byrd."

I pulled the Sig from my belt again, held it behind my back and opened the door with my left hand. He was standing sideways on, wearing a trench coat and a fedora, like a character from a Bogart movie. He had a cigarette in his mouth and he was leaning into the flame from a match. He turned and raised an eyebrow at me, and spoke as he shook the match and released smoke from his mouth.

"Harry Bauer?"

"Yeah. Who are you?"

"Captain Russ White, US Air Force. May I come in?"

"You got some ID?"

He reached in his coat and pulled out a brown leather wallet. In the transparent flap was his Common Access Card. I took it, pulled it out and had a look. As far as I could see he was who he said he was. I handed it back and stood aside.

"Come on in, Captain."

He stepped through the door, took off his hat and smiled. "Any objection to first names, Harry? I'm not big on formalities."

"None. You want a beer?"

"Sure." He grinned. "But I'd prefer a Scotch if you have one."

I took his coat and gestured at a chair. "I have one. Ice?"

He lowered himself into the chair. "Two rocks."

I went to the kitchen, took two tumblers and a bottle of The Macallan from the cupboard and filled a cereal bowl with ice. Then I carried the whole lot to the living room and set it on an occasional table between his chair and mine. I don't like coffee tables. They are designed to trip you up and graze your shins.

I poured in silence, gave him two rocks of ice and had mine neat.

"Cheers." He raised his glass and sipped, then smacked his lips and sighed. "The Macallan, a rare treat. A crime to put ice in it, but bad habits die hard."

I nodded, gave him a moment and asked, "How can I help you, Russ?"

He took another sip and regarded his glass like he was particularly proud of it.

"Ever heard of Zak Lee?"

"No. Who is he?"

"Heilong Li, Westernized his name to Zak Lee. He's a Chinese chemist, emerged from obscurity some five or six years ago to become head of viral research at UCP, that's United Chinese Petrochemicals, an umbrella company that handles about fifty percent of Chinese chemical and medical research and development, under government control and supervision, naturally."

"We don't like him?"

"Not a lot, no. At a conservative estimate we figure he is directly responsible for somewhere in the region of one hundred and twenty thousand deaths in Africa alone: Senegal, Cote d'Ivoire, the Congo, Gabon, Angola, Namibia, and South Africa, possibly other places too. Women, children… Men go without saying."

"What do you mean he is responsible for their deaths? How?"

He shrugged. "The west coast of Africa is like his personal testing lab. Testing on human subjects in China is not impossible, but it is difficult. It is a restrictive regime, not anarchic at all. President Xi Jinping is a man with a lot of power, and a lot of personal privilege, but his power comes from the system. The system is supreme in China and he must operate within it.

"So what UCP does, and the system turns a blind eye, is pay large bribes to West African regimes that *are* anarchic, where the system is simply an extension of the man in power, and they are granted permission to experiment on live human beings, whole villages and towns, where basically nobody gives a damn what happens to the people."

I didn't answer. I sipped from my glass while he rattled the rocks in his. He set his glass down and sighed. "He turns up, usually in person but sometimes it's his students and assistants. They are supported by armed guards and they force an entire population to take a so-called vaccine, or a cure for some local disease." He gave a dry laugh. "Of course the objective is not to kill these people. Labs don't make money by killing their customers. The purpose is to establish what the side effects are of the products they are researching, before feeding them to people who *do* matter. So in some cases entire villages have died in a matter of a few weeks. In others the majority of the subjects have gone blind.

"In one case, in the village of Massonde, four hundred miles southeast of Luanda as the crow flies, five hundred and fifty by Angolan road—and the last fifty of those through dense jungle—these *doctors*, for want of a better name, were sent in, protected by armed thugs in uniform, to provide vaccines against the flu. Within forty-eight hours half the town had become psychotic, hallucinating, screaming, running naked through the village square..."

He shook his head. I said nothing, watching him, waiting. He pointed at the bottle and made a question with his eyebrows. I said, "Sure, don't ask. Just help yourself. What happened?"

He spoke as he poured. "The soldiers mowed them down. And anyone who showed symptoms was systematically shot. The town is now a graveyard."

I nodded. "You said there might be other places outside Africa."

"Sure, Latin America, other parts of Africa, remote parts of Mongolia, the Far East... We suspect, but we can't be one hundred percent sure of our facts."

"So you'd like me to pay him a visit."

He smiled, gave a short laugh. "You spent a lot of time with the Brits, right?"

I returned the smile. "A bit, yeah."

"You have their flair for understatement. Yeah, we'd like you to go and blow the bastard's brains out."

"Good. Consider it done. I'll need all the intel you have, obviously."

"Obviously. But it's a little more complicated than that. He's here in New York. So it's important it looks like an accident, or at the very least a mugging or an act of terrorism..."

"You want deniability. That goes without saying."

"Yeah, but there's more, Harry. Zak Lee is here talking to a UN delegation, a delegation from the European Union, and there are US representatives meeting with him too. The brigadier would really like to know what they're talking about."

I frowned. "I thought that wasn't our job. That's what the Feds are for, or the Firm."

"Sure," he sipped, "but let me ask you something. When the big unknown here is China's chemical warfare capability, and the man who's responsible for developing it is in New York, at the United Nations, talking to American companies that are part of the military industrial complex, do you feel relaxed and comfortable leaving things to the CIA and the FBI?"

I nodded and sighed. "I guess not."

"It's a bit like having Dennis Rader break into your house, and you don't do anything because it's the cops' job."

"I get the point. So what does the brigadier want me to do?"

"He's convinced, and some of his advisors agree, that Lee's research has reached a critical point and he may be mobilizing resources to deploy it."

"You mean he fears he's preparing a dirty bomb?"

He shrugged. "That's partly what we need to find out. A bomb is simply a means of delivery. The problem is, the brigadier fears he may actually have something to deliver. If he has, then we need to know what, and where, when and how he plans to deliver it. The consequences could be very serious."

"And you say I have a gift for understatement." I drained my glass and set it on the table. "OK, so I need to know who my targets are, their exact location and any other intel."

"Your primary target is Heilong Li, Zak Lee, your secondary target is Yang Dizhou, no Westernization. He is Zak's personal assistant. He is also a very accomplished scientist and was Zak's student and disciple for many years, then became his assistant. He takes care of business for Zak. He has to go too.

"They're staying at the Oriental Suite, at the Mandarin Oriental, on Columbus Circle. Chinese taxpayers to foot their comrades' bill at fourteen grand a night, power to the people, comrade."

"They don't make Communists like they used to. So who else is on the list?"

"He has a number of meetings scheduled at the UN, plus a couple of private meetings with US scientists from Colombia at the hotel, which I suspect is just cover, and then a couple of dinners with bankers and industrialists from the petrochemicals industry. It's a busy schedule."

He reached in his pocket and pulled out a manila envelope which he handed to me. I opened it and inside were a couple of A4 documents stapled together. I examined them and saw that it was a list of times and dates showing where Lee was going to be, and what he was going to be doing while he was there. There were also a couple of photographs, one of Zak, the other of his assistant.

Zak was in his mid-sixties, bald as an egg, very thin, with hollow cheeks and large ears. He was tall, maybe six two, with a long, thin neck, long thin arms and big, bony hands.

Yang was shorter, thick set, with heavy, bottle-base glasses, receding gray hair and a pencil moustache. Somebody must have told him that was a good idea. I asked without looking up, "He in the same suite?"

"Yeah, and May Ling, the personal assistant's personal assistant."

I glanced at him. "I don't kill women or children. I'm funny that way."

"Relax, that's company policy. Besides, she's not on the list."

"So what about these delegates he's meeting with?"

"OK," he drained his glass and crossed one leg over the other, "that's part of your brief."

"What is?"

"Decide which ones to recommend for termination. You run your list by the brigadier, and the management decides which ones to execute."

I nodded and looked back at the pictures.

"OK. This is going to be expensive. I'm going to need serious expenses. I'm going to need to get inside and recon this place. I need to be invisible…"

"Sure." He reached in his jacket again and pulled out another, fatter envelope. In it was an expensive leather wallet containing five thousand bucks, a driver's license in the name of Auberry Winchester, a Centurion Amex and a Black Visa. "You have absolute operational autonomy," he said. "Do what you have to do. Keep the brigadier in the loop as much as you can, but he likes you and he trusts you, so you have pretty much a free hand." He grinned. "Don't let him down."

"I won't."

He sighed, put his hands on his knees and levered himself to his feet.

"Thanks for the whisky. A rare treat."

I let him out and stood smelling the damp, night air as I listened to his steps receding down toward Barkley Avenue. A few seconds after they had faded I heard the soft hum of a motor, which in turn blended into the night, leaving only the distant call of a foghorn, and the desultory chatter of a bird, fooled by the streetlamps into believing it was day.

I closed the door and went back inside. I picked up the papers he'd given me. Auberry Winchester. I smiled. It was like something out of Scott Fitzgerald meets P. G. Wodehouse. I'd have to go clothes shopping for blazers and cravats. But first I'd have to digest and memorize Zak Lee's schedule for the next few days, and do some observing from a distance. My window of opportunity was small, and I was starting from zero, but it was as important to go slow and steady at this stage, as it was to act lightning fast when the time came.

Zak Lee's first appointment was the next morning, Monday the 30th, ten fifteen at the United Nations building. I figured I didn't need to follow him inside because there was no way I was going to make the hit in there, but I could follow him there and follow him back, see what route he took, what kind of transportation he used and what his security was like.

A guy like him might have real tight security, or he might choose to keep a low profile. He wasn't exactly famous, and the people who might want to kill him were probably too poor to leave their villages, let alone their countries. Either way I didn't want to make assumptions. It was better to keep an open mind. We'd see tomorrow.

I scanned his schedule again and saw he had a lunchtime engagement in his rooms with a Professor Moricone from Harvard, and then a dinner appointment at nine PM. This appointment, instead of being in his suite, was in the restaurant. That struck me as curious.

Either he was not at all shy, or he had a purpose for arranging a public meeting. He must know there were people in the international intelligence community who'd be watching him. I filed that away under "answer later."

So between lunch and nine I'd have a few hours to buy an expensive wardrobe, an expensive watch and expensive shoes. I figured I should get an expensive haircut, too. Expensive people notice that kind of thing. Finally I figured I should hire an expensive car for the week. That made me smile. What the heck, Cobra might need it again for another job in the future. It might be cheaper just to buy one.

This hit had definite pluses to it.

THREE

I was up at six the next morning, went for a ten-mile run, spent an hour training in the backyard and had a breakfast of spelt waffles and honeycomb at nine thirty. Then I showered and dressed and went out to my old beat-up 1999 VW Golf GTI. It was the kind of wreck people made a point of not noticing, but under the dented, scuffed chassis, there was nothing wrong with the tweaked engine or the suspension. I had done some work and jacked it up from a hundred and fifty brake horsepower to two hundred and fifty by taking out the old engine and dropping in an Mk6. I'd had to tweak the suspension and the wheels too, but it had worked out nice. The 1999 model only weighed two thousand eight hundred pounds, compared with the three thousand four hundred of the Mk6, so with the extra power and torque it was doing naught to sixty in four seconds, which was nice.

I climbed behind the wheel, stuck the old-fashioned key in the ignition and enjoyed the low growl and rumble of the engine. Personally I like a stick shift because it gives you more control over the engine and the revs. You drop from sixth to third at a hundred MPH and your revs go through the roof. If you need a burst of speed or power, you can do that with a stick shift. With an automatic you're stuck with what the car thinks you ought to be doing. And if it's a German car, two gets you twenty the car will think you should be obeying the rules.

And the trouble is, a lot of the time I'm breaking the rules, doing stuff I ought not to be doing.

It was a half hour drive from my house to Columbus Circus. I approached down the West Side Highway and West 56th, then turned north onto 8th Avenue. I followed the circus round to West 60th and parked outside the post office, where I had a good view of the entrance to the hotel, and the hotel underground parking. There I killed the engine, adjusted the mirror and settled in for a wait.

It wasn't a long one. At fifteen minutes to ten a black Audi Q8 emerged from the hotel underground parking. A moment later two men exited the hotel and walked quickly toward the Audi. They were Heilong Li and Yang Dizhou. The chauffeur climbed out to open the rear door for them and at the same time a guy the size of a small barn got out of the front passenger side and stood staring up and down West 60thth Street, like he really didn't like West 60th Street at all. He and the driver were both Chinese, with real short hair, dark suits, dark shades and wires in their ears. They were about as conspicuous as my car was invisible.

Once their charges were in the vehicle, they climbed back in and took off. I followed them at a leisurely pace onto Columbus Avenue and down West 57th, all the way to Second Avenue. There they turned south as far as East 40th, where they finally turned onto First Avenue and then into the United Nations compound and underground parking.

As events go it wasn't much, but it told me something important. That was the most direct, obvious route they could have taken to get to the UN, and they had not been a bit shy about it. They had been bold to the point of being showy, and were making no effort at all to be discreet. Which meant that either they did not expect trouble, or they didn't care if they got it. Either way it suited me fine.

I decided not to waste time following them home. I had their schedule and I was keen to get my shopping done. So my first stop was Hickey Freeman on Madison Avenue, where I spent just short of ten grand on two suits, an evening suit and a handful of shirts. After that, I went to look for a suitable car at Cooper Classics on Perry Street, in the Village. I called before I went. When the sweet girl on the other end answered I told her, "Hi, what's the most expensive, cool car I can walk away with this afternoon?"

She took a moment to answer, then laughed and said, "The car I'm in love with right now is a replica."

"A replica?"

"Of the AC Cobra. Factory five, Oxford blue period color, silver Le Mans stripes, cream leather upholstery, VX220 seats, ProCharged four twenty-seven CI SBF stroke engine putting out seven hundred and fifty bad-ass horsepower, stainless-steel headers, four-barrel Holley, Carter fuel pumps, fully lined engine bay in polished alloy, Edelbrock rocker covers, electric power steering, high torque starter motor, ProTech shocks all round, electroplate brake calipers, Smiths instruments, period radio, power steering drives like a dream, complete build portfolio. Man, I'm getting horny just telling you about it."

A Cobra? How could I say no? I smiled into my voice and told her, "Yeah? I think you just sold it. Hold it for me, will you? I'm on my way."

It was a very sweet ride and worth every one of the

fifty thousand dollars I paid for it. And when I turned up at the Mandarin Oriental that evening, that replica kit car was going to look just as sweet sitting next to the Bentleys and the Ferraris as it did in the showroom at Cooper Classics. In fact, my only worry was whether the brigadier would let me keep it when the job was done.

I arranged to collect the car later that afternoon and took my purchases home in the VW, along with Dashiell Hammett's *Glass Key*, which I had a feeling I might need at dinner. Once home I made a reservation for a week at the Mandarin, packed a suitcase with a false bottom with all the things I thought I might need, showered and dressed, and made an appointment at the Pall Mall Barbers at 10 Rockefeller Plaza. By the time they'd finished with me, I not only had a name out of a P. G. Wodehouse novel, I looked like a character out of a P. G. Wodehouse novel too.

I'd taken a cab from Throggs Neck to Manhattan for my restyle and a wet shave. One hundred and twenty bucks lighter, I had then taken a cab to Coopers and collected my Cobra. From there I had finally rolled up at Columbus Circus in my gleaming automobile, tossed my keys to the valet, allowed a buttons to take my case and strolled into the foyer to check in.

Once registered, the buttons led me to my room, threw open the curtains, showed me where everything was and stood smiling and expectant at the door. I took fifty bucks from my wallet and handed it to him.

"Say, I heard there was some kind of Chinese scientific delegation here. Am I right?"

He smiled and gave his head a little dance. "Well, it's not exactly a delegation. That's Mr. Heilong Li. I'm never sure which is the first name and which is the surname, they do it the other way around over there. But he's here with Mr. Yang Dizhou and a couple of assistants, on business at the United Nations. 'Course, we get a lot of people here from the UN, because it's very handy for them, just down the road as it is."

"I imagine so." I gave a small laugh. "That's a dangerous business!" I said. "A guy like you who's a little bit awake could pick up a lot of useful gossip on the airwaves."

He gave me a careful smile. "Dangerous is the word, sir. Gossip is a double-edged sword. You're not wrong that there are clients who are willing to pay serious bucks for snippets of information. But you start playing that game and in no time at all you start losing people's trust. And then you're screwed, if you'll forgive my French."

"Sure, I get that. Trustworthiness is one of the five most valuable commodities. But it is, at the end of the day, a commodity that can be bought and sold. And a guy who knows how to work the market can choose his customers and sell *them* his loyalty and trustworthiness. Am I right?"

I was watching him carefully. There was only one thing I was really interested in right then, and it was whether he looked uncomfortable. He didn't. He looked wary, but he didn't look uncomfortable at all. He had been here before and he had negotiated these particular rocks with success.

He gave a small shrug with his eyebrows. "I guess that's true, sir. For me personally, it would take a lot for me to betray a confidence, or something I had overheard from a customer. I'm no saint and I guess if the price was high enough… But the price would have to be very high, or it would have to be a matter of national security or something like that. It's not just that I could lose my job, there is also the issue of self-respect, right?"

I nodded and tried to look sage while I did it. "I hear you." I pointed at him like my hand was a gun. "And I like what I hear. National security is never more at risk than when it is in the hands of diplomats."

He nodded, and there was a hint of resignation and obedience about it. "Yes sir."

I leaned my backside against the desk that was up against the wall and folded my arms.

"Diplomats," I said, "and big business interests, like the big pharma and petrochemical companies. I, personally, have seen senior management and CEOs of large multinationals, who would have sold their own mothers down the river for a lucrative contract, and these guys were already worth several million dollars apiece." I gave a short, dry laugh and his eyes told me he really wanted to get back to his job. I ignored what his eyes said and drove on. "They would have sold their mothers, but in some cases they actually *did* sell their country down the river for huge payoffs from hostile nations. You know what line of work I'm in, kid?"

"I have no idea, sir, but I am guessing it is something patriotic."

"You're not wrong. You're a bright kid. What's your name?"

"Bobby, sir."

"Well, Bobby, I won't tell you what my job is because then I'd have to kill you…" I laughed noisily and he made a real effort to laugh with me. When I was done I made a real serious face and told him, "But you should know that I am involved in issues of national security and I am here precisely for what you observed, this hotel's proximity to the United Nations. Now, I am well aware of how useful an ambitious young man like you, who cares about his country, can be. So I would like to make an ally of you…" I knew damned well that buttons in luxury hotels have high expectations and don't work for peanuts. So I peeled another fifty bucks out of my wallet and handed it to him. "…and ask you, if you see or hear anything, anything at all, that you think might be of interest to me, let me know."

I held up both hands and made a motion like I was slowing him down. "Now, I am not going to ask you to make an evaluation of intelligence and decide what is useful and what is not. That is not your brief, and it is not a skill I would expect you to have. You just give me anything that comes up concerning Heilong Li and Yang Dizhou: change of schedule, heightening of security, sudden change in his breakfast menu, a call girl who stayed the night…" I spread my hands. "You hear me, right?"

"Yes, sir."

"And not only will you get to feel good about yourself, young man, but you will also find that Uncle Sam can be very generous when he is grateful."

"I have nothing right now, sir. But I will keep my ear to the ground and let you know if I hear anything."

"Addaboy."

At the door he hesitated a moment and turned back to me.

"There is one thing, but I don't know if it's of any importance."

I had my wallet halfway to my jacket pocket. I paused. "Let's find out."

"Well." He made a face of uncertainty that was almost a wince. "We're pretty used to a high level of security here at the Mandarin, as I'm sure you know, sir. But the setup in the Oriental Suite goes a little beyond what you would expect."

"Yeah, how's that?"

"Well, inhouse hotel security is pretty tight. We have the latest in alarm systems and video surveillance, plus security guards and detectives. Most people who are security conscious add to that a bodyguard and, or, a couple of men at the door." He shrugged. "If you're on the top floor of a Manhattan skyscraper, nobody's going to come in through the window, right? Not unless it's Ethan Hunt."

"OK, so?"

"So Professor Li has two men on the outside of the door, two men on the inside of the door, plus his personal chauffeur and bodyguard, and then he has two men on the roof above his suite. And that is all in addition to the hotel's own electronic security system, which is cutting edge."

I thought about it a second, then nodded. "OK."

His face told me he didn't want me to miss the point so he went on.

"I mean, that's a lot of security, right? But the vehicles he uses are part of the hotel's own fleet. They're top of the line and bulletproof glass, but I'm pretty sure he could get something more..."

I smiled. "I get it. It's a good observation." I pulled a C note from my wallet and handed it to him. "Anything else, keep me posted."

"Of course, Mr. Winchester."

The door closed and I sat a while with my ass against the desk staring at a point six inches above the floor, but seeing only Heilong Li's two guards outside the door, two inside the door and two on the roof. And Ethan Hunt, what film was it? I shifted my gaze to the dark window, with the sparkling lights of the city outside the black glass, and tried to remember for a while.

It didn't really matter. The important thing was the six guards, and where they were placed: two outside, two inside and two on the roof. I smiled to myself, then went and had another shower, and dressed for dinner.

At eight thirty I went down to the cocktail bar, stopping briefly for a chat with Bobby the buttons, and ordered myself a martini, dry. Just for the heck of it I told the barman I wanted it shaken, not stirred. He must have heard it before because he didn't flinch. He just said, "Naturally, sir," and went ahead and shook me a martini dry. By the time he'd finished I had located Heilong Li and Yang Dizhou. They were sitting at a table in the corner with two men and a woman, none of whom looked Chinese. The woman was in her forties, attractive, blonde, well-dressed in an expensive, dark blue suit with diamonds that appeared to be real around her neck and in her earlobes. Her eyes were a pale blue that looked dangerous and her makeup was discreet but effective. I figured that probably summed her up. She was quiet, watching, listening, holding a gin and tonic but not drinking it.

On her right was a big man, six two or three, running to fat. His head was big and enhanced by jowls. His eyes peered suspiciously from pouches and his large lips moved constantly, like he was savoring the air. I estimated his weight at an easy three hundred pounds. Even his thousand-dollar suit couldn't make him look elegant. For all I knew, he might have had a beautiful soul, but he looked like a greedy, arrogant slob. Make that a greedy, arrogant, dangerous slob.

The third guy with them was in his sixties and you could see he worked out and ran his two miles every morning before breakfast. He was lean, well-dressed and wide awake. His gray hair had cost as much to cut as I'd spent on my handmade shoes. And his handmade shoes had probably cost as much as my suit. He had ruthless and predatory written all over him and I had a bad feeling that what was going down among cocktails at that table, among those five people, might have wide-reaching repercussions for a lot of other people, other people who could not afford thousand-dollar, handmade shoes.

As I pretended to read messages on my phone, a waiter from the restaurant entered the bar, approached Heilong Li and bent to mutter in his ear. Li's only acknowledgment was a brief nod. Then he smiled at his guests and said something, and they all rose and left the bar.

FOUR

I sat at a table close enough so I could eavesdrop, but far enough away to be inconspicuous. I ordered a salmon, beetroot and avocado salad to start with, with a glass of dry Manzanilla, and a T-bone steak with a half bottle of claret which I told the wine waiter to recommend for me. While I waited I had another martini and sat and pretended to read The Glass Key, while I listened carefully to my prey.

For a moment I was back in the hills above Sulfur Springs, lying motionless in the shadows of the pines, smelling, watching, listening, while the bull elk grazed peacefully unaware that death was grazing with him in the meadow.

But it was a moment, no more, and I put the thought out of my mind. You can't think that way when you're putting together a hit. Your thinking has to be here, and now.

Heilong Li was doing most of the talking. He had the calm authority and arrogance that comes with believing you are invulnerable. His English was almost accent free. He was saying:

"What we can offer you is a license limited by territory. And the territory must be within the geographical and jurisdictional limits of the United States. You are free to set your own price, but CF Inc. takes a cut of between ten and twenty percent. The higher your price, the higher the percentage, with fifteen percent falling somewhere in the mid range."

The fat guy laughed noisily and drained his cocktail. As he set his empty glass down on the table he belched. "And China comes in playing hardball. You're dreaming and you know it. For starters, why the hell should you limit us geographically? Why the hell shouldn't we have Western Europe too? We can distribute there as easily as anybody. In the second place, fifteen percent, kiss my sweet fanny. You'll take seven percent and be grateful we don't just go right ahead and develop our own vaccine."

Heilong Li and Yang Dizhou exchanged a few inscrutable words, and though they were expressionless and incomprehensible, the contempt was palpable. Once he'd allowed the fat guy to palpate it for a while he turned to him and spoke.

"Mr. Gutermann, we are of course delighted to entertain you as our guest. However, our purpose tonight is to speak about business, and the time we have at our disposal is limited..."

He left the words hanging and smiled amiably as he watched Gutermann's cheeks flush red. The woman stepped in by rattling the ice in her glass and, before sipping, then said, "Mr. Heilong, Peter raises a reasonable point as far as I can see. Our resources are among the best in the world. There is nothing to stop us developing a vaccine ourselves, with no need to pay what are, after all, exorbitant license fees."

Heilong Li screwed up his face in what turned out to be a silent laugh.

"Exorbitant. My English nanny used to say, 'Is as

does!' 'Is as does!' I would say to her, 'Nanny! That is not fair!' She would reply, 'Fair is as fair does!' I would complain, 'Nanny! This food is not good!' She would reply, 'Good is as good does!' I never did know what it meant! Then, one day, after she was dead, I realized what it meant..." He leaned forward, leering at the woman. "You know what it meant, Ms. Goldbloom? It meant, 'I have the power, so fuck you!'"

His laughter was shrill and startling, like the spasmodic shrieking of a parrot in a tropical rainforest. In a curious echo to Gutermann's reaction, Ms. Goldbloom's cheeks colored a delicate pink. The third guest's voice was quiet and measured.

"Don't you think you're overstating the case, Mr. Heilong? After all..."

But Heilong Li was already shaking his head, holding out the palm of his left hand in front of the man's face in a bizarre, "talk to the hand" gesture.

"Please, Mr. Browne, let's not waste any more time. The big issue here, which you are carefully trying to ignore, is the fact that I can develop my products a *thousand* times more quickly than you, because I have experimental resources that you have not. I have the vaccine, and I know, as you know, that it will take you years to develop it to a point where you can get FDA approval and start marketing it. So what you need to be asking yourselves is not how much money will you lose with my licensing agreement, but how much will you lose if you don't jump on the wagon right now? It is a simple choice. You have to choose between losing fifteen percent and losing one hundred percent." He gave another one of his parrot shrieks. "We can sit here and pretend to argue, but you know that in the end either you accept my terms, or somebody else does."

Two waiters approached my table. One carried my salmon and avocado salad, the other a chilled glass and a bottle of *Manzanilla*. He set down the glass, poured and went away. Meanwhile a gang of waiters had descended on Heilong Li's table and the conversation had died away.

I carefully set my bookmark in my book, smelled and sipped my wine and set to on the salmon, then returned to reading while I chewed and sipped. By the time I had got halfway down the page there was a pop and a moment later the flock of waiters had left and the table of five was tucking into a bottle of Pol Roger and five dozen oysters. They ate in silence and I phased out everybody else in the dining room until all I could hear was the clatter of shells on china, the desultory slurp of oysters being sucked from those shells and the clink of crystal flutes.

I ate too. If camouflage in the mountains was remaining motionless in the shade and undergrowth, here it was eating and drinking as one of the herd. Eventually, Mr. Browne leaned back in his chair and dabbed his mouth with his handkerchief.

"We are familiar with your…," he hesitated a moment, then gave a small shrug before picking up his glass, "your exceptional facilities, Li. And I for one am not going to pretend that we have anything comparable on this side of the Pacific. I will say, however, that I am by no means sure the FDA will approve your vaccine…"

Li didn't let him finish. He restrained a splutter of amusement into his champagne flute and waved his left hand at Browne across the table.

"My dear Browne, please, that is the least of your worries. The FDA will approve it. The president himself will take care of that."

Browne arched an eyebrow at him. "Yours or ours?"

Li said something to Yang Dizhou in Chinese and they both laughed. Shortly after that three lobsters were brought to the table along with two more bottles of champagne. My plate and glass were cleared away and my T-bone steak was delivered with a bottle of *La Fleur de Petrus*, Pomerol, 2014, which he had opened earlier to allow it to breathe. He poured me half an inch which I swirled around like I knew what I was doing, sipped, thought about it and nodded. He poured me another two inches, bowed and went away on quick, silent feet.

I stroked the T-bone with my knife and it opened up, succulent and slightly bloody on the plate. It was exquisite and I sat back to savor it and the wine while Li started to talk again.

"It is very rare, Browne, very rare, that a person should find himself completely out of options." He nodded a few times. "But it happens. The man who falls out of a window twenty stories above the ground is out of options. The woman who is in the path of a high-velocity bullet is out of options. If that asteroid the doomsayers are always talking about ever shows up, we will *all* be out of options." He laughed, but nobody else at the table did. "The fact is that sometimes karma catches up with us and becomes fate, destiny, whatever you want to call it. And when that happens, we run out of options. This..." He opened his hands like he was opening a large book and gestured at them all around the table. "This is where you are at right now. You are not completely out of options, not exactly. But you have only two options left. Only two. They are, accept my terms, or walk away."

Gutermann had been lost in his own fat world of

sloppy, oral delight, chewing and sucking on hunks of lobster which he held with short, conical fingers. Now he picked up his napkin and wiped his face with it.

"And if we walk away?"

Li shrugged. "It makes no difference to me. I have cornered the market. Your antitrust legislation does not affect me. You are convenient to me so that I can break into the North American market, but if you do not like my terms somebody else will." He suddenly leaned back and let out his strange, parrot-like laugh again. "Yesterday Hillary was on the phone to me, begging for a piece of this action." The laughter faded from his face and he reached for another piece of lobster. "But they are a spent force. I would rather work with you. So I offer you this opportunity. However, if you will not work with me, she will."

It was the woman, Goldbloom, who answered. She sighed loudly and shook her head. "There's only one thing I hate more than getting screwed over, and that's wasting time. That's what we're doing here right now. I don't know if we are out of options, but I am damn clear what our best option is. We will take over distribution of your vaccine in the USA and Canada, on your terms, but there is one condition I will impose, and this is not negotiable."

Li didn't answer, but he looked at her with the kind of inscrutable expression that usually precedes a great deal of pain. She held his gaze for a count of three while she sipped her champagne. Then she told him what her condition was.

"We need access to your testing labs."

"No."

"Think long term, Li. Make long movies in your head. You have the upper hand today in this negotiation, but you know that down the line, someday, you will need our good will. We need access to your testing fields, and that is the condition. Otherwise I will personally make sure the FDA does not approve your vaccine. Take it or leave it."

I had to smile. He was quiet for a long while. Finally he said, "Through our agents and supervised by our agents."

She shrugged. "You got yourself a deal, Li."

They all raised their glasses and toasted. I read on about the political corruption in America back in the '20s and '30s. Their conversation shifted to more mundane subjects like illegal hunting in African nature reserves, the latest shows on Broadway and prostitution in Bangkok. I ordered a black coffee and a Macallan, and sat and thought while I pretended to read.

I hadn't learned a lot more than I knew already. I had added detail, but not much more than that. Except that there was a deal going down; a deal in which a corporation represented by Gutermann, Goldbloom and Browne would be granted exclusive distribution rights across North America for a vaccine manufactured by the Chinese. The brigadier had asked for information, if I could get it. I wondered if this was the information he was after, and whether I should now focus on the kill. I turned a page and stared unseeing at the print.

Something told me the brigadier would not be satisfied. He would want more. He would want to know, a vaccine against what? Either way I would need to get into the suite. Whether it was to collect intel or kill these bastards, I would have to get inside. Like Li had said, sometimes you run out of options. Killing him inside the UN was out of the question—security was too tight and getting away would be almost impossible. That left the route from the hotel to the UN complex, and on that route the risk of collateral damage was unacceptably high. That left the hotel and the suite. As there was no way to predict his and Yang Dizhou's movements within the hotel, my only realistic option was to break into the suite. Whether I did that to get information on the deal, or to kill them, at this stage made little difference. I had to get in, and then I had to get out.

I sipped some coffee and followed up with a slug of whisky which I rolled around my mouth for a while, enjoying the thought of how much Cobra would be paying for that sip.

There were six possible points of access to the suite, and most of those could be eliminated straight away. I could enter through the floor, through the ceiling or through one of the side walls from a neighboring room. All those four options would entail some form of demolition and could therefore be eliminated immediately. That left just two points of access: the front door and the window.

Going in through the front door would mean avoiding hotel security, which I had already been told was cutting edge, neutralizing the guards on the outside, opening the door, then neutralizing the guards on the inside. That would leave the bodyguard and the chauffeur, and May Ling. Though they would have to be faced sooner or later whatever my point of entry was.

Which left the window. Entering through the window, if done correctly, could mean getting direct access to Heilong Li and Yang Dizhou without having to tackle the guards on the door. But it would also mean approaching up, or down, a sheer steel and glass wall, fifty-four floors above ground level.

An interesting prospect.

I called the waiter, signed my bill and took my book up to my room. There I tossed it on the bed and dialed a secure number on my cell. It rang twice, then the brigadier's voice spoke.

"Harry, tell me."

"I'm at the Mandarin. I followed Heilong Li and Yang Dizhou to the UN this morning and I've just had drinks and dinner about fifteen feet away from them."

"I hope you're being discreet. This is not Afghanistan."

"Yes, sir. I will also remember to brush my teeth before I go to bed."

"What have you learned?"

"He had dinner with three people aside from Yang Dizhou. A big slob called Gutermann, a woman in her forties name of Goldbloom and a guy in his sixties, name of Browne. They discussed a licensing contract for a vaccine..."

I reported the content of their conversation and he was quiet for a while. Finally he said, "There was no mention of what this vaccine was for."

"None. I know you said you wanted intel, now I'm wondering whether this was the intel you were after, or whether you want more. You stressed to me once that we are not an intelligence gathering agency. Our job is to execute people."

"That's quite true, Harry." He said it like he'd never thought of it that way before.

"So you want me to execute these bastards or you want me to find out what color panties they wear?"

"Let me ask you a question. In your honest opinion, do you think they have electronic files in their suite relevant to this vaccine?"

"Of course."

"Then I think we have little choice but to collect it. But don't let that take precedence over your primary mission. Execute them and collect whatever intel you can find in the form of documents, paper or electronic."

"OK."

"Have you a plan yet?"

"Yes."

"When do you plan to execute it?"

"Tomorrow night, when I'm not weighed down by a T-bone steak and half a bottle of 2014 Pomerol."

"I see you're making good use of the company expense account."

There was no trace of sarcasm in his voice and that made me smile. I let the smile show in my voice. "Camouflage, Brigadier."

"All right, I'll be waiting for your report. Be careful."

He hung up and I stood looking out at the night, with the constellations of New York City lights scattered against the black sky. I'd be careful. I had no other option. I was out of karma and in the hands of fate, climbing down the sheer face of a glass and steel building, fifty-four floors above Columbus Circus.

FIVE

The Oriental Suite was located immediately below a vast terrace, roughly trapeze shaped, that overlooked Columbus Circus. It was about a hundred and twenty feet across at its widest point, a hundred and twenty at its deepest and just thirty-six at its shallowest. There was a broad lawn at its center and the general idea was that the terrace would be used for parties or outdoor events. I had learned from Bobby the buttons that right then the terrace was closed for cleaning and repairs.

My copy of Heilong Li's schedule told me that from nine PM till late he and Yang Dizhou would be at a private meeting with the delegates from the European Union's External Action Service at their offices within the United Nations complex. Exactly what kind of delegates was not clear, but that didn't worry me. You didn't need to be a genius to work it out. What the intel didn't supply, my imagination could make up. They were the kind of delegates who bought and sold licenses and privileges in the "national interest" of the emerging European Federation. The important thing was that Heilong Li and his bodyguards would not be in the suite at that time.

So that morning I had taken the Cobra to Eastern Mountain Sports, on Broadway, and I had bought a few things I hadn't packed: a harness, thirty yards of mountaineering rope and a set of suction cups for my hands and feet. I had also bought a black, woolen hat which could be easily converted into a balaclava, some black pants, sneakers and a sweatshirt.

I spent the rest of the morning in the gym, had a light lunch and in the afternoon I reviewed my plans, read *The Glass Key* and slept, and generally stayed out of sight.

I rose at seven, had a cold shower and dressed. From my suitcase I took out a few things from the false bottom: a set of night-vision goggles, a pair of latex gloves, my Maxim 9—an internally suppressed 9mm semiautomatic—which went in a holster under my arm, my Sig Sauer P226 TacOps, which went in a holster on my right thigh, and my regimental Fairbairn and Sykes fighting knife, which I slipped into my boot.

Over my shoulder I hung a canvas bag for anything I might want to bring back with me.

And into my pocket I slipped a diamond-tipped glass cutter.

Next I pulled on my coat, stuffed my woolen hat in my pocket and stepped out into the passage at around the time that Heilong Li was stepping into his private reception with the EU delegates.

It was an eight-floor climb but I didn't take the elevator. I slipped into the service stairwell and took the stairs at a steady run. I came out of the stairwell on the fifty-fourth floor into a long passage. The lights were off, but sixty feet to my right I could see a faint glow. I made a sprint in that direction and came out into a broad lounge, maybe forty or fifty feet square. There were scattered nests of armchairs and low tables, large potted palms and a bar. Under the high ceiling, the place seemed vast, silent and still in the darkness. The only illumination was the light from the city, which filtered in through the enormous glass plates that made up the wall on my left. Through it I could see the terrace, littered with sacks of sand and cement, bricks and other pieces of construction material. Against the wall, partially covering the glass, was a huge frame of scaffolding. And on the right, set in a steel frame within the glass wall, was a door.

I crossed the floor on silent feet, hunkered down by the door and examined the lock. It was set in a steel plate clamped to the glass. There were no cables and no sensors. I stood, stepped back, pulled the Maxim 9 from my holster and blew out the lock.

There was a *phut!* A hard smack of lead on steel and the splintering of glass. I stood motionless, listening. No other sounds came to me, except the sigh of night air and the quiet hum and wail of city noises as the door swung slowly open. I stepped out into the night.

I found a sack of cement and placed it against the door to keep it closed, then made my way to the parapet. There I identified Heilong Li's suite, marked the spot and went to secure one end of my rope to the scaffolding. I took off my coat, pulled on the harness, fitted the rope to the clamps and returned to the parapet.

Heights don't bother me, but looking down the sheer, dark face of the building into the void, for a moment I felt the lurch of a hollow, empty sickness in my gut. I ignored it, pulled the balaclava over my face, attached the cups to my boots and my hands and slipped over the side. I was fifty-four floors up with only emptiness beneath me, and the suction cups keeping me attached to the sheer, shiny glass wall.

Progress was agonizingly slow. One suction cup at a time: right hand, clamp to the glass, suck out the air and seal; left hand, release the vacuum, slide the hand down, clamp to the glass, suck out the air and seal; right foot release the vacuum, slide down, clamp to the glass, suck out the air and seal; left leg... And all the while the sense of emptiness behind and beneath me grew more intense, as the parapet receded above me, farther out of reach.

I focused my mind, following my personal mantra, "concentrate attention through observation," and pretty soon I had descended some fourteen feet to where I had calculated, according to the specs I had found on Google, was Heilong Li's bedroom. There I bent my knees to my chest, locked the suction cups on my boots to the glass, side by side, gripped the rope with my left hand and, with the glass cutter, cut a wide circle, describing a circumference around my body.

When I was done, I fixed the suction cup on my left hand to the glass in front of my belly and gave it a sharp smack with my right fist. I heard the brittle crack as the cut yielded to the force of the blow and, controlling the give of the rope with my right hand, I slid gently, by degrees, through the hole I had cut in the glass.

It was an awkward landing. It was very dark and I discovered, by touch and error, that there was a small, round table just below me and, to either side of it, an armchair. It didn't help that I had four-foot glass disks attached by suction pads to my left hand and both my feet.

I released my right foot, managed to get purchase on one of the chairs, settled the glass on the chair beside my foot and released the other boot. I let go the rope by degrees till I was squatting on the chair beside the glass, then stepped to the floor, released the last suction pad and pulled the night-vision goggles over my eyes. The world turned black and green and shapes began to emerge.

Six feet away was an emperor-sized bed. I froze. In

the bed there was a form, a person, sleeping. The hair and shape slowly resolved themselves into a woman. Her back, a shapely, attractive one, was turned to me. On the bedside table, on the far side of the bed, was a silver bucket, glinting green, with a bottle of champagne in it. Two glasses stood beside it. One very slow step took me to within three feet. I was thinking, hard and fast.

It was not yet ten o'clock, and this woman was out cold. That was unusual. For a second I considered it might be a trap, but dismissed the idea. It was too elaborate and nobody but me knew I was coming. Another step took me to the side of the bed and then I saw the mirror and the silver box. Coke, champagne and who knew what else. This girl was out for the count. Even so, it affected my plan.

My plan had been to take out the four guards by stealth, search the suite at my leisure for information on the vaccine, and then take out Heilong Li and Yang Dizhou when they got back—after any interrogation which might seem necessary. But now, with this girl sleeping in the bed, the risk of her waking up while I was at work was too high. My priorities had to change and adapt. First priority now had to be securing any documents, electronic or otherwise, that might shed light on Heilong Li's vaccine, before executing the hit. I could not risk waking the girl.

I scanned the room. It was maybe twenty foot square. Beyond the bed there were a couple of armchairs and beyond them a long, six-door wardrobe. To the left of the wardrobe was a passage that I figured led to the en suite bathroom and the bedroom door. Up against the wall, about twelve feet from the end of the bed, there was a desk. A black leather swivel chair was pushed up against it, and on the desk was a laptop computer. I crossed the room, unplugged it and slipped it into my canvas bag. Then I hunkered down and, one by one, carefully pulled open the drawers in the desk.

In the first there was just hotel stationery, a couple of pens and a few boxes of Montblanc ink cartridges. I slid it closed again and opened the one below it. Three A4 lined notebooks with nothing written in them. Still squatting, I took a long step to the other side of the desk and opened the bottom drawer. It was empty. I closed it and heard the girl in the bed sigh and move. I froze and waited until there was only silence, then slipped open the top drawer. Inside it was the jackpot: a detachable hard drive and a diary. I put the hard drive in my bag and opened the diary. The pages were crammed with Chinese characters. I closed it and dropped that in my bag too, wondering what my next move was.

As it was, that decision was taken out of my hands. A piercing scream tore the darkness apart and was rapidly followed by another, with promises of a third on the way.

I rolled and came up on one knee with the Maxim in my hand. The girl was sitting up in the bed with her hands plastered to her cheeks, her mouth gaping open and her eyes screwed shut. She drew a deep breath and another hysterical scream tore from her throat. I jumped to my feet, ramming the Maxim back in my holster. Two long strides got me beside her and I clamped my right hand over her mouth and my left against the back of her head. I pressed hard, hurled her back on the bed and put one knee on her belly. I pressed my face close to hers and hissed, "*Shut up!*"

She wasn't listening and screamed into my hand, trying at the same time to bite my palm. I leaned closer and rasped again, "*Shut up!*" Then her right hand, armed with inch and a half long nails, was clawing at my face through the balaclava, threatening to tear the damned thing from my head. I released her mouth. The scream that came out of it then was like a long, silver needle, piercing and deafening. I pulled the Maxim from my holster again and shoved it in her face. She screamed again. The door burst open and light streamed in down the short passage, casting a luminous wedge along the white wall, bisected by two huge dancing shadows.

I swung the weapon around as the shadow melded with the vast bulk of a man in a brown suit who came barreling around the corner. I double-tapped. The Maxim spat silently and one slug hit his throat while the other tore into his forehead. Both erupted almost simultaneously from the back of his skull in a shower of black blood and gore. The girl screamed and kept screaming.

Then three guys were in the room and charging at me, big black forms stumbling over the dead hulk of their comrade. I tried to fire but the screaming, hysterical girl was clawing at my face and the shot went wide. Then a fist-like hunk of rock smashed into my chest and hurled me against the bedside table and the wall. The lamp fell to the floor and I went after it.

Then it was chaos. A guy was shouting in Chinese. In my peripheral vision I saw the girl, luminous and naked, jumping from the bed. One of the guys was going after her. Two giant shadows loomed over me on the floor. A foot rose to stamp on my chest and I knew I would die. My right hand, still holding the Maxim, was pinned under my body. I squirmed, shifted and fired.

It was luck fueled by desperation. His right foot was raised high, ready for the stamp. The slug tore into his left shin just above his ankle and shattered the bone. He screamed and fell back, with his foot twisting away at a grotesque angle.

Then from the mêlée a massive fist gripped my shirt collar and dragged me to my feet, while another equally massive right fist pounded at my face. I tried to weave and duck, but it was impossible and the blows hurt like hell. Three punches grazed me and I knew if the fourth connected I was dead. I rammed the Maxim in his face, but this guy knew what he was doing. He grabbed the barrel in his left and levered it back toward me. I released the trigger, went with the flow of his movement and smashed my right elbow into his jaw. It was a blow that would have put most men's lights out. He grunted and took a step back.

I didn't waste time. I delivered a side kick to his right knee and followed with a roundhouse kick to the side of the same knee. I heard it crunch and he let out a weird noise that was all about pain. I leveled the Maxim at his head and was hit in the side by a freight train that hurled me across the room and smashed me against the mahogany foot of the bed, knocking all the air out of my lungs. I dropped to the floor and needles of pain shafted through my chest, paralyzing my arms and legs.

In the dim light I saw the guy I'd kicked trying to hop one-legged toward the wall, keening with pain as he went. And the guy who'd charged me standing over me, leering. Like the others, he was big, barrel-chested, almost bald, with powerful arms and legs. I tried to raise my hand to shoot him, and realized too late my hand was empty. He said something in Mandarin I did not understand, but I knew it was bad. He was going to hurt me, and he was going to enjoy it.

He reached down with his left hand and, instead of grabbing the scruff of my neck, like his pal had done, he clutched my throat, lifted me to my knees and began to squeeze. I could feel the blood pressure rising in my head and my lungs were suddenly screaming for air. His leer turned to a broad grin as I felt my tongue swell and my eyes start to pop. I was seconds from death and I knew it. His eyes said he knew it too.

I read somewhere once that if you focus on somebody's hands when they are strangling you, you will die. In a millisecond I realized that both my hands were clenched around his wrist, and they were doing sweet FA there. With milliseconds to go, I dug the nails of my left hand deep into his wrist. His face twisted with the pain, no longer grinning but determined not to let go. That was enough, because he was focusing on my nails and the blood seeping from them, and he didn't notice my right hand drop to my boot.

The hard, cold handle of the Fairbairn and Sykes touched my fingers, and, in what should have been my dying breath, I rammed the razor-sharp blade up, deep into his armpit and dragged the blade down along his arm, severing his brachial artery and the cephalic vein. He didn't scream. He gasped with shock. And instantly a powerful jet of blood sprayed across the room, spattering the glass wall with black blood. His hand released my neck and I struggled to my feet, wheezing painfully and noisily as air ripped at my bruised throat. He staggered away, gripping at his arm with his right hand, but the damage I'd done was catastrophic and after a couple of steps he keeled over and hit the floor with a massive thud.

I ignored him. Still wheezing painfully, I made for the guy with the broken knee. He was standing in the shaft of light from the open bedroom door and I could see terror, bright and wet in his weeping eyes.

I stood in front of him, let him see the rage and pain in my eyes, and looked down, first at his broken knee, then at his good one. He shook his head and muttered something I didn't get. I said:

"Do you speak English?"

He was sweating hard and I knew he was in serious pain. "Rittoo," he said.

"I will let you live, you understand? I will let you live, and get a doctor. OK?"

He nodded very slowly and very cautiously. "OK..."

"But you, tell me, where is the safe?" I made the shape of the safe with my hands, and mimicked turning the knobs for the combination. "Safe, where?"

He looked like he was going to cry. My eyes told him what was coming next and he held up a hand and shook his head. Then he pointed to the wardrobe. I went and grabbed a chair, dragged it over, frisked him, pulled his Glock from under his arm and sat him down.

"Where is the girl?"

"Lock in room."

It made some kind of crazy sense. That was why they hadn't come in shooting, so as not to hurt her. But they couldn't let her run either, because Heilong Li would lose face.

I nodded and went and pulled open the wardrobe. The safe was there, in the wall. I looked at him. "Combin-ation. Number. Pin."

His shoulders shook, his face crumpled and he started to weep. Through his sobs he said, "Two three, zero one, two zero, two three."

I punched the numbers into the screen and the

door clunked and swung open. There was a stash of cash, I figured about fifty grand. Spoils. I put it in my canvas bag. There was also a notebook and a USB drive. I bagged them too. Then I stood, picked up his Glock and handed it to him. He stared at me a moment, and there was something like gratitude in his eyes.

He took the gun, cocked it and aimed at my head. I shot him between the eyes.

SIX

I stood a moment, uncertain. I'd expected hotel security to have busted in by now. But there was no sign of them. I figured maybe Heilong Li felt if anybody came after him and broke in, he'd prefer to deal with them himself, on his own terms, rather than have the local authority step in. Having the local authorities involved could have two serious downsides. First would be the publicity he and the Chinese government might be exposed to; and second was the fact that whoever broke in, might actually be working for the local authorities. So he beefed up his private muscle and dealt with security himself.

What didn't seem to have occurred to him was that somebody might break in, take on his four gorillas and actually beat them. That was what had happened, and it had left me with the question of what to do with May Ling, if that was who she was.

I flipped on the light, stepped over the bodies and went to the bedside where I had seen the mirror and the silver box. I opened the lid and saw there were still a few grams of the white powder in it. I picked it up, with the mirror, and carried it out of the room.

I was in a short passage. The first door on my right was a bathroom. Opposite it was a door with a key in the lock. I pulled the balaclava from my head and stuffed it in my back pocket. Then I unlocked the door and eased it open.

She was still naked, sitting cross-legged on the bed, shivering and crying. She might have been pretty, even beautiful, but there was something jaded and joyless about her eyes. She was watching me with something between resentment and fear. I had the Maxim in my right hand, and the silver box in my left. I showed her the box and smiled like I was a nice person.

"You speak English?"

"Of course."

"Good, then we can get along fine and understand each other. I don't want to hurt you. I want to get you away from here, and I don't want anybody ever to know you were here in the first place. So far, I figure we want the same thing, right?"

She nodded. I went on. "When the cops get here, if they find you, even if you don't get framed as an accessory or an accomplice, they are going to be all over you like a rash. And I am figuring maybe there are things you would rather they did not know about you. Am I wrong?"

She shrugged. "No."

"Are you May Ling?"

She thought about it, then shrugged again. "Yeah."

"So, you come with me, and I will introduce you to some people who will be very interested to know you, and will probably pay you lots of money to talk to them about Heilong Li. You get to take all his coke with you, and the cops need never know a thing. The alternative is I kill you in the next three seconds. One..."

"No problem, I'll go with you."

I smiled. I had no idea what I would have done if she'd let me count to three.

She dragged on some jeans, a sweatshirt and some

sneakers, found what looked like a kilo of coke from the lounge, and we stepped out into the corridor.

There we pushed through the fire doors into the service stairwell again and ran down the sixteen flights to my floor. I peered into the dimly lit, carpeted corridor. It was empty, as you'd expect. At that time just about everybody was at dinner, and we made it to my room without being seen. I slipped the card in the door, the light went green and I pushed it open, then shoved May Ling inside and closed the door behind me.

She turned to face me. Her face was tight and there was childlike fear in her eyes. "Are you going to be nice?"

I gave a small nod. "I'll be nice." I pointed up at the ceiling. "But you just keep remembering that I just killed four very dangerous men upstairs. You know what that means?"

She sat on the bed and nodded. "You're four times more dangerous than they were."

"Good. So you stay put, you shut up, you do everything I tell you to do, and you don't do *anything* I don't tell you to do. We clear?"

"Very." She shook her head. "I am not dangerous at all. I'm a good secretary and a very good lover. That's why I'm here."

"That'll do just fine. Now shut up."

"Can I have a snort?"

I pulled my cell from my pocket and dialed. "No."

"Can I have a drink?"

I jerked my head at the bar. "Yeah. Fix me a whisky while you're at it."

The brigadier's voice said, "Yes."

"We need to talk in person. I have May Ling here."

"You *what?*"

"She's willing to talk to you."

He was very quiet, then said, "What about the rest of it?"

"A mixed bag. I don't want to talk right now. The shit's about to hit the fan and we need to disappear. You need to send in the cleaners and get me and May Ling the hell out of Dodge. And you need to do it now."

"Just answer yes or no."

"No."

"Shut up, Harry. Did you hit the main targets?"

"No."

"Either of them?"

"No."

"Well for God's sake, what *did* you do?"

May Ling stood close and handed me a glass with lots of whisky in it. I took it, set it down on the desk, put a finger on her chest and pushed her gently away. Into the phone I said: "That's not a yes-no question. Quit wasting time. Send a car. I'll settle the bill. The Oriental Suite is a mess and you need to insulate me, May Ling and yourself."

"Did you get anything?"

"Yes."

"Fine. There will be a car there in fifteen minutes."

I hung up and started to strip. I pointed at the wardrobe. "Give me a suit. Get the case. Pack everything into it. When you're done, get a towel and wipe down every damned surface in the bathroom and the bedroom. Do it now."

Fifteen minutes later I was dressed and I had double-checked all the surfaces where there might be prints. The two glasses were washed and polished and we were on our way down in the elevator to the lobby.

May Ling was eyeing me sidelong with no expression but plenty of curiosity in her eyes.

"Who are you?"

"Nobody you want to know."

She turned to face me and there was defiance in her eyes. "How do you know that?"

The elevator slowed to a halt. I gave her a humorless smile. "By the way you screamed. Come on, shift your ass."

As we walked toward the reception desk I was surprised to see the brigadier sitting in an easy chair, watching me. I steered May Ling toward him and he stood to greet us. He didn't look very amused. I spoke before he could say anything. Smiling in a way I thought was urbane and debonair, I said, "Brigadier, what a pleasure to see you. May I introduce May Ling?"

His smile was thin the way a black mamba is thin, and his eyes said he would shoot me later. He shook hands with May Ling, asked her how she did and turned back to me.

"I believe there were some things you needed to explain to me…"

"There are indeed. Thing is, we are in a bit of a hurry. I suggest you take May Ling somewhere…," I fixed him with my eyes and gave the word just enough emphasis, "*appropriate*, and I will join you as soon as I have settled the bill."

He nodded once. He was mad. "You've been to my country house."

"Sure."

"We'll be there." His eyebrows rose slightly. "Have you got business to finish here before you join us?"

I shook my head. "Not no way. I think things are

going to get a bit busy around here, Brigadier, and we would be smart to get moving. I'll see you there." I went to move but paused. "You got your chauffeur?"

"Yes. Why?"

"Just as well, and by the way, in case anybody asks, May Ling and I were together all evening." I smiled at her. "Right?"

She winked and returned the smile. "You bet."

The brigadier offered her his arm. "Shall we go? And I should tell you..." He leaned into her, close and confidential, and murmured in her ear. "My friend here is old-fashioned about not hurting women. I have no such scruples. So you'd be well advised to behave."

They made their way to the main door and I went to the reception desk, where I settled my bill and asked for my car to be brought to the door. So far there was no sign that the bodies had been found or that the alarm had been raised.

I paid the bill, then stepped out into the evening to wait for my car. Down the road I saw a dark Jeep pull away and head north. I knew the brigadier was as mad as a grizzly with a hornet up its ass, and I was also aware that I had screwed up. But hanging around to finish the job now was a bad idea, and would just lead to further screwups. We needed to step back and reassess the situation, and that was what I was going to tell him when we got to the HQ.

The kid brought the Cobra round, I gave him twenty bucks, climbed in behind the wheel and took off after the brigadier.

It was a forty-five-minute drive, north through the bright lights of Manhattan, over the Henry Hudson Bridge and deep into the growing dark of the suburbs and semi-countryside of Yonkers and Westchester. Eventually I came to the winding lanes and woodlands of Pleasantville, where I followed the searching, yellow funnels of my headlamps out of town and along Bedford Road, where trees and mailboxes sprang out of shadowy lawns, throwing black shadows leaping across the roads like inky daemons, until I found Apple Hill Lane and the big, iron gates of Cobra HQ.

There, voice recognition and iris-scanning technology reassured security that it was, probably, me and the gate swung open to let me in. Ten minutes after that I was stepping across the checkerboard floor of the entrance hall toward the study-cum-library where the brigadier was waiting for me with May Ling. When I opened the heavy, walnut door and went in, I found they weren't alone. Colonel Jane Harris was there too, in a dark blue suit, watching me from a burgundy chesterfield by the open fireplace. She had what looked like a gin and tonic in her hand, and the expression on her face said she'd like to skin me alive and roll me in coarse salt.

The brigadier had been in the chair opposite hers, but now he stood and turned to face me. His face wasn't a lot friendlier than the colonel's.

"Harry, you know Jane, of course. Come in, help yourself to a drink. Have you eaten?"

"No." I shook my head and stepped toward the bar. "Contrary to popular rumors, I have not been sitting on my ass blowing bubbles. I have been working. Pretty hard." I poured myself a large Macallan and turned to face the chief. "May Ling can attest to that, she was part of the hard work I was doing. I wouldn't say 'no' to a couple of cheese and ham sandwiches. If you think I deserve them, of course."

I might have told him I'd had a fun day fishing.

He remained expressionless and pulled an old-fashioned cord that was suspended from the ceiling, then returned to his chair. I sat on the sofa, next to May Ling, who'd been watching me with a small smile.

"Nobody," said the brigadier, "is accusing you of slacking on the job, Harry, but you must recognize that the results tonight are extremely disappointing, and I should like to know why. Though first...," he gestured to May Ling, "I would like to know what you mean by exposing May Ling to our operation, and vice versa."

I reached across and handed him the canvas bag containing everything I had collected from Heilong Li's suite, except the fifty grand which were acknowledged spoils of war.

"In there you have Heilong Li's notebook, his diary, his laptop and his USB drive." I gestured to May Ling, "And right here you have his personal assistant's personal assistant. Though—" I turned to look at her and gave my head a little twist. "If I am not very much mistaken, most of the assisting was done in the bedroom, and for Heilong Li. Is that right?"

She nodded. "I was offered the job as a PA, but really I was Heilong Li's live-in sex worker."

I turned back to Brigadier Buddy Byrd, carefully ignoring Colonel Harris. "I broke in, found May Ling asleep in the bed, she woke up and raised the alarm, I killed the four guys he had guarding the suite, and my options were to either kill May Ling as well, or bring her in on the off chance that she might be able to provide us with valuable, firsthand information. Obviously I was not going to kill her. So I took what was to me the only viable option."

The colonel sighed loudly and spoke to the brigadier like I was not there.

"Alex, he is a liability. I told you from the start he would be a liability and that is exactly what he has become."

Buddy regarded her a moment and turned back to me. "May Ling was present?"

"Of course. She raised the alarm."

He turned to her. "What kind of information can you provide us with?"

She thought about it for a moment, gazing at the logs burning in the fire.

"Probably more than you'd expect. I was with them all the time when they were having their most intimate conversations. They thought I was just a dope and didn't understand. But I figure, if we have a few conversations, and you give me the right kind of incentives, things I heard that don't make a lot of sense to me, might make a lot of sense to you."

There was something of the smart aleck about the way she said it, and Colonel Harris gave a bark that might have been some kind of a laugh.

"You have got to be kidding me."

I studied her for a couple of seconds. "Colonel, you want to play a dirty game, but you want the players to play clean. If I know anything about prostitutes, and I do know something about prostitutes, Colonel, May Ling probably has useful information which she knows is useful, and a ton more she doesn't know is useful. Get a couple of experts to debrief her and you'll end up being grateful for my professional incompetence."

Her face flushed red to the roots of her platinum hair. "Mr. *Bauer!* You are..."

I interrupted her: "In the real world, Colonel! You think May Ling is offended because I called her a prostitute?"

I turned to May Ling and jerked my chin at her. She was watching the colonel and smiling. I started to ask but she interrupted, keeping her eyes on Harris. "I'm a high-class whore, Colonel Harris. It's what I am, and I'm damned good at it. Satisfaction guaranteed. But I am not as stupid as you think I look. I have information I *know* you will find useful, but I am also sure, like Harry says, that I have information that I do not realize is useful. I don't know who you are, or what you think useful information is. I don't care either. But you are welcome to all the information I have. All I'm saying is, like everything else, it has a price. Your call."

"My call." It was the brigadier. The door had opened and a man in a dark suit stood waiting in the doorway. Buddy Byrd turned to him and gave him his instructions.

"O'Connell, have Alice bring up a plate of cheese and ham sandwiches for Mr. Bauer, he hasn't had supper yet and he is hungry. Have her bring up a couple of beers for him as well. I think the Marston's IPA should do. Meanwhile, have Ramirez and Jones come and collect Miss Ling, will you."

"Of course, sir." O'Connell gave a small bow and left.

May Ling was looking worried. "Who are Ramirez and Jones?"

"They are professional interrogators, but don't worry, we left the techniques they use in China behind a very long time ago, particularly in a case such as yours, where we are not fighting against national loyalty, ideology or anything of that sort. All we need to do is persuade you that your interest runs with ours. Am I right?"

"Completely. So why do you need to hand me over to these bozos? And, am I going to get paid? I need money, a new identity, somewhere to live..."

He smiled. "Yes, you'll get paid, and you'll be taken care of. And I am handing you over to these gentlemen because they, like you, are good at what they do."

The colonel got to her feet and crossed to the bar to pour herself another drink. "I'm getting nauseated by the stench of testosterone in this room."

I stood also and went to stand with my back to the fire. I watched her a moment.

"Colonel," I said, "in 1936, when the Spanish Civil War broke out, you know one of the reasons why it was so easy for Franco to march into Spain?" She sighed, but I didn't give her a chance to answer. "There were two Spanish Navy destroyers lying off the coast of Valencia. They could both have made it to Cadiz, where the invasion had taken place, in a matter of a few hours, and helped halt the invasion before it even started. But, believe it or not, at that time, every battleship in the Spanish Navy was a cooperative, and the crew of each ship had to sit down and vote on whether or not to head for Cadiz and engage Franco's troops. Not surprisingly they voted not to, and Franco's men, assisted by the Foreign Legion, swarmed over Andalusia and marched steadily north, toward Madrid."

"Thank you for that history lesson, Mr. Bauer. What's your point?"

"That when you have a job that needs doing, it's not helpful to get sidetracked into ideological debates and soul-searching about who has what rights and why. When planning an operation, you need to leave your 'isms' at the door."

The brigadier cleared his throat. "Can I suggest you have your very interesting conversation somewhere else at some other time? There are a couple of things I need from May Ling before she leaves us for the night. Are you willing to answer a couple of questions for me now, May Ling?"

"That depends on the questions, Buddy. I told you there's a price."

"You will be paid for the information you give us, May Ling, and we will ensure your safety, but there is a degree of urgency about this and it affects your security as well as our operation. Once they discover the carnage and theft in the suite at the Mandarin, Heilong Li and Yang Dizhou will leave New York posthaste. Have you any idea where they will go?"

She nodded. "Sure, I know exactly where they're going to go."

I said, "Where?"

"Casablanca, in Morocco."

"Why?"

"There is a lab out in the desert there, where they are working on a vaccine or something."

Colonel Jane Harris stepped toward her. "What kind of vaccine, May Ling? A vaccine against what?"

May Ling smiled. "You know what? This is fun, but I think I'm getting Alzheimer's, because my memory is going all kinds of foggy."

There was a knock at the door. The brigadier barked, "Come!" and two guys in jeans stepped in. A pretty girl in a French maid's uniform slipped past them and delivered to me a tray with beer and sandwiches on it. I gave her a wink and my thanks and she blushed and scurried away.

The guys were both in their thirties and both had the look of soldiers about them. Ramirez was shorter, olive skinned with intelligent eyes. Jones was bigger, black and had the patient smile of a guy who's seen it all and knows all the plays. They stood waiting, looking at May Ling with interest. I said:

"When Heilong Li and Yang Dizhou see she's gone they'll assume she's talked and they'll change their plans. There's only one thing we can do."

He nodded.

"We have to kill her and have them find the body."

Her eyes went wide like saucers and her skin went very, very pale.

SEVEN

Fortunately she didn't start screaming again. She went very pale and the brigadier hastily explained to her that her death would be faked if she would just give them her fingerprints on some latex pads and a sample of her DNA. She agreed and Ramirez and Jones led her from the room.

When the door closed the brigadier turned to me. His face was hard and his eyes would have made penguins shiver.

"Would you mind explaining this almighty cock-up to me, Bauer? As I recall, it was a fairly simple operation. Go in, get what intelligence you could, kill the guards, kill Heilong Li and Yang Dizhou and get out."

I nodded and sighed.

There is something about officers like Buddy Byrd, who never lose their cool and are always fair and even-handed. When they do get mad, they make you feel like shit.

"I went down the outside, cut a hole in the glass and went in. Believe me, I studied all the alternatives and that was the only viable one.

"The intel I had said May Ling was Yang Dizhou's assistant, not Heilong Li's playmate. There was nothing at all to suggest she was sleeping with Li. But when I got through the window the first thing I found was May Ling sleeping in Li's bed, an empty bottle of champagne, a mirror and a silver box of coke."

The colonel swore under her breath like it had been my incompetence that had May Ling screwing Li and snorting coke. I ignored her.

"Obviously the mission was immediately compromised. At that time of night and as Yang Dizhou's assistant, she should have been with him at the UN. Now, one thing would have been lying in wait for Heilong Li and Yang Dizhou in their suite and taking them out with a suppressed weapon, while everybody else in the place was dead. Quite another was seeing the operation through with a stoned, unconscious woman in the bed, who could wake up at any moment."

The brigadier said, "And I assume that is what happened."

"I decided to take what intel I could, while she slept. Eliminate the two guards on the inside of the suite, but leave the two guys outside so as not to raise the alarm. Then, provided everything went to plan..."

The colonel barked, "You should have aborted immediately!"

I looked at her a moment, then turned back to the brigadier. "Provided everything went to plan, I would gag and bind the girl and wait for Heilong Li and Yang Dizhou to show and take them out with the Maxim 9."

"But?"

"But May Ling woke up while I was going through his desk."

The colonel snapped, "You woke her!"

"She woke!"

"Oh, come on!"

I turned to the brigadier. "Am I being accused of

lying, sir?"

He shook his head. "No, certainly not. Colonel, you are out of order. If this man says he did not wake her that is good enough for me. But even if he did wake her, he was operating in near impossible conditions." To me he said, "What happened next?"

"She started screaming hysterically. I tried to gag her but it was too late. The four guards stormed in."

"The two from inside and the two from outside."

"Yes. They were tough and well trained."

The colonel's face said she didn't believe a word of what I was saying. Her tone of voice agreed. "And you killed all four of them..."

"Yes. I got the combination for the safe from the last one and acquired the USB and the notebook. That was when I called you. I knew I couldn't make the hit in those conditions, but I figured that with May Ling and the information I'd gathered we might be able to set up a second hit."

He nodded. "Yes, you did well."

The colonel's jaw dropped. "Excuse me? He screwed up the damned operation!"

He sighed. "Jane, any operative who had gone in at that time on that day, would have encountered the same problem. Perhaps we should have foreseen that May Ling was a prostitute..."

"Yes!" she snapped. "You should have!"

I blended a frown with a smile and offered it to her. "Based on what? What intel was there to suggest that she was a prostitute sleeping with him?"

She drew breath to tell me it was something we should have assumed, but I cut her short.

"Should we also have allowed for the possibility

that Heilong Li and Yang Dizhou were sleeping with each other? Or with one, some or all of their guards?" She saw too late that she'd backed herself into a corner, but I didn't let up. "Or should we have assumed that just because May Ling was a girl she was also a prostitute? Isn't that a bit sexist?"

The brigadier spoke quietly. "I won't have this infighting on my team. It stops now. The fact is that right or wrong, we did not foresee that May Ling might be in his bed at that time of the evening. Now, the damage is done but we have also acquired a great deal of information which needs to be analyzed before we make any firm decisions. Has anyone got some positive observations or suggestions to make that do *not* involve blaming anybody?"

I bit into a sandwich and said, "Yes."

"Go ahead."

"I fly to Casablanca tomorrow, or as soon as possible, and start looking for this lab. Whatever you get from the documents or from May Ling you can feed to me while I'm there. We need to strike while the iron is hot and before they have a chance to recover. One thing seems obvious to me. They can't move the lab. If he was due to go there, he still has to go there. Maybe he'll be a bit more careful, that wouldn't be hard, but he still has to go. I should be waiting for him there."

"Colonel?"

She thought for a moment and sighed. "I agree. The damage is done, we need to exploit what we have managed to salvage from the operation. So yes, going to Casablanca as soon as possible is the right thing to do."

"Fine." He drained his glass and stood. "Tomorrow may be too soon. I think you need to have a conversation or two with May Ling and with her interrogators before you go. We also need to prepare you a new ID. We'll talk tomorrow over breakfast. I'm off to bed. Good night."

We wished him a good night and he left. I sat chewing and staring at the flames in the fire. Beside them Colonel Jane Harris stood holding her gin and tonic, looking at the ice and the piece of lemon as they bobbed around in circles. Finally she said, "Why are you hostile to me, Mr. Bauer?"

I sighed and took a pull on my beer. "I'm not."

"That's a lie!"

"Again?"

She closed her eyes. "It is obvious. The hostility comes off you in waves."

"Look, I look at you and I see a uniform. I see a colonel. If I disagree with you, I tell you. If you were a guy that would not be a problem. But you, you look at yourself and you see a woman dressed up as a colonel."

"Why you...!"

"Shut up and listen to me. *You* see a woman. I don't. *You* see a woman dressed up as a colonel. And if you say something I disagree with and I tell you so, it's not two guys disagreeing over weapons, tactics or strategy, it's a misogynistic grunt giving a female officer a hard time because she's a woman. So if I have anything against you it's this: when the going gets tough, you play the sex card. You can't do that."

I stuffed the last of my sandwich in my mouth and washed it down with the remains of my beer. She watched me do it without saying anything. When I had finished I stood.

"I have fought side by side with men of every race on earth. Some of them were great soldiers, others were not. All of them got upbraided, dressed down and humiliated at some point, just as I did. None of them ever played the race card, because they were all soldiers and they all understood, you can't turn an operation, where everybody is fighting for their lives, where everyone depends on everybody else for survival, into a self-indulgent, poor-me whinge about your own private insecurities. We all have baggage, Colonel. In the Regiment, we all carried our own. We didn't expect anybody else to carry it for us. You're a colonel. I respect your rank. I don't give a damn whether you're a man or a woman. Good night."

I went out into the checkered hall and climbed the old, mahogany stairs to the second floor. There, at the end of a long corridor in the west wing, I found my room. It was large, with a six-foot-square fireplace and massive oak beams supporting the ceiling. In the far wall, two narrow lancet arch windows overlooked the apple orchards.

I hung my jacket in the freestanding oak wardrobe, stripped and went to the en suite bathroom to shower. After ten minutes under the piping hot water I emerged, toweling my hair, and heard a soft tapping. I wrapped the towel around my waist and opened the door. I wasn't all that surprised to see May Ling leaning on the jamb smiling at me. She had a bottle of single malt in her hand.

"Quite a day, huh?"

"I've had quieter."

"You killed four guys."

"I've had busier, too."

She grinned. "You're a bit of an asshole, aren't you?"

"I've been called worse."

She arched an eyebrow and it made an already attractive face desirable. "You want a drink or not, Harry?"

"Sure. Do you come with the drink?"

She shook her head. "I usually take a little longer than that."

"That's funny. Come on in."

She moved through the door and I heard a footfall outside. I stepped out to look and found myself staring into the colonel's blue eyes. She was maybe seven or eight feet away and stopped in her tracks. A hesitant smile played over her lips. Then she seemed to make up her mind and drew closer until she was barely two feet away.

"Bauer," she said, "I... Harry, I wanted to talk to you."

I raised an eyebrow in an odd echo of the way May Ling had looked at me just seconds earlier. "Can it wait till I'm dressed?"

She glanced at the towel and then into my face, searching for something she wasn't going to find.

"Perhaps I could come inside while you..."

I watched her gaze drift past my shoulder. Her face hardened and her cheeks flushed red. I heard May Ling's voice, an amused, insolent drawl, "You going to be long, Harry?"

The colonel's eyes found mine and locked onto them. Her face was tight with anger and humiliation.

"It can wait, Mr. Bauer, until you are less busy. Good night!"

She turned on her heel and I watched her walk quickly away toward her own room, in the east wing.

I turned and smiled at May Ling. "You going to pour those drinks, or do I have to pour them myself?"

"Do I have to apologize, Mr. Bauer? Have I been a very bad girl?"

I went back into my room and closed the heavy oak door behind me. May Ling removed the towel.

* * *

I rose late, showered and dressed, and went down for breakfast at ten AM. May Ling was still sleeping. I found Brigadier Alexander "Buddy" Byrd and Colonel Jane Harris having coffee on the patio by the east lawn, under a very blue sky. The brigadier smiled amiably as I approached. The colonel looked away at the trees. He said, "Good morning, how did you sleep?"

"Like a log. Now I am hungry." I sat. "I saw O'Connell. He's bringing bacon and eggs. How about you?"

"Superb. I always sleep well." He said it like it was an achievement. It probably was. I poured myself some coffee.

"We have a plan yet?"

The colonel answered without looking at me. "Ramirez and Jones didn't get long with May Ling last night. She was apparently otherwise engaged."

"Busy girl. What about all the other material?"

The brigadier said, "It's being analyzed. I agree with you, Harry. I think we need you on the ground there ASAP. We have an address for Heilong Li's office in Casablanca, and we have an approximate location for the lab in the desert. I want you out there snooping, gathering information and setting up the hit. I want to know if Heilong Li and Yang Dizhou are there. If they are not, I want to know when they arrive, and what they do when they get there. And above all I want them eliminated."

I nodded. A French maid had appeared at my shoulder and set a plate of bacon, eggs, beef sausages, fried mushrooms and toast in front of me, along with a knife, a fork and a linen napkin. She smiled at me and left. I asked:

"What about Gutermann, Goldbloom and Browne?"

"We're tracing them, as far as we know they are still in New York."

I cut into the bacon and skewered it to a piece of toast which I dunked into an egg yolk.

"Have we any idea who he met with yesterday at the UN?"

"Yes, our friends at the Agency sent us the names. But you don't need to know that right now."

I grunted and drank strong black coffee.

"When do I go and who am I?"

"You go tomorrow, JFK to Madrid, Madrid to Casablanca. Your documents will be delivered sometime today. You are Guy Patinkin, a travel writer, working on a series of articles for the *New York Times*. 'The Other Side of Islam.' You're traveling around the Muslim world looking at ordinary Muslims, their ordinary values blah, blah blah."

"Good, that will give me an excuse to nose around without drawing too much attention."

"Exactly, and if you're sympathetic to Muslims, you may actually get a little friendly support."

"Have we any friends out there?"

He nodded, then shrugged. "We have a chap who can fix you up with hardware. But aside from that I don't think you need any help. It should be straightforward, Harry. Locate and destroy."

"What about the lab?"

The colonel answered. "At the moment, the lab is no concern of yours. The only reason the lab should concern you is if Li and Dizhou stay there, rather than in Casablanca. The most likely scenario is that they will stay at a hotel and visit the office and the lab. So there is no need for you to go anywhere near the lab. We don't want a repeat of New York."

I frowned. "We don't want to know what's in there?"

"Yes, we do, but right now that's not your job. Your job is to take out the targets. If that changes I'll let you know."

I glanced at the brigadier and he blinked twice. For a man who never blinks that is a significant message. I nodded.

"Sure, understood."

He said, "As to Gutermann, Goldbloom, Browne and the European delegation, we need to study the intelligence and analyze it. Then I'll let you know."

"What about this hardware supplier? I'm going to need weapons."

"We have a man out there. Make a list of what you need, give it to me this afternoon and I'll pass it on."

"Yeah? What kind of stuff can he get?"

"Most things."

I smiled at my bacon. When an ex-commanding officer of the SAS tells you an arms supplier can get you most things, you know he means the supplier probably can't get you a thermonuclear device. The colonel was watching me with hard eyes and asked:

"What are you likely to need? You're taking out two men. You need a gun."

I mopped the egg off my plate with a piece of bread and smiled at her like I meant it.

"You see, Colonel Harris, that's why you're an administrator, and I'm carrying out the hit."

I wiped my mouth with the white linen napkin,

dropped it beside my plate and stood. I looked at Buddy Byrd and said, “I’ll see you later, sir.”

I crossed the lawn and went in search of the gym.

EIGHT

We touched down in Casablanca at nine AM, I spent twenty minutes collecting my car, which was unfortunately a Mercedes, slung my luggage in the trunk and took the N11 into town. The road, such as it was, snaked through surprisingly green fields, where men and asses labored side by side under an unforgiving sky inhabited by a jealous, unforgiving god. Even in that comparatively lush area, the dust was pervasive and the heat, at that time of the morning, was becoming oppressive.

Casablanca is for me, much like Morocco, a place of constant and consistent disappointment. It is not, and probably never was, the iconic place depicted in the movie with Bogart and Bergman. Today it is just like a thousand other cities across the Mediterranean, with broad streets flanked by identikit apartment blocks five and seven stories high: vast and luxurious for the small elite, cramped and with paper-thin walls for the immense, impoverished populace. Both united in the conviction that somehow, all the ills of their country are caused by the West under the evil leadership of the United States; and that Allah will eventually lead them to a glorious victory over the Great Shaitan, and all their ills will be converted into blessings.

The N11 became the N1 and I followed the *Route D'el Jadida* onto *Boulevard Brahim Roudani*. With the soft top down and the sun and the breeze on my face, I could almost kid myself I was in the south of France. But this place was like Lyon, or Bordeaux, with all the joy and fun sucked out of it. It had the French colonial architecture, the graceful, tree-lined streets, but where the French, the Spanish or the Italians—let's face it, anyone on the north shore of the Mediterranean—would have had the pavements sprawling with terraced cafés and restaurants, the most exciting thing *Brahim Roudani* had to offer was an abundance of cell phone shops and tea shops selling cakes so sticky they were best used for trapping flies.

I eventually came to the *Boulevard Moulay Hassan I*, where I made an illegal U-turn and pulled into the Hyatt Regency and handed my bags and my car over to a couple of kids in burgundy uniforms who looked like they should still be at school.

My room was large and comfortable, and unremarkable. It had a panoramic view of the intersection of the *Boulevard Hassan I* and the *Avenue des FAR*, with the old clock tower overlooking the hooting, honking chaos.

I had known I was going to arrive in the morning, so I'd made a point of sleeping for most of the flight, in order to beat the jet lag. I had a quick shower to wash the long flight out of my muscles, changed into a cream linen suit and stepped out into the bright sunshine: an American abroad, taking a walk in the city.

We had learned from May Ling that Heilong Li and Yang Dizhou had several times mentioned an office in Casablanca from which they conducted the administrative business related to the lab out in the desert. She knew it was close to the port and, as far as she could recall, it was called something like, "Rosh New-ah." Half an hour with a map of the port area of Casablanca produced a small street that connected *Avenue de l'Ambassadeur Ben Aicha* with *Rue de l'Ocean*. It was called *Roche Noir*. It was confusing at first because *Roche Noir* was an arrondissement of Casablanca. Turned out it was a small street as well.

That street was about two miles from the hotel. An enjoyable stroll after so many hours cooped up in airplanes. I wandered down the *Avenue de l'Armee Royale* as far as the *Place Zallaga*, taking photographs like a real tourist. Then I continued up *Avenue Pasteur*, stopped for coffee and very sticky cakes, and moved on to the *Avenue de L'Ambassadeur Ben Aicha*, where I started to become interested in the little side streets on my left, like they were cute and quaint and the sort of thing we didn't have back home.

Finally I came to *Rue Roche Noir* and stood on the corner looking, as though the architecture was special. It wasn't. Like pretty much everything else I had seen that morning, despite the fact that it was sitting on the shores of the Atlantic, it was standard, post '60s Mediterranean apartment blocks and office blocks, and could have been anywhere from Malaga to Haifa.

There wasn't much to see on the street, a bank and a couple of apartment blocks at the near end and a large, walled yard at the far end on the left, with a few shacks and tumbledown buildings contained inside it.

I entered the street and continued my stroll toward the port, scanning the walls for security cameras. The only ones I saw were on the walled yard, angled in from either side above a large, solid steel red gate, big enough to allow a large truck through. It bore the legend, "TRANS ARABIAN TRANSPORTATION CO SL."

The buildings opposite were the kind of thing

you'd expect in a rundown, semi-industrial quarter: a mechanic's garage, a builder's yard, a guy making wooden furniture out of a small, dark shop that smelt richly of pine. I passed them all with interest, and noted at the same time that there were no fresh tire tracks in the abundant dust that had accumulated around the Trans Arabian Transportation Company's gate.

On the *Rue de l'Ocean* I turned left and walked past the north wall of the site. There I saw a smaller door, also red steel, with another CCTV camera angled over it. A glance at the lock told me it was clean and not rusted. A glance at the bottom of the door and the sidewalk told me it was in use and frequently transited.

I turned back and returned to the *Rue Roche Noir*. There was no other building on the street that had the slightest possibility of being Heilong Li's offices in Casablanca. There was the *Banque Populaire* on the corner of *Avenue de l'Ambassadeur Ben Aicha*, which was not a realistic possibility, and aside from that it was either a one-man car mechanic's operation, a one-man carpentry shop, a builders' yard where the office was barely big enough to hold the accounts ledger, a one-man plumbing shop or a hairdresser's.

If Heilong Li had his offices in this street, they were at the Trans Arabian Transport Company.

I made my way back to *Avenue de l'Ambassadeur Ben Aicha* and turned south and west, the way I had come. I pulled out my cell and called the brigadier on a secure number.

"Yes, what have you got?"

"The Trans Arabian Transportation Company, SL."

"A little unoriginal."

"Yeah, that was my first thought too. It's the only

business on the street that is likely to be a cover for their operation. You got anyone here in Casablanca who might know something about them?"

"Maybe, we have a contact in the *Police National Judiciaire*, if we ask nicely they might be willing to help. I'll talk to him and get back to you. Anything else?"

"Yeah, I'm going to go and take a look at the lab. But I don't want to do that till I have my weapons. Did you get the OK from your man yet?"

"Yes. *Allée des Jardines* and *Boulevard Moulay Slimane*, it's on the beach. You'll find a big empty lot, and just beyond it, heading east, a dilapidated villa surrounded by a high wall. He has date palms in his garden. There is an electronic gate with an intercom. I'll give him a call and tell him to expect you today. When you buzz on the intercom you tell him you are looking for M. Gilbert Gordon. He will tell you there is nobody of that name there. You ask him if he knows where you can find him and he will ask you to wait a moment. Then he'll come and open the gate to you."

"Seriously? Will Q be there to give me a laser pen?"

"It's tried and tested, Harry, and it saves lives. No laser pens, only the stuff you asked for."

I made my way back to the hotel. Had another shower, changed my clothes again and had the boy bring my car around. My stomach was telling me it was lunchtime, but my stomach was going to have to wait. I was not going to be able to relax until I had a P226 under my arm and a Fairbairn and Sykes tucked in my boot.

The North African heat had been building through the morning and despite the Atlantic breeze, it felt like a hundred easy in the shade. I put the soft top down, tried to imagine I was driving an Aston Martin, and roared down the *Avenue de l'Armée Royale*. It took me pretty much all the way along the route I had just made on foot, and then beyond. I drove past the *Rue Roche Noir* and kept going until snatches of beach started to appear on my left, broken up by large warehouses and the kind of ugliness only governments who don't give a damn know how to create.

Then there was a small patch, a brief flash, of what was left of old Casablanca, a jumbled hive of white walls, flat roofs, domes, winding, narrow streets and steps, swarming with people and improvised markets. A glimpse of a way of life all but dead, ill-equipped and unable to survive against the relentless, standardizing drive of globalism. A drive that set a universal standard of living by quantifying quality of life.

It soon passed and faded in my rearview mirror. A few minutes after that the warehouses were replaced by houses with walled gardens and lawns, and then it was there: a broad expanse of dirt, a hundred yards square, with the beach beyond. And just past it, the house the brigadier had described.

Palms and eucalyptus trees rose above a white wall maybe eight or ten feet tall, and among the trees, red gabled roofs and a domed copula. I drove past it, made a U-turn and pulled up in front of the house.

The intercom outside his steel gate had an incorporated camera that lit up blue when I pressed the call button. It bleeped for fifteen seconds and then a deep, lazy voice said, "Allah is great. Who is it?"

He said it in English so I figured he already knew it was me.

"I'm looking for Gilbert Gordon."

"I am sorry, you are mistaken. There is no Gilbert

Gordon living here."

"You know where I can find him?"

"Maybe. Wait. You have come by car?"

"Yeah. Why?"

"Maybe you want to put something in the boot. I will open the gate to the carport. You can reverse in."

Twelve or fifteen feet from where I was standing was a large, double gate with spikes on top. It clunked suddenly and started to roll open. I returned to the Merc, put it in reverse and, spinning the wheel to full lock, I backed the car through the double gates, down a path with dense subtropical gardens either side, and into the dark maw of an underground garage.

There, inside, by the door, I could see a heavy, dark, bearded man in slippers who was standing holding a remote control. And as my nose slipped through and my trunk was sucked into the shadows of the garage, the gates started to close again, shutting out the street and the world beyond.

The gates clanged shut and the guy with the beard started to beckon me back farther. Lights flickered and flooded the garage space with stark neon on bare concrete. Against the far wall, maybe twenty or thirty feet away, in my mirror, I could see a Range Rover, a Mercedes AMG GT Coupe, and an Audi A5 Coupe. I figured weapons trading was thriving in North Africa.

The garage door started to roll down, the guy raised his hand to signal me to stop and I killed the engine and climbed out. He approached me with a big grin, a big belly and his big hand stretched out in front of him.

"Good afternoon my dear friend, I am Ali ben Mohammed. It is a great pleasure for me to make your acquaintance. Any friend of Buddy's is a brother to me. I am at your service."

I took his hand and we shook. "Sure. Likewise. Good to meet you. You got something for me, Ali?"

"Oh, yes!" He gave me a look like a kid who's been practicing a magic trick and is about to perform it for his favorite uncle. "I definitely have something very special for you."

He beckoned me over to the Range Rover and I now saw that beside it was a small stack of cartons, some small and some large. As he walked he spoke.

"Buddy and I go back a long way. His father and mine met during Suez. Tragic. Britain had to leave, to make room for America and Israel, what can you do...? Here we have it. Please inspect it with care."

We hunkered down and he handed me a large shoebox. Inside it was a holstered Sig Sauer P226 with an extended magazine. My personal favorite handgun. He grinned at me as I looked it over.

"No such thing as too much ammo. Am I right?"

"You're right."

The next box was larger and contained a Heckler and Koch 416, one of the two best assault rifles you can get. It came with four thirty-round magazines.

"Because," he said, wagging his finger at me, "sometimes you just haven't got the time to refill, but with a hundred and twenty rounds, we must hope God will have blessed you with victory before you are out of ammunition!"

He said this as he handed me another shoebox. This one contained the Fairbairn and Sykes fighting knife, which I immediately strapped to my calf. He was still talking.

"Of course, in Europe and America it is hard to find

weapons such as these. Here I am afraid it is all too easy, if you have the right connections. Here…" He handed me another box, slightly over three foot square. "It is the bow. Take down, as you requested, sixty-five pounds draw weight at thirty-one inches, and twelve wooden arrows, goose fletched with razor-sharp broadheads." He made a face and nodded, shrugging at the same time. "Death is almost instant, and largely painless."

I nodded while I examined the bow and the arrows. They were good and I packed them back in the box.

"And now," he said, "something a little special. This is EPX 1."

I nodded. "I know it."

"It has been around since 2015, but has not been used much. Its sensitivity to impact and friction are about the same as C4 or Semtex, but it has a significantly higher detonation velocity than any other plastic explosive. You wanted twenty pounds of C4; I have taken the liberty of procuring ten kilos of EPX 1. You will use it in the same way, but you will get…," he paused and giggled like a child, "more boom for your bang."

I smiled. "That's good. It's funny. What about detonators?"

"You have here a dozen remote detonators which work with a mobile telephone, a cell phone to you. You have also half a dozen micro trackers which will connect with your laptop or your cell via the internet." He grinned. "It looks, my friend, as though you are going to have a great deal of fun. My heart aches with memories of the many good times I shared with Buddy. If I can help you in any way, you know where to find me."

I thanked him and refused his offer of coffee and a little something a little stronger. We put the goods in the trunk of the Merc and he opened the garage door and the gates for me. I pulled out and turned onto *Avenue Moulay Slimane* again, headed east.

NINE

I didn't go back to the hotel. What I had in the trunk was too hot and I needed to get it somewhere safe fast. Fast meant before anyone noticed me, before I came to anybody's attention. I had been in Casablanca just a few hours. So far only Ali ben Mohammed had actually noticed me. To everybody else I was just another anonymous Westerner in a fancy car. But by this afternoon there would be at least one police officer, in addition to Amin, who would be aware of me and my presence, and the list would steadily grow. As a rule of thumb, it is best not to have cops aware of you when the trunk of your car is packed with lethal ordnance. I needed the Heckler and Koch and the EPX 1 to be safely hidden before any more people started to become aware of my presence.

So I took the A7 south out of Casablanca, stopping on the way to buy a spade, and floored the pedal from the A5 interchange, past the airport, past Berrechid and Settat, where I started to climb into arid highlands, and hit a hundred and ten and a hundred and twenty miles per hour through land that was increasingly made up of dunes of red, yellow gray and black sand. Until I came at last to the exit for Ben Guerir and the R206. I followed that, through harsh, scorching desert for another twenty miles where, after about ten minutes, I came to a broad valley, and within it, the tiny village of Aracha. Aracha was about all there was in it, for as far as the eye could see.

Now I slowed right down. Because now I was searching for the ideal location for my stash. I cruised out of the village, and, after three and a half miles of sand of every shade between black and red, through gray and brown, I came to an intersection. There I stopped, killed the engine and climbed out.

Straight ahead the R206 cut through shimmering, wavering dust with scattered, parched fields, toward El Kalaa des Sraghna. To the right the road was a beaten earth track that ran in a gentle curve through miles of flat, desiccated clay toward a minute hamlet called Commune Lamharra. Here, in this area, May Ling had said she believed they had the lab.

I climbed back in the car and turned down the dirt track, rolling slowly at ten or fifteen miles per hour under the scorching sun, raising a huge dust cloud that lingered and trailed behind me on the still air.

After a little over a mile I came to a smaller track on my left, just wide enough for one vehicle, that wound away into the heat haze. On my right the land rose gently into low dunes, and my gut told me I wasn't going to find anything better than this. I spotted a narrow goat track and slowly inched the Merc up to the crest of the dune, and then gently down the other side. The rise was probably no more than eight or ten feet, but it was enough to conceal me and the car from the road.

I climbed out and stood by the hood, looking around me. I was pretty sure I was hidden from view from all directions. I also noted that between the dunes on my right and left, the ground was flat clay, with small shrubs, and extended featureless for a good distance. The place was ideal.

Here I set about digging a hole in the dry earth,

which is not an easy thing to do. Fortunately it only needed to be about six foot by three, and two and a half feet deep. In it I laid the twenty-two pounds of EXP 1, the HK416 assault rifle, and the extra ammunition. This I covered with dirt and laid a rock on top so I'd be able to locate it later. Then I climbed back in the Merc and slowly ground my way back up the goat trail and down the far side to the road.

There I paused and got out again. There was not a soul in sight, only baking, hot stillness as far as you could see. Even with shades on, the glare was blinding. The land was barren and without features save for the dunes, but I was sure, in my gut and in my bones, that somewhere within two or three miles of where I was, was the lab where Heilong Li was producing the vaccine he was trying to license to Gutermann, Goldbloom and Browne, and the EU Commission. May Ling had identified this area from what she had overheard, and from what I had seen, it felt right.

My choice right then was either to have a prowl around and try and find the place, or go back to the hotel.

I did neither. I pulled my cell from my pocket and sent my location to the brigadier's secure number. Then I called him.

"You take risks," he said. "A secure number is not an invulnerable one. What do you want?"

"I think I'm within a couple of miles of the lab. I've sent you my location. Can you get some satellite imagery? Something a little better than Google Earth. I'm on the P2113. There's a dirt track that runs south of where I am, and my gut is telling me that track leads to the lab."

"OK, I'll see what we can do. Harry?"

"What?"

"Wait for the images. Go out tonight. Or dine at the hotel with an escort. You are a playboy visiting Casablanca. Play the part. I do not want you going off half-cocked. If we can't get the imagery you come back and recon the place yourself by night. Understood? Don't go charging in unprepared."

I nodded as though he could see me. "Yes, sir. I won't."

"We have a lot of intel yet to come. Just take it easy for a bit."

"OK. I hear you."

"Good."

By the time I got back to town, a hot copper sun was hanging low over the ocean. I hadn't eaten yet. I was hungry and thirsty and I had gritty dust clinging to just about every part of my body, except where it had been washed off by the sweat. I badly needed a shower, a beer and a meal.

In my room I stripped off my clothes and stood under a hot shower for fifteen minutes, washing away the desert and the heat of the day. By the time I'd rinsed off the soap and the shampoo and stepped out to towel myself dry, I was beginning to smile at the prospect of a cold beer, a steak sandwich and a couple of martinis.

I'd pulled on my pants, thinking of the brigadier's instructions and planning my evening in my head, when there was a knock at the door. It was the kind of knock that expects to be answered. I grabbed my shirt and called, "Who is it?"

The answer had the kind of authority only French fascists with pencil moustaches know how to command.

"Police Judiciaire!"

I frowned to myself and went and opened the door.

There were two of them. They were both short. They were wearing light linen suits that might have been made in the local bazaar, and they were both looking up at me with an air of generalized resentment. The one directly in front of me had the pencil moustache I had imagined, plus tightly curled black hair and the kind of big, brown eyes that smiled when people got hurt. I figured he was a hundred and thirty pounds fully dressed, in his mid-thirties.

The guy behind him was bigger, fatter and lazier. He also sweated more. His hair was turning salt and pepper over unshaven cheeks. His suit was brown, for some reason only he could explain, and the whites of his eyes were slightly yellow. They were both smirking, like they'd caught me red-handed putting my shirt on, and didn't realize that wasn't a crime. I said:

"What?"

It's not smart to be polite to fascist cops with pencil moustaches.

Moustache said, "You are Guy Patinkin?"

"You came to my door, pal. How about you tell me who you are first?"

"I tell you! We are *Police Judiciaire!*"

"Yeah, and I'm Kate Winslet. Name and badge, pal. Name and badge!"

He said something ugly in French to his partner and they both pulled badges from their breast pockets. I inspected them and handed them back. Moustache was Amin ben Abdullah, and his partner was Mustafa ibn Suleimani. "What do you want?"

"I want answer to my question, *monsieur*, are you or are you not..."

"Yeah, I'm Guy Patinkin. So what?"

He shrugged a couple of times with his eyebrows like he was mad and stood on tiptoes a few times. "*Monsieur*, you may dispense with the bad attitude, we are here at the request of your *Monsieur* Buddy Byrd!"

"Oh," I nodded and stood back, "Sure, come in. Drink?"

They looked at each other as they shuffled in, smirked, shrugged and waved their hands around a bit. "Well, perhaps, in the spirit of international harmony and cooperation, a little whisky..."

I found a couple of miniature Johnny Walkers, dropped them into a couple of tumblers over a couple of rocks and handed them one each. Then I gestured at a couple of chairs by the window. They sat and I turned the chair at my desk to face them and sat. I smiled.

"You can't be too careful these days. You never know who you're dealing with."

It was Amin who did all the talking. "This is a great truth, my brother. We must all be very careful. But Buddy Byrd, he is a man of much respect. He ask, 'Please, tell my friend Mr. Patinkin, what about the Trans Arabian Transport Company?' And I know this is something that I am must to do for him."

"I am very grateful. So what can you tell me about this company?"

"I can tell you, my friend, that we are very interested in this company ourselves!" He leaned forward with one eyebrow raffishly arched. "One thing is clear, the thing that they do, that they do not do at all, is transportation!"

I fought my way through the tangled lianas of his grammar, narrowed my eyes and nodded. "No transportation, huh?"

He raised an urgent finger. "Not none, my friend! Not none...but..." He snapped his fingers. "Very little!" He sat back, smiling and nodding. "And to the trained mind of a detective, this, *this*, is *bizarre*." He pronounced it the French way, like he was gargling the word. "Because, if there is no transport, *alors!* The company it is *faillite...*"

He snapped his fingers at me three times in rapid succession, demanding the word in English. I said, "Bankrupt."

"*Voila!* If it is making transport every day, every week, then *tout normal!* But if he is making the transport," he looked incredulously from one wall to the next, searching for a shred of logic in a mad world, with his hands raised and his shoulders hunched, expostulating, "now in March! Now in September! Now not for a whole year! And then again in March! He must go bankrupt! But he does not!" He fell back in his chair, shaking his head and laughing complacently. "Nooo, *mon ami!* This is not normal. This is *bizarre!* And so, it has my attention!"

I nodded like I thought he was smart. "So when they make a shipment, what size is it, and where does it go?"

He pointed a finger at me. "These are the correct questions! How big are they, and where do they go? *Voila!* How big are they? One container. Never 'ave I seen anything bigger than one container! Where do they go? South! Always south! Mauritania or Algeria. Sometimes they have filed for permission to go through Western Sahara, but that... *C'est pas possible*. So, always they go through Mauritania or Algeria."

"Final destination?"

"*Eh bien*, I can tell you what the manifest say, but the manifest...Ha! *Il peut dire la masse*! He can say the mass, it does not mean it is true. Eh? Where does it go? I don't know!"

"What does the manifest say, apart from mass?"

Mustafa suddenly spoke up. "I 'ave seen Senegal, Cote d'Ivoire, Gabon, Angola, also the Congo, *Namibe... toute l'Afrique du sud-ouest.*"

"All of southwestern Africa?"

Amin nodded. I echoed his nod. It made perfect sense according to what the brigadier had told me.

"What about the company? Who runs it? Who manages it? What about the personnel?"

"Ah!" He wagged his finger in the air again. "The company is owned by another company, International Holdings Incorporated, based in Gibraltar. International Holdings Incorporated is owned in turn by an umbrella company, the Belize Intercontinental Investment Company, which is a subsidiary company of the BHIB, the Beijing and Hong Kong Investment Bank.

"The local manager is Hassan ben Hassani, who was released from prison it makes three years, after serving seven years for murdering an American tourist whom he accused of blaspheming against Allah. Hence the relatively light sentence. He employs an accountant, Musa and Musa, and a number of freelance drivers, all whom have some kind of criminal record."

"OK, cool." I went to the bar and cracked two more Johnny Walker miniatures, then handed them to the two cops. "What about visitors? Do they ever receive visitors?"

It was Mustafa who answered again. "Yes, Dr. Stuart Chen, and Dr. Ling Wei. Both from Hong Kong."

I scrolled through my phone and found pictures of Heilong Li and Yang Dizhou. I showed them to Mustafa.

"This them?"

He nodded and glanced at Amin, who was leaning in to look. Amin echoed the nod. "*Oui*, that," he pointed at Heilong Li, "is Dr. Stuart Chen, and this," he pointed at Yang Dizhou, "is Dr. Ling Wei. They visit two or three times every year."

"Good, and they go out of town a lot, right?"

"Yes, mostly to Marrakech."

"You follow them there?"

He shook his head. "We do not have resources for that. But we gather from conversation, from waiters, from whores…"

"You never followed them?"

"But we know they leave town via the A7, they have told Aicha or Rachida they are going to Marrakech, then we can be sure they are going to Marrakech."

"Aicha and Rachida?"

"*Putes,* prostitutes. They give us information, we allow them to provide an essential service."

He gave a smile you could fry bacon in. I smiled back.

"Sure. One last question and I'll let you gentlemen get back to work. Are you aware of any kind of medical or scientific facility in the desert south east of here, say near the lake, *Barrage al Massira?*"

His face went suddenly hard. I saw Mustafa frown and glance sidelong at his partner.

"What kind of medical or scientific facility, Mr. Patinkin?"

I smiled, like I was surprised at such a stupid question coming from such a smart guy. "I don't know," I said. "That's why I'm asking."

"What makes you think there might be one?"

I sighed. "The men you call Dr. Stuart Chen and Dr.

Ling Wei, are in fact Heilong Li and Yang Dizhou, both eminent Chinese scientists in the field of biochemistry. Now, if they are connected with the Trans Arabian Transportation Company, and they are making occasional trips with large containers down into western Africa, it's a fair bet they are manufacturing some kind of biochemical product up here which they are shipping down there. That would imply some kind of laboratory or similar facility. If the company base is in Casablanca, where would be the ideal place for the lab…?"

I spread my hands. He didn't look convinced, but he looked like he was open to the possibility.

"If you were to know of such a facility, Mr. Patinkin, or to discover such a facility, we would expect to be informed immediately."

"Naturally. You don't need to tell me that, Detective Amin. I am aware that this is a cooperation of goodwill and mutual trust. If I come across any information at all that I believe you believe I should know you would want to know about, you will be the first to know about it. You have my unconditional assurance of that."

He almost winced. "I hope so." He rattled the ice in his glass and stared at it like he didn't believe it was really ice. "Mr. Patinkin, why are you asking about the Trans Arabian Transportation Company? What do you plan to do with this information?"

I smiled. "The only thing I plan to do tonight, Detective Amin, is find a beautiful woman and take her out to dinner, then dancing and then who knows? As to the Trans Arabian Transportation Company, I plan to do exactly nothing. I am here gathering information, nothing more. If they are doing anything they should not be doing, then I will leave it to those who have the appropriate jurisdiction to do something about it." I spread my hands and shrugged, implying that was the only answer I could possibly give. "I do not aim to cause anybody problems, Detective. All we want is to cooperate, and if possible, help."

He stared at me for a moment with the kind of face you'd use to force your kid to eat spinach, then suddenly smiled and spread his arms wide. "Of course! *Of course!* We are all brothers. So, you want a beautiful woman? Elegant, nice, you can take to a restaurant...?"

I was about to tell him no, that I was fine, but something made me stop. He turned to Mustafa and rattled something in French. Mustafa pulled out his cell and started searching for something.

"Here, here! Uff!" He laughed and danced his head around. "Good woman! I cannot afford! Name is Rachida! Good woman, very beautiful!"

He handed me the phone and I copied down the number. Shortly after that I saw them to the door and bid them farewell, promising to stay in touch. As I closed the door behind them I was thinking that Rachida was one of the two names they had mentioned as the girls who informed them about Heilong Li and Yang Dizhou. I dialed the number and it rang three times before a dark chocolate voice said, "*Oui*?"

"Is this Rachida? Do you speak English?"

"I can speak English if you want. Do you want?"

"I do want. Detective Amin ben Abdullah gave me your number, and I was wondering whether you would like to have dinner with me."

"That depends where you are going to eat."

"Where would you like to eat?"

"You are American?"

"I am."

"Then there is only one place we can go."

I raised an eyebrow. "Where's that, hell?"

She laughed and it was a nice sound. "No, silly. To Rick's Café. An American in Casablanca must go to Rick's Café."

TEN

Casablanca was not shot in Casablanca, it was shot on the Warner Bros. lot in Hollywood, so Rick's Café was not the actual Rick's Café, but it was close enough to get you in the mood to start talking with a lisp and calling dames "shweertheart." And Rachida was about as similar to Ingrid Bergman as Cassius Clay was like Rudolf Nureyev. In heels, she was half an inch shy of six foot. Her skin was on the brown side of black and her hair was an unashamedly retro, Afro globe of curls that made you want to bury your fingers in it and do all kinds of things well brought-up boys don't do. But she was beautiful and glamorous and I was open to calling her "shweetheart" before the night was out.

She refused the offer to pick her up and met me in the cocktail bar at the hotel. She was dressed in a silver satin number that was low cut to good effect at the front, and plain outrageous at the back. She wore just enough makeup to highlight eyes that were vast and almost black, and lips that were too well shaped and too sensual ever to be described. To say she was the most beautiful woman I had ever seen would be trite. She was the most stunning specimen of womanhood I could ever imagine encountering. She was as hot as a Carolina Reaper in wasabi sauce.

Hyperbole? Pal, you didn't see her.

I found her sitting on a stool at the bar sipping a

Manhattan. She regarded me as I approached, with slow, intelligent, amused eyes while she bit into a maraschino cherry.

"Rachida?"

"Guy Patinkin, and dressed in a black evening suit. You know how tired I get of seeing men in cream tuxedos?"

"It must be exhausting. Do you also get tired of men telling you you're stunning?" Before she could answer, I told the barman, "A Macallan, double, straight up."

She held my eye a moment, smiling, then said, "Never."

The barman poured my whisky. I sipped it and took some peanuts and popped them in my mouth.

"I feel duty bound," I said, "to tell you that I had ulterior motives in inviting you to dinner."

"I don't know whether to be worried or relieved. What were your motives?"

"You know Dr. Stuart Chen."

"You ever heard of client confidentiality?"

"Are you a lawyer?"

"No, Mr. Patinkin. But do you know the difference between a lawyer and a high-class whore?"

"I'm hoping you're going to tell me."

She winked. "Lawyers are mainly men." She sipped her drink. "There are only two things on this planet that are more expensive than a woman's body."

"You're an endless source of fascinating facts, Rachida."

"Do you want to know what they are? I think you should."

"Hit me."

"That's extra."

"Tell me, then."

"Violence and information." She set her glass on the bar and raised an eyebrow at me. "Right now, as far as you are concerned, I have a monopoly on two out of three. If you want either, you're going to have to pay. Are you willing and able to pay, Mr. Patinkin?"

I nodded several times. "Oh yes. Yes, I am both willing and able."

She grinned with lots of teeth. "We have client confidentiality, Guy, but, like lawyers, absolutely no loyalty. Show me your money, and ask me your questions."

I studied her a moment while I sipped my drink. "Are we in a hurry?"

"I'm not. Are you?"

"Never. Time is all we have, it's best spent wisely."

It was a balmy night, freshened by a sea breeze touched by the silver light of a fat, translucent moon. We could have walked, and I would have enjoyed taking a detour to watch the dark green ocean with its luminous foam from the marina. But dressed the way she was dressed, looking the way she looked, I wasn't about to risk letting her loose.

I had phoned ahead for them to hold a table in the gallery, and we took a cab. Our table was ready when we got there and we climbed the stairs to the galleried landing where our table was set overlooking the central patio. There was a lot of white linen and polished crystal, there were Moroccan wall lamps, chandeliers and potted palms, and the music was, unsurprisingly, big bands of the 1940s. I enjoyed it and Rachida fit right in with the décor—at least that was what most of the men at Rick's Café seemed to think.

She ordered another Manhattan and I had a martini dry. We sipped in silence and studied the menu while Billie Holiday worried about that old devil called love. When the waiter returned Rachida ordered the *escalope de foie gras pommes Lorraine*, and I ordered a goats' cheese salad with figs. For her main she ordered *magret de canard avec chutney de fruits* and I had the T-bone steak. The waiter recommended a bottle of ice cold white *Muga* for the *foie gras* and the goats' cheese, and *Marques de Riscal* for the duck and the steak. I figured he probably knew what he was talking about.

The orders out of the way, we took a moment to stare at each other over our drinks to the sound of Ella saying she'd take Manhattan, the Bronx and Staten Island too.

"You're an intelligent woman," I said after a while. She didn't look pleased. She looked pissed but made an effort to hide it.

"Am I supposed to be pleased that the great white warrior thinks I am smart?"

I went cold inside. "Warrior?"

"That's what you focus on? I found your comment patronizing..."

"I was thinking aloud. And I'll tell you what I was thinking in a moment. First explain to me why you called me a warrior."

She gave her head a small shake and sighed. "We are the buffer here between the peace, abundance and complacency of the northwest, which starts at Gibraltar and Cadiz, and the madness and anarchy of Africa, which starts at the western Sahara. Our principal industry, in this desert, is tourism, because we do not impose Islam upon our visitors, and because we peddle a particular style of cheap, sexual tourism you don't get in Miami and the Costa del Sol. So we get two main types of tourists here. The assholes from Spain who come to buy grifa and hashish, and the mercenaries from Africa who come north on leave to spend their hard-earned money on obedient, chocolate-skinned girls who will do just about anything for a dollar."

"And that's what you think I am?"

"I recognize a mercenary when I see one."

"Clearly you don't." I smiled. "You recognize a soldier and you mistake him for a mercenary. I was in the Army, now I write articles for the *New York Times*, and, with a bit of luck, books."

She wasn't sure but opted for caution. "It makes no difference to me, Guy. You asked why I called you a warrior. I called you a warrior because I recognized a soldier."

I drained my glass and set it down on the table. "Which confirms what I was thinking. When I said you were intelligent, I was not patronizing you. I was thinking that Amin and Mustafa, and Dr. Stuart Chen, all had you down as a dumb broad..."

"A what now...?"

"Archaic American English from about the time this movie was made..."

"I know what a dumb broad is, Guy. I'm just having trouble believing anybody still says that."

"But you're about as dumb as you are short, fat and ugly."

"See, now that is not patronizing."

"And you must have picked up a lot from hearing Stuart Chen and Ling Wei talk."

"I don't speak Chinese."

"Don't bullshit me, Rachida. I am sure they talk among themselves in Chinese, but to their clients they speak in English. And those were the times when you and Aicha would have been there."

She nodded. "Yes."

"And there must have been pillow talk, too."

"Some."

I smiled. "I want it all."

"I am not a dumb broad, Guy. Nor am I a crazy dame. I am an intelligent professional, raised in the ghettos of Casablanca, forced into this profession at eleven years of age. I learnt the hard way how to take care of myself, and that the only person in the world who ever will take care of me, is me."

"Is that where you learnt to speak perfect English, in the ghettos of Casablanca?"

The waiters arrived with an ice bucket and a bottle of white *Muga*, Rachida's pate and my goats' cheese salad. They went away and we started eating. As she spread *foie gras* on a small piece of toast she said, "No."

I looked up and she went on.

"I learnt to speak English in England. I moved there when I was sixteen, with an English sugar daddy. That was the closest I ever came to loving a man, and I didn't love him, believe me. But I liked him and I was grateful to him. He set me up in an apartment on Bayswater Road, near Notting Hill. He paid for me to learn to drive, he bought me a Mini, he paid for a couple of private tutors to teach me English and English literature, so that he could take me to fancy parties and I would not let him down. I was there for seven years. I returned to Casablanca...," she thought for a moment, "about five or six years ago."

"So why'd you come back?"

"He died. He had a stroke and died. He left me a few

thousand pounds in his will." She laughed. It was a beautiful sound. "I know what you're thinking. I could have gone to university, got a degree, built up a career..."

"So?"

"Do you know how often I have sex?"

"You'd be surprised if I said yes, wouldn't you? Of course not. I have no idea. Often?"

"About four times a year. That's about all I need. And that is with men of my choice. I make a lot of money —and I do mean a *lot* of money—from keeping company and, above all, knowing how to listen. I choose my clients, and the clients I choose can no longer get it up. So, I do the same work as a psychoanalyst, with a fraction of the training and a fraction of the skill, with none of the professional responsibilities or restrictions, and for four or five times the fee." She gave a small shrug. "The best of it is, I never had to go to college or train. So why the hell would I want to go to university in London, live in digs, share a fridge with drunken, disgusting students, working my ass off to pass exams, when I could be dining at the Savoy and living in an apartment in one of the best neighborhoods in the city?"

"No reason, but you neatly avoided answering the question. What made you come back to Casablanca?"

She shrugged. "My clients pay London and New York prices, I pay Moroccan prices. I live like a queen. And that, by the way, is my point."

"You expect me to pay London and New York prices for the information I want from you?"

She chewed and swallowed while watching me, then sipped cold white wine, still watching me. When she put down the glass she said, "That's right."

"So how much do you want for everything you

learned about Dr. Stuart Chen and Ling Wei?"

She laughed again. "I still haven't decided how much you're willing to pay."

"Well, that has to depend on how useful it is." We ate in silence for a while. When I had finished I wiped my mouth and dropped the napkin beside my plate. "I'll give you five grand. Tell me half. If it's good I'll want the other half, and I'll pay you another five grand for it."

She shook her head. "No." She laughed, leaning back in her chair with her head thrown back. "No way. You know damned well I'll save the best for last. Five for starters, and if what I give you is good, ten for the rest. You know that was what you expected to pay anyway."

"How do I know the rest will be any good?"

She leaned forward and her eyes were intense, black coals. "How do *I* know you won't kill me if it isn't?" I didn't say anything, and after a moment she went on. "Don't think I can't see it in your eyes. I have seen it before, and I am seeing it now. Fifteen grand is cheap at the price, but I am playing it safe, soldier."

I nodded. "Done." I reached in my pocket and pulled out my wallet. "I have two grand on me. Can we talk? Come back to the hotel with me after dinner and I'll give you the rest."

She shook her head again and smiled. "Give me everything when we get to the hotel. I believe you. What do you want to know?"

I put my wallet away and thought a moment while the waiters came and took away our plates and glasses, and replaced them with Rachida's duck and my T-bone. The wine waiter gave me a glass to taste, I acted like I knew what I was doing, he poured the wine and left us. I watched Rachida poke some duck in her mouth and asked her:

"What was Dr. Stuart Chen shipping in his trucks?"

She took a deep breath and let it out through her nose.

"I'm going to give you an answer you don't want to hear. Then I'm going to tell you something more." She sipped her wine and carefully set down the glass like it made a difference where she put it. "I don't know what he's shipping. They never discussed that in front of me. Any time they talked about what it was, they talked in Chinese."

"That's the part I wasn't going to like, right?"

I poked a piece of beef in my mouth and chewed, watching her.

"Yeah, but I *can* tell you that each shipment went to a different place, and that each one progressed south..."

I frowned. "What does that mean?"

"The first went across Mauritania to Senegal. The next, a few months later, went, again across Mauritania, to Cote d'Ivoire. A year later it went via Algeria to Cameroon, and three months after that to the Congo..."

"So each shipment went a little farther south."

"That's right. Now, the thing is, a lot of the girls I have worked with in the past, and many of the girls I know now, come from these very remote countries, and a couple of them began to compare notes and they noticed a pattern. Wherever Dr. Chen sent a shipment, within a month or two there was some kind of outbreak in a remote area, barely reported in the press, and several hundred people died." She shrugged. "At first I put it down to paranoia and a Third World predisposition to explain away all their ills with conspiracy theories. But eventually I saw that it was true. Wherever the shipment went, there was some kind of outbreak."

I scratched my chin. "Amin said he didn't know the final destinations of the shipments. How come you didn't tell him?"

"I keep Amin sweet because he can be useful. But he doesn't pay, so he gets the sweepings."

"Right." I cut into the meat, watched the blood ooze onto the plate and mix with the oil, and put another slice in my mouth. It was tender and succulent. "So your reading was that he was using these remote, impoverished countries as a kind of real-world lab."

She shrugged. "I didn't intellectualize it that much, Guy. But I guess you could put it that way."

"So, if that's right, the chemicals he was experimenting with must have come from Morocco."

"You're asking me to speculate." She said it with her mouth full, talking around the food.

"No." I shook my head. "I'm asking you if you ever heard him talk about a factory, a lab, any kind of facility of that sort in Morocco."

She thought for a long time, then shook her head, pulling down the corners of her mouth. "No."

"You're lying."

"I am? How so?"

She didn't look fazed but she wouldn't meet my eye. I smiled.

"It was a trick question, Rachida, and there will be more. I happen to know for a fact that he did talk about the place where they manufactured the stuff. And now I am real curious about why you didn't want to tell me about it."

She laid down her knife and fork. "Does this mean I don't get paid?"

"I'm undecided. It all depends on how you respond to this first embarrassing situation. What are you going to do? Are you going to redeem yourself, or dig yourself deeper into the hole?"

"Who are you, Mr. Patinkin?"

"I told you, I'm a writer. I also told you I used to be in the Army. Maybe you assumed I was some kind of grunt, but I never told you what regiment I was in, or what rank I attained."

"You're a writer..."

"An investigative journalist. I'm writing a piece for the *New York Times*, but that's just a cover. What I am really working on is an exposé of Chinese-sponsored criminals like Stuart Chen."

"And here and there you plant a question to which you already know the answer, to see if I am lying to you."

I leered at her as I pushed a chunk of meat into my mouth.

"I've conducted a few interrogations on characters a lot tougher than you."

"Is that what this is, an interrogation?"

"Would I have to pay extra for that?"

She shook her head. She wasn't smiling. "I don't play that kind of game."

I drained my glass, then refilled hers and mine.

"I suggest you stop playing any kind of game, Rachida. I made you a generous offer, which you accepted. Quit trying to play me and give me the goods I'm paying for. You've got yourself into a very dangerous game, and believe me, you are much better off having me on your side than against you."

"Is that a threat?"

"Yes. Now quit stalling and answer my question.

What did he say about the lab or factory here in Morocco?"

She pushed her duck around with her fork for a bit, then flopped back in her chair.

"I heard him talk to several people about a plant in the desert, just north of a town called Lamharra. Access was via the A7, but then you had to turn east into the desert, at Ben Guerir. As far as its location goes, that is the best I can do. As to what they were making there, they always spoke about a vaccine."

"A vaccine against what?"

"A plague."

"A plague? What kind of plague?"

She shrugged and shook her head. "One that he was convinced was coming."

ELEVEN

We'd finished the main course, and the last of the *Marques de Riscal* with a plate of goats' cheese. Now she was holding a large balloon of cognac and I was sipping a glass of The Macallan and trying not to think about how good she looked by lamplight.

"You said they had clients who used to come and see them. Where was that? Did they stay at an apartment? How come you spent so much time with them?"

"Dr. Chen and Dr. Wei have always rented a suite at the Casa Diamond. When they were in town they always called me and Aicha. Sometimes they called a couple of other girls too. They'd be in town for a week, maybe ten days, and we would stay with them for that period. They pay serious money."

"And their clients would come to the suite to see them?"

"Mostly, yes. Sometimes they'd go out to the plant."

"But you never accompanied them there?"

"Is that a trick question, Guy? I already told you I don't know exactly where it is."

"Can you remember the names of any of these guys? Were they only ever men?"

She thought for a while, with her bottom lip stuck out.

"Yeah, there was a woman, about a year ago,

blonde, well-dressed, smart. She didn't look Jewish, not the stereotype, but she had a Jewish name...Goldberg? It wasn't Cohen or a 'stein' name."

"Goldbloom."

She nodded, "Yeah, Goldbloom. That's right, and the guy was elegant, a gentleman, also smart, but serious and reserved. His name was Browne. He wined them and dined them for a week, and one day they went to the plant."

"There was no third guy with them?"

"No." She shook her head again. "More recently there was a group from the European Commission, or a department of the European Commission..." She paused to think, looking up at the ceiling. "The European External Action Service. There were four of them: Padraig O'Hanlon, Hans Grinder, Ruud van Dreiver and Michelle des Jardins."

"You have a good memory."

"No. For people who might be useful, I have an exceptional memory."

"And you thought these people might be useful?"

"People who are rich, or wield a lot of power, are always useful, Guy. You know that."

"So when will Stuart Chen be back in town?"

She stuck out her lip again and gave a small, elegant shrug. "I don't know." She saw the skepticism on my face and added, "He hasn't been in touch."

"Will you tell me if he does?"

She considered her cognac for a while, tipping the balloon this way and that. Her brows contracted slightly and she spoke to the glass. "I'm having trouble seeing how that would benefit me." She raised her eyes to meet mine. "What you're paying me for this information is what this man might spend on dinner. I'm sorry, I like you, for some reason I can't quite explain, but you are not in the same league."

I allowed a smile to touch the side of my face. "You don't know what league I'm in."

She giggled at her cognac, then threw back her head and gave a surprisingly delicate, feminine laugh. When she'd finished she tilted her head on one side and smiled. There was a hint of genuine compassion in it.

"Oh, please," she said, then gestured at me with her open left hand. "Nice suit, well cut, but off the peg, not bespoke. The shoes, two hundred dollars? Two fifty tops. You're staying at the Hyatt, a nice hotel, but it's *not* the Casa Diamond Suites. You drive a Mercedes. Nice car, but it's not a Ferrari, a Bentley or an Aston Martin. So you are good at what you do, you make money from it, but you are not big league. Not even fringes of." She shrugged. "Sorry."

I was still smiling. "Take it easy, you'll hurt my feelings."

"You're a soldier. You don't have feelings."

"So what would it take for you to tell me when you next hear from Chen?"

She thought for a long time, like she was wrestling in some internal conflict. Finally she frowned again and narrowed her eyes at me. "Why are you so interested in him, really?"

"I told you. I'm writing a book."

She sighed, gave a humorless smile and shook her head at her drink.

"When I lived in London with…with my sugar daddy. I met a lot of artists. He moved in a very artsy circle. And you know one of the first things I noticed?"

"Tell me."

"Artists talk all the time about images, colors and textures. Musicians talk all the time about sound, texture and rhythm. Poets and philosophers talk all the time about concepts, and especially meaning." She paused to look at me. I knew what she was going to say and I was struggling for an answer. She said it: "And writers are obsessed with words. You? You're blunt, direct, hungry for information, but you don't give a damn about words. I don't know what you are, but I know for sure you're not a writer."

I laughed. "What about journalists, what are they obsessed with?"

She wagged a finger at me. "Good try. But I'll tell you what journalists are obsessed with: quoting. They are always quoting politicians, celebrities, statistics. They are always showing off their knowledge, showing off how much they know about this man, that woman and the other company or organization. In all the time we have been together you have not quoted a single thing. In fact, all you have done is bribe me, try to seduce me and subtly threaten me. You, Mr. Patinkin, if that is your name, are a soldier."

"That is no secret. I already told you that."

She shook her head. "No, you said you *were* a soldier. I say you still are a soldier. I'll tell you what it would take for me to tell you if Dr. Stuart Chen gets in touch with me again."

"What?"

"I want to know why you want him, and why you're after him."

I raised my hand and called the waiter. When he came over I asked for the bill and told him to call me a cab. Rachida looked a little surprised, watched the waiter leave and shifted her gaze to me.

"Unilateral decision? Do I get a say?"

"No. We go back to the hotel. I give you your money, and we are done here."

"Have I offended you by calling you a soldier? I didn't think journalists were that sensitive."

I shrugged. "I just don't believe you have any more to tell me. You have carefully shifted the conversation from answering my questions to asking questions of your own. That tells me you have nothing left."

"Wow. That's cold."

I chuckled. "This from the woman whose personal relationships are predicated on who provides the most in terms of power and money."

"Come on, Guy!" She sat swirling her cognac a moment, without looking at me. "You read people as well as I do, and you know that's a front." She glanced at me. "A protective shield. I just don't want to hand over a man who has been good to me to some hired gun who's going to shoot him just to get his hands on some formula."

"You read too many spy novels."

The waiter arrived with the bill. I paid by card and left a fifty-dirham tip, then stood. Rachida looked like she was annoyed, but trying to hide it. The waiter brought her coat and helped her on with it, and as we went down the stairs she said, "I have to admit," and there was ice in her words, "This has never happened to me before. I doubt I'll ever forget this date."

"I'm flattered. I'm glad I wasn't like all the rest. But I told you, Rachida. I *was* a soldier, now I am doing investigative journalism, using a set of skills few other people have. You don't want to believe me, that's your problem, not mine."

We stepped out into the night. The moon had slipped below the horizon, leaving the once silver ocean black and deadly. There was a *Grand Taxi* waiting, a Mercedes-Benz W126, its white paint tinted amber by the lamps outside the restaurant entrance. I opened the door, she climbed in and I went around the other side to get in next to her.

To the driver I said, "Hyatt Regency." He grunted something and took off. To Rachida I said, "I think you ran out of information. I don't believe you know any more than you already told me."

"All right, Guy, you made your point. I won't argue." She was quiet a moment, watching me as orange light and shadows slid over her face, and the Moroccan streets slipped past outside. Suddenly she said, "So who were you with, the Marines? The SEALs?"

Some guys in the Regiment keep it a secret. Some guys get "lent out" to friendly governments and others do a bit of moonlighting, so it pays to keep their identity quiet. We never advertise who we are, we never wear tattoos with "Who Dares Wins" woven around a dagger. That would be stupid. But neither have I ever felt the need to keep my years with the SAS a secret. I don't tell everybody I meet, but I don't hide it, either.

"I was with the British Special Air Service for eight years."

Her mouth formed a silent "O" and she nodded once slowly, like everything made sense now. I frowned.

"That mean something to you?"

"No, not really. Just, while I was in London, you read a lot about them in the press, you heard about them on TV... You know, they're kind of legendary over there.

It's a tough gig, I know that. It sort of explains..."

She trailed off and gestured at me with her open hand.

"Yeah? Well, like all legends, a lot of it is exaggerated and overstated, but a lot of it also falls well short of the truth."

"I can imagine. So what happened? Why'd you leave. You're young."

"It's a long story." I smiled at her. Her eyes looked huge in the close darkness of the cab. "And I don't need a psychoanalyst, especially one with no training."

Her smile held a trace of sadness. It might have been genuine. "That was uncalled for." I didn't answer. "And besides, are you sure it's true? Maybe that's exactly what you need." She gave a giggle that was kind of naughty. "I mean, I'm sure you have no trouble getting it up, but you look to me like a man who could use a cuddle and a talk."

I shook my head.

"Come on, Rachida. Don't play games with me. Five grand for a night's work isn't bad, even by your standards. I'll pay you what I owe you, then we each go our own way."

She looked away, watched the almost empty streets drift by in the night. After a minute she said, "I guess I deserve that."

I didn't answer. We turned off the *Avenue de l'Armée Royale* and pulled into the hotel forecourt where a young man in a uniform came down to open the door for Rachida. I paid the driver and he drove away, muttering something in French that involved my mother, a camel and a number of other animals. Maybe I should have tipped him more.

I climbed the stairs with my wallet still in hand,

and Rachida linked her arm through mine. I said, "I think there's an ATM in the lobby." She turned to me and there was a little bit of ice and a little bit of rage in her eyes.

"Do you mind," she said, "not paying me off in the lobby, like a common whore? I haven't serviced you sexually, and in fact all you have done is take me out to dinner and pick my brains. I don't think there is any need to insult me and humiliate me publicly."

"Sure." We crossed the lobby to the elevators, where we stepped in and I punched the button for my floor. Then I turned to face her. It was hard to get past how stunning she was to look at.

"You came on pretty strong at the start of the evening, Rachida. You went out of your way to underscore that this was all about money. Now suddenly you're changing your tune. What's going on?"

She didn't answer. The elevator eased to a stop and she followed me to my door. I opened it and she went in. I followed and closed the door behind me. I didn't look at her. I went to the safe in my wardrobe, opened it and pulled out five thousand dollars. When I turned to give it to her, she was sitting on the edge of the bed, watching me. I held up the money.

"Five grand, as agreed. I don't believe you have anything else to give me. I hope this won't be a problem."

"It won't be a problem, Guy. Why are you doing this?"

"Doing what, exactly, Rachida? You don't want the money now?"

"You know what I mean. We were having a nice time, getting to know each other, enjoying a drink. Then suddenly you couldn't get away fast enough. We were having fun, laughing, flirting a little... Then you're all uptight, paying the bill, get a cab, on your feet. What happened?"

"What are you doing, Rachida? You wanted to keep this on a business footing."

"Do you have to be so..." She waved her hands at me. "...cold and distant and *unfriendly?*"

"Cold and distant? You want us to be best friends now? What the hell has got into you?"

She shrugged. "I guess I'm not used to rejection."

I laughed, put the money in an envelope and handed it to her. She stared at it a moment before taking it.

"You're a very attractive woman, Rachida. You're intelligent and skilled too. You don't need my validation. You made a damn sight more money tonight than I did. And that's how we measure success, right?"

"Is it? I suppose so." She still wouldn't look at me. I said, "You want a nightcap?"

Now she looked up. "Sure. As long as I'm not keeping you from something more important."

I gave a private laugh and poured her a cognac. As I handed that to her I said, "If it's any consolation, I am not rejecting you. You must know already I find you very attractive. In fact..." I turned back to the bar and poured myself a whisky. "In a sense," I went on, "it's you who are rejecting me." She looked surprised and I shrugged. "You said it yourself. I can't afford you. And besides, apart from a couple of adolescent experiments, I don't pay for my women. It's a matter of self-respect."

"That's supposed to make me feel better?"

"You said you weren't used to rejection. I'm not rejecting you."

She looked away. Then her eyes travelled around

the room. She said, “Have you got some music here? We could listen to some music.”

She leaned back, stretched across the bed and grabbed the remote control from the bedside table. I stood sipping and watched her lie back against the pillows and scroll through the channels on the TV till she found some jazz.

She watched me back for a while, in silence, then said, “I’m getting a headache, turn down the lights, will you?”

I went and turned them down, then leaned against the wall. “What are you doing?” I asked again.

“Why do I have to be doing something? I told you I don’t like rejection. Can’t I just react like a normal woman? Can’t I just be Rachida, reacting to an attractive man?” Her voice was suddenly slightly slurred. “Do you know how attractive you are?”

“No.”

“Well you are.”

She swung her legs off the bed and she was like a sinuous silver snake. Then she moved around the bed until she was standing in front of me, an inch away, and I could smell the expensive cognac on her breath. Her black eyes were huge, her lips were full and I could feel the warmth of her body. I wanted badly to hold her.

“I told you,” she whispered, “three or four times a year, I need a man. This is one of those times. Help me to get this dress off, will you?”

I knew it was a really bad idea. But then, I told myself, some of the best ideas are. And besides, life is too damn short.

TWELVE

At four AM she rose from the bed, like a dark snake, with the silver light of the nighttime city touching her breasts and her legs in the shadows. I watched her move to the window and sit, coiled in the chair, and stare out at the night. At six she rose from the chair, a tall, slender Afro silhouette against a red sky, where the sun was burning night from the heavens. I watched her cross to the bathroom, and I heard the hiss of the shower.

I swung out of bed and poked my head around the door. I could see her dark, misted form through the glass of the cubicle, arched under the stream of water. I went to her bedside table and rifled through her purse till I found her driver's license. Her name was Rachida Ait. I picked up my phone, photographed it, sent the pictures to the brigadier along with a list of four names: Padraig O'Hanlon, Hans Grinder, Ruud van Dreiver and Michelle des Jardins. Then I leaned against the windowsill where I could see the open bathroom door and called him. He answered immediately.

"Yes. Who is this woman, and who are these names?"

"Have your backroom boys got anything for me?"

"I gather you are not alone."

"I agree."

"But you can talk right now, I imagine, or you

wouldn't have called."

"This would be a more productive way to move forward."

"Me asking and you answering monosyllabically?"

"Yup."

"Are you under duress or being threatened?"

I smiled. "No, not really."

"You're not giving me a lot to go on, Harry. Did you pick up this woman last night?"

"Yes, she came with a recommendation, but I was surprised at how communicative he was."

"OK, one thing at a time. Recommendation from whom?"

"OK, I see that, sure. You said you were going to talk to some guy for me, remember?"

"In the police?"

"Hell, you're the editor! First person singular and a preposition. Try that for size."

"Am...in. Amin?"

"Yup. You're quick. That's good."

"And he recommended this woman?"

"In a manner of speaking. But I'm telling you, Ed, I need more background. Right now I am in a blind alley, the desert location is looking like a dead end and I am on the brink of jacking in the whole project."

"Are you serious?"

"No, not at all, but get this. This is what I need you to focus on, right?"

"Yes."

"The guy in the picture..."

"The woman in the photographs you sent me?"

"Precisely, that guy has intimate, personal knowledge of the subject. He did a PhD or something."

"Are you telling me she lived with Heilong Li?"

"On and off, several times."

"Who is she?"

"That's what I'd like to know, Ed."

"Why do you keep calling me Ed?"

I growled, "Because it's your job!"

"Oh. I see, yes. I'll run her through face recognition and a couple of databases, see if she pops up anywhere. What about these names? Who are they?"

The hiss of the water in the bathroom died away. I said quickly, "From the European Union's External Action Service, allegedly."

"Oh, that's interesting. Has she been able to provide you with anything else?"

"Like hell. The account is dry. Which, you know, makes me wonder. And Ed, I am going to need you to pull your finger out and help me out here. It's been an expensive few days for me, pal, and I need some results."

"I'll have some photographs for you this morning, and I am having a meeting with Colonel Harris and our analysts at ten. I told you to relax and be a playboy for a few hours."

"I did." I glanced at Rachida, who had stepped out of the bathroom wrapped in a towel. I smiled at her and said absently, "It was fun. I have to go. And, Ed, get that damned contract sorted for me, will you? I'm hemorrhaging money here. Make it happen, pal."

I hung up without waiting for an answer. She dropped the towel and started pulling on her panties. I said, "What are your plans?"

"Plans?" She held her dress by the sleeves and stepped into it, then shrugged the sleeves over her shoulders. "I'm not sure what you mean."

"You're going home?"

She stood in front of the mirror, running her fingers through her wild curls. "Of course." She glanced at me and grinned. "It was fun, Guy, but I have to get back to my life."

"What about Dr. Chen and Ling Wei?" She made a question with her face, took her lipstick from her bag and started doing her face. I said, "Will you let me know when they get in touch?"

She sighed and pushed her lips in and out. Then started applying pale blue shadow to her eyelids. "I don't know, Guy. I'll think about it and let you know."

"Don't call me, I'll call you?"

She put her makeup away in her purse and came around the bed to where I was still leaning naked against the windowsill. She gave me a kiss on the mouth and whispered in my ear, "Another life, another world, maybe..."

Then she was half-running across the room in her heels. She pulled open the door, closed it with a "clack!" and she was gone, leaving a vacuum of silence behind her.

I stood a while, looking at the closed door, thinking, running things over in my mind. Then I went and showered for twenty minutes in piping hot and freezing cold water. Toweled myself dry and dressed in jeans and boots. After which, I went down for a breakfast of rye toast and strong black coffee.

With breakfast done, I went to the concierge and said, "I want to hire a plane."

"A plane, *monsieur*?"

"Yeah, a small Cessna or something. I have a license. Sometimes I like to take up a kite. The views along the coast must be spectacular...."

"Indeed. A kite, *monsieur*?"

"Yeah, a kite, a plane. It's a hobby. I like to take up a plane sometimes and fly around. I have insurance, I have a license. If there's a club in Casablanca..."

"I will make inquiries, *monsieur*, and let you know as soon as I have found somewhere."

I slipped him a twenty and thanked him. Then I returned to my room where I opened my email and found an encrypted file with satellite pictures of the desert around Lamharra. They weren't great.

The first couple showed a building, or a complex of buildings, roughly a mile and a half north of the P2108, about four and a half miles east of Commune Lamharra. The next couple of pictures were closer in, magnified, but they were grainy and the detail was blurred. They showed an L-shaped building, probably four stories high, with the long section running west to east, and a fat "foot" section running from north to south. Contained in the angle of the "L" was a concrete parking lot. Across the lot, to the east of the main building, there was a long, low, blue nave or hangar with a red, gabled roof; and some fifty yards or so to the south, there were what looked like four large tanks or reservoirs, sixty to seventy feet across and maybe eighty to a hundred feet long, lying in a straight line and filled with a deep, green liquid which might have been water. I could see vehicles, mainly Jeeps and Land Rovers, but no people.

The third set of two photos showed close-ups of the building. The quality was better but still not good. There was the blurred image of a person crossing the parking lot toward the outbuilding, but it was impossible to identify anything about the person, even whether it was a man or a woman. It was pretty much what I had expected at short notice. Aside from giving me some very basic information about the location and shape of the place, whatever it was, it offered me no useful information at all. I could not even be one hundred percent sure this was the lab May Ling had spoken about. And if it was, there was no sign of guards, armed or otherwise.

I went down to the hotel gym and spent an hour training, and by the time I'd finished in the sauna and was making my way back to my room I got the call from the brigadier.

"Can you speak."

"Yes."

"The woman you picked up, Rachida Ait, she doesn't show up on any databases. We've made an informal request to the Moroccan authorities and all they have is that for the last five years she has been living in Casablanca, working as a high-class prostitute."

I punched the button for the elevator. "That fits with what she told me. Where was she before that?"

There's no record of her before that, Harry."

"None at all?"

"Nothing, but they tell me that is not unusual. There are a very large number of unregistered births there, and many, especially among the remote desert villages, who only ever register their children with the local mosque."

I grunted. "She claims she was seven years in London with a sugar daddy who kept her in style and had her taught English and English literature, a kind of Professor Higgins who turned her into a knockout he'd be happy to take to meet the Queen. Her English is flawless and she is very smart. You'd be forgiven for thinking she was the product of a good university."

"That doesn't mean much. Given the right conditions, intellect will rise to its own level, Harry. She may be exactly what she claims to be. Don't get sidetracked."

"OK." The elevator doors opened and two men and two women emerged laughing and talking loudly in Arabic. I stepped in, pressed my floor and the doors closed. It began to rise.

"Listen, the satellite pictures are pretty much useless. They tell me there is a four or five-story, L-shaped building with a big outhouse and three water reservoirs. Nothing else."

"I know."

"I can't even be sure it's the place."

"You'll have to do a recce. Do you need backup?"

I thought about it while the elevator slowed to a stop, then shook my head. "No. Not yet, anyway. I'm going to hire a plane and do a flyover."

I stepped out and made for my room, knowing what he was going to say.

"You know what I'm going to say. That will alert them…"

"Yeah, it will alert them, but they won't know to what. And by the time they act on it, it will be too late." I opened my room and went in, walked to the window and stood looking out. "There is one thing I need to know, sir. One thing above all others, and I was hoping Rachida would be able to tell me, but she wasn't."

He was ahead of me. "Where Heilong Li and Yang Dizhou are, and when they will arrive in Casablanca."

"Yeah. I'm pretty sure they aren't here yet. Have they left New York?"

"The intelligence we have is that Li and Dizhou left New York bound for London Heathrow eighteen hours ago..."

"So they touched down in London about eleven hours ago." I glanced at my watch. It was twelve noon. "One AM. Morocco time is the same as the UK. Two gets you twenty they chartered an air taxi and they are here in Casablanca right now. You have an operative here?"

"No, but we have a couple of PIs we can use. You want the Trans Arabian Transportation Company watched?"

"Of course. There should have been a man on it twelve hours ago, sir."

"There was. Keep your knickers on and let me finish. They touched down by air taxi in Casablanca International at five fifteen this morning. They were followed to the Casa Diamond where they checked in and have not emerged yet."

"Good."

"I'm glad you approve. Now, are you still listening?"

"Yes."

"The group she told you were attached to the European External Action Service, Padraig O'Hanlon, Hans Grinder, Ruud van Dreiver and Michelle des Jardins. They are not employed directly by the EEAS, they consult for them."

"Convenient, they provide deniability."

"Precisely. They are independent researchers of an extremely high academic caliber within the field of biochemistry. Ostensibly they are on a mission from the EU to liaise with China in the field of research and cooperation. Our analysts believe that they are instructed to buy this vaccine, or more precisely the right to distribute it within the EU area."

"Your analysts are right."

"Yes, and it would be very interesting to know precisely which company or companies would get to benefit from that arrangement."

"More interesting even than that, sir, would be to know exactly what this vaccine is for: a vaccine against what?"

"We have advised the CIA to dispatch agents to western Africa to investigate those outbreaks and see what caused them…"

"Yeah, that's great, but I think I may have a quicker way."

"I'm quite certain you have, but don't tell me about it, Harry. Just give me the results when you have them. Soon, please. Either way, Harry, you are not to consider these people targets at this point. Understood?"

"OK. Sure. Listen, have your private eye contact me as soon as Heilong Li is on the move. Have him follow them wherever they go, except if they head out south along the A7. If they do that he is to call me immediately and liaise with me."

"Fine. What is your plan?"

"Track them to the lab. Fly over, do a recce, establish where they are. Go in, kill them, destroy the research and leave."

"What about the plane?"

"When I leave the lab compound I will report by radio that I can see smoke in the vicinity of Lamharra. There will be nothing to tie me to the killing. By the time they make the connection, if they ever do, I will be long gone."

"Good, go ahead. Focus on Heilong Li and Yang Dizhou, forget about everybody else for now. Contact me when you're done."

"Ten four."

I hung up and called down to reception.

"*Oui*, Monsieur Patinkin?"

"Did you manage to get me a plane?"

"*Oui,* Monsieur Patinkin! I was just about to make you the telephone call. I give you now the details of the plane and the location of the airfield, and you can go anytime to sign the papers and take the aero-plane for the flying. They, naturally, require your identity and your pilot's license. 'Aving this, *voila!* The plane is yours!"

He gave me the details. I memorized them and sat thinking for a while. Then I took my laptop, stuffed it in a rucksack, grabbed a few other things I was going to need, and went down to the street to look for a cab to take me to the Casa Diamond Suite Hotel.

THIRTEEN

The Casa Diamond Suite Hotel achieves the near impossible, by being even more grotesque on the inside than it is on the outside. The main difference, apart from the degree of sheer bad taste, is that where on the outside it looks like a Soviet-era apartment block wrapped in neon spaghetti, on the inside it looks like a psychotic jihadist on a bad acid trip had tried to cram every conceivable piece of high-gloss marble, brass and glass into a rococo palace and score all of it with octagons.

I stepped into this mind-boggling nightmare and made my way to reception. The concierge made an expression that hung like wet washing between a smile and a wince and wished me a good afternoon. I didn't care if he had a good afternoon or not, so instead I said:

"Call up to Dr. Stuart Chen and tell him Miss Rachida is here and needs help to carry up his gift."

The wince became dominant and he asked me, "And you are…?"

"Miss Rachida's driver. Anything else you need to know, pal?"

He arched an eyebrow and shook his head all at the same time, then picked up the phone. I went outside and leaned against the *khrushchyovka* wall in the sun, with my cell in my hand, to wait and see if my long shot would pay off. It did.

Ten minutes after I'd stepped outside, Heilong Li's driver came out in a pale gray suit and stood on the sidewalk gazing this way and that, looking for Rachida and her driver. I didn't wait. I set off at a quick pace, staring down at the screen of my phone. I collided with him, hard. He staggered back and I stumbled, grabbed at his jacket to stabilize myself, dropped my cell and fell to my knees grabbing at his legs and shoes as I went.

He spouted a mouthful of Chinese abuse and even lashed out a kick at me as he stepped back and away. I held up both hands, apologizing profusely in English, grabbed my cell and got quickly to my feet.

"I am sorry, so sorry. I apologize. Please, I am so sorry..."

He gave me more Chinese abuse and, for good measure, spat at me and screeched, "You born from egg, fuckin' snake!"

I held up both hands, still apologizing, and backed away toward my Merc. I clambered in, hit the ignition and made a speedy exit. In my rearview mirror I could see him. He had stepped into the road and was watching me drive away. I wondered if he'd made a note of my license plate. I didn't think I'd given him the chance.

The airplane rental office the concierge had given me was located at the international airport, and I headed south now on the A7, driving fast and keeping my eyes peeled for cops. The last thing I needed was to get pulled over for speeding right then, but it was equally important that I was in position and ready when the call came that Heilong Li was on the move, headed for the lab.

My plan had been crude, and I was well aware that my ruse to plant a bug in Heilong Li's driver's shoe could cause extreme suspicion. But it was a risk I was prepared to take. Because I was pretty sure of how it would play out.

His driver would tell him what happened. They would check his pockets to see nothing was missing, and nothing had been inserted. They would find he was clean. They would contact Rachida about the alleged gift and she would, worst-case scenario, tell them about me.

And right there was the billion-dollar question: what would she tell them?

Two got you twenty I had convinced her that I was smart but incompetent. The way soldiers are who operate effectively under a good command, but are incapable of commanding themselves. It was odds on that she believed I was probably exactly what I said I was, a wannabe investigative reporter, and that would be what she told Li.

But there was, in addition, another, deeper reason why she would play down my importance: if I was a real threat, and she had led me to them, then there would be a price to pay. A high price. So she would be at pains to downplay how serious a danger I really was. The incident with the driver would be put down to a bungled attempt to get his cell, or something of that sort.

As well as that, I was curious to see how Heilong Li and Rachida interacted, and what the nature of their relationship really was.

Aside from that, bottom line, as I had told the brigadier, once I was in that plane and I had done my reconnaissance, they would have had very little time to react before I struck. Death was on their doorstep, and they did not know it.

I arrived at the Moroccan Air Club twenty minutes later, left my car in the parking lot and went inside. Twenty minutes with a pretty girl in a blue blazer brought to light that my pilot's license was British and had to be validated by the Moroccan *Direction Generale de l'Aviation Civile*. Two hundred bucks, a wink and a nudge took care of that, and half an hour later I had my flight plan submitted and I was settled in a Cessna 182 Skylane, rising above the vast patchwork of fields south of the airport, with the town of Berrechid sprawled out ahead of me.

I climbed steadily to seventeen thousand feet and settled at a comfortable hundred and forty knots, roughly a hundred and sixty miles per hour, on a bearing fractionally east of south. The lab and the weapons stash were about eighty miles away, so my ETA was in half an hour, fifteen minutes after four PM.

I opened my laptop, opened the tracking app and saw that Heilong Li's driver, or at least his shoe, was still at the hotel in Casablanca.

After Settat, the terrain became rapidly more arid as it started to climb toward the desert highlands. After fifteen minutes the vast body of water which is the *Barrage al Massira* appeared, glinting green in the afternoon sun, and slid gradually beneath me, to the steady drone of the engine.

Five minutes after that I began a steady descent toward the shallow, sandy valley of Aracha. I came in low, looking for the intersection of the R206 and the P2113. I found it, did a low flyover, forty feet above the ground, saw there was no traffic in sight, turned back and touched down on the flat, level ground between the low dunes where I had buried the weapons. I killed the engine and came to a gentle stop just fifteen yards from where I had put the stone marker. Then I swung down from the cockpit.

I worked fast in the intense heat, with the dust sticking to the perspiration on my face and chest. I moved the HK416, the ammo, the bow and arrows and, most important of all, the EPX 1 high explosives to the small cargo bay in the plane and stuffed them in the rucksack.

Just as I was finishing my cell rang.

"Yeah."

A voice I didn't know answered with a strong French Moroccan accent.

"*Monsieur,* your friends are driving on the A7. I think you are want to know this."

"Thanks."

I hung up and checked the laptop. The brigadier's private eye was right. Heilong Li was on the move. He had left Casablanca and was on his way to the lab along the A7. It was just before five. He would be here just after six, as it was growing dark.

In the burnished, dying light of the later afternoon, I taxied back to the dirt track that was the P2113, accelerated hard and took off steep, turning west and south in a sharp climb toward the big, blue dome of the sky. I kept climbing to the Cessna's service ceiling at about eighteen thousand feet, and then turned southeast again to fly over the expanse of red, black and yellow earth where I knew the lab was.

It soon came into view and, having located it, I began to descend for a closer look. From the first flyover, taking it steady, I could make out a perimeter fence, which covered about a quarter of a mile square. It didn't look sophisticated, just barbed wire strung between posts, maybe six to eight feet high. I figured it was probably electrified, but it was impossible to tell from this distance.

The lab complex itself was easier to see now than it had been in the photographs. It was four stories high, made of concrete and large sheets of pale green glass. It had a flat roof and as I flew over I could see two men there, motionless, probably staring up at me.

I decided to come in for a low fly-past. It was, once again, a calculated risk. I was one, small, private Cessna. I didn't believe that would be enough to send Heilong Li scrambling back to his hotel. From what I had seen of him, this guy was bold and aggressive, and supremely arrogant. And it would take more than a small plane to set him off course. On the other hand, it could provide me with invaluable intelligence if I rattled their cage right now, and that was what I intended to do—before Heilong Li arrived there.

I turned into a steep dive, approaching from the south, like I was coming in to spray crops. Now I could see the wire fence, and beyond it the three large water tanks. The fence was simple barbed wire, but I could also make out a second set of cables that told me the wire was electrified. The fence was a good eight feet high, and would be difficult to get through without raising an alarm.

I shot over the fence and saw now that the big water tanks were flat, at ground level and covered in some kind of transparent plastic sheeting. Before I could take in any details, they had passed and I was hurtling toward the building.

There were three saloon cars in the parking lot, plus two Range Rovers and a soft-top Jeep Wrangler. For a couple of seconds I could see people through the plate-glass walls and windows, staring at me. Three men came out the front door into the lot to gaze up at me. One was in a suit, the other two in lab coats.

I rocketed over the building and tore across the desert, kicking up a storm of sand and dust. I climbed to three hundred feet and did a circuit of the grounds, searching for men and dogs. There was nothing, just desert, dunes and a few scattered shrubs.

To the north the ground sank slightly toward a shallow valley, and I figured that area would be out of sight to the lab complex. So, in the dying sun, as it sank toward the horizon, I did another low flyover, kicking up as much dust as I could, and then came in for a slow, bumpy landing close to the north perimeter fence.

There I killed the engine and swung down from the cockpit. I slung the HK416 over my shoulder, stuffed the EPX 1 in the rucksack and hoisted that on my back. I grabbed the bow and the pack of twelve arrows and set off at a steady run directly south toward a position which I had fixed in my mind, two hundred and fifty yards east of the lab.

Running through sand is exhausting, but if you keep your mind focused on only the next step, you can keep going for a surprisingly long time. Either way, after a couple of minutes I heard the grind and whine of a Jeep, and I saw the glow of headlamps through the quickening dusk. I dropped to my belly, lay flat and motionless and watched the headlamps move past in the direction of the plane.

The plane was my plan A for getting out of there. Plan B was stealing one of their vehicles, but I really didn't want to do that. So I got on one knee, nocked an arrow and stuck the fingers of my right hand in my mouth, to emit a piercing whistle.

I saw the red taillights stop. I figured they were fifty yards away. Then there was the distinctive whine of reverse and the taillights moved momentarily toward me, then swung to my right and the headlamps glowed bright, obscuring everything around and behind them. Next thing there was a shout and they were charging at me, jerking, bouncing and wobbling. I knew they couldn't shoot me, not moving the way they were. And I could not aim. This shot would not be down to aim. This had to be calculation. My arrow would be the fixed point, and they would come to meet it.

It took all of two seconds. I drew, estimated their distance and the height above the left headlamp, and loosed. And the Jeep drove the driver's chest right into the barb. The Wrangler wobbled and swerved, there was a shout and the vehicle careened off to my right. By that time I was already running, with another arrow nocked on the string, toward the bounding vehicle.

It struck a couple of rocks violently, swerved again and came to a halt. Darkness was closing in fast and it was hard to see clearly. I had the night-vision goggles in my rucksack, but no time to get them. I saw the silhouette of a man, partially backlit by the headlamps, stagger to his feet from the passenger side and stumble down from the vehicle. He was about twenty yards away, dazed and probably in pain. He stopped, paused and looked around. It was the last thing he ever did.

I drew and loosed in one fluid movement, and the razor-sharp hunting broadhead punched through his rib-cage and sliced deep through his heart and out his back.

Another few steps took me to the vehicle. I killed the engine and the lights, hunkered down and waited, listening, smelling the air. Far to my left a light appeared. It seemed to waver in the dark, swell and shrink. Then, like an amoeba, it stretched and broke into two and became a pair of headlamps. Outside the compound. Maybe a mile away, but closing.

Heilong Li.

I closed my eyes, listening hard, focusing on the lab, then on all the darkness around me. Nothing. Nothing but the growing sound of the approaching car.

I ran. I ran fast, disregarding the risk of loose rocks and potholes. I had to get to the lab before the car, and I had to get there unseen and unheard. My boot landed on a rock. The rock gave and rolled, my foot twisted and I went down with a wrenching pain in my ankle. I bit back the shout as I hit the ground, rolled and scrambled to my feet, ignoring the piercing, stabbing pain in my joint. I could not allow myself to hobble. I could not allow myself to limp. I had to run, and I had to run hard and fast.

At fifty yards I dropped on my belly, pulled the goggles from my rucksack and fitted them over my eyes. I scanned the side of the building, looking for CCTV cameras. I found one on each corner of the building, coupled with a spotlight, at about fifteen feet, angled down toward the ground, and in toward the wall. The one on my right was my problem. If I flattened against the wall it would see me.

There was a concrete path along the wall, bordered on the inside by flowerbeds and on the outside by a row of azaleas set among a strip of lawn. I crawled another ten paces closer to the flowering shrubs, got on one knee and took careful aim at the lens. The shaft whispered, arched through the air and the hardened steel tip bit deep into the concrete three inches from the camera, then dropped silently to the ground.

I took another arrow, nocked it, adjusted my aim and loosed. Again I watched it arch through the black and green darkness, but this time it smashed into the lens, tearing it from its housing.

Then I was on my feet, sprinting hard, my ankle screaming with the throbbing agony. In a few seconds I was flattened against the wall, inching toward the corner of the building.

I peered around the corner and swore softly. I was too late. The black SUV swung through the gate a hundred and fifty yards away to the southeast, flooding the area with its lamps. Then it was speeding toward the building, slowing, pulling into the parking lot, skidding to a halt in front of the door.

The doors opened almost instantly and the driver and his pal climbed out to open the back doors. Heilong Li climbed out the near side. Across the roof I just about recognized Yang Dizhou, who slammed the door behind him. And then, after a couple of seconds, somebody else climbed out, somebody tall and graceful in jeans and a silk blouse, somebody with a wild head of Afro hair.

Rachida.

FOURTEEN

For a fraction of a second I considered it. I could probably take all four of them with the P226. I had the element of surprise. Heilong first, then his driver, Yang Dizhou over the roof and the bodyguard would make a run, take him down as he went. Tie Rachida to the steering wheel. Lay the charges and get the hell out of there. Take Rachida back for interrogation.

It went through my mind in the time it takes to blink, and I discarded it. It was not a thought, it was an instinct. If what they were doing here was so valuable, worth so much on the international market, there was no way security could be this lax.

So I didn't move, and, as they went inside, two armed guards in uniform came out and turned the corner toward where I was standing in the shadows. One of them was carrying a telescopic ladder. I knew they were coming to fix the camera. I picked up the broken arrow and stepped back behind the azaleas.

A few seconds later the two guys in uniform appeared, staring up at the shattered camera. They were muttering to each other in Arabic, gesturing and shrugging a lot. They set up the ladder, rested it against the wall and after a moment's debate, one of them started to climb. I nocked another arrow, stood silently and in one, fluid movement I drew, aimed and loosed.

The guy at the foot of the ladder frowned as he watched the feathered, wooden arrow whisper above his head and bury itself in the back of his pal's neck, severing his brain from his heart and his lungs. Death was almost instant, and the last thing he saw as he fell back from the steps must have been a very dark sky peppered with brilliant, cold stars.

By that time I had kicked his friend's feet from under him and slammed his back on the hard concrete, partially winding him. I had knelt on his solar plexus and placed the razor tip of the Fairbairn and Sykes against his throat. In Arabic I said, "*Taharuk watamut!*" Which roughly translates as "move and die." I followed that up with, "Do you speak English?"

He swallowed and said, "*Quoi?*" and then, "*Je ne veux pas mourir!*"

He didn't want to die. That was fine. I put my finger to my lips and whispered, "OK, *combien?*" Which as far as I remembered meant either how much or how many. I jabbed my thumb at the building and assumed he'd get what I was asking. "*Combien soldats?*"

He flapped his hands a bit, shaking his head. "*Douze, non! Non! Quatorze! Deux dans la Jeep!*"
He held up two fingers and made a driving motions with his hands to tell me there were fourteen soldiers, and two of them were in the Jeep.

In a swift motion I cut his carotid artery and his jugular. Death was quick and painless, and pumped copiously into the flowerbeds. I ran to the corner. I had to move fast. If I delayed or thought too much I would be trapped. I still had the element of surprise and I had to use it.

I peered around the corner. There was no one

there. Another sprint took me to the next corner where I had a clear view of the main door. Through it I could see Heilong Li, Yang Dizhou, Rachida and the two guards in a broad lobby. They were talking to the man I had seen earlier in the suit and another man in a white coat. The smart thing would have been to take them all out, including Rachida, right there and then. But that's not my style. Call me sentimental, but I don't kill women.

The guard had said fourteen men. But there was no damned sign of them. Where were they? There was a paid assassin slipping into their damned facility and they had no idea. It was wrong. My heart was pounding and my belly was on fire because it was wrong and I felt I was sinking into a trap, but I had no reason but fear to pull back.

There are only two things you can do with a trap. Retreat, or act unpredictably. I opted for the latter.

I moved back silently to where I had left the guard's body. I took a cake of EXP 1 from the rucksack and tore it in half. I molded it, pressed it against the glass side of the building, inserted the detonator and returned to the corner from where I could see the main door. I peered around. They were still talking, but they had moved farther inside. I dropped the bow and the arrows, pressed number nine on my phone and all hell broke loose.

The explosion rocked the ground. The glass in the windows above me cracked and shattered. At the side of the building, where I had laid the charge, a billion tiny shards of glass showered into the night, illuminated by the spots. Inside the building I saw the small group stagger and drop to the floor, covering their heads with their arms.

I sprinted, covering the distance to the door in a

couple of seconds with the 416 in my hands. I burst through the door with the weapon at my shoulder. Heilong Li and Yang Dizhou were lying facedown, still in shock. Beside them was Rachida. The chauffeur and the bodyguard were struggling to their feet. I took them both out with a couple of double taps. Heilong Li began to stir, Yang Dizhou was struggling to his knees and Rachida was on all fours. There was too much movement and if I fired now I might hit her. I bellowed, "*Rachida! On your feet! Move!*"

She turned and stared at me. Heilong Li's eyes were wild. Yang Dizhou screamed, a horrible, inarticulate noise, and next thing the whole damned group were clinging to each other and running toward the stairs and the elevators. I went after them, still shouting at Rachida to move away. But my words were lost among the hysterical screams and shouts.

They hammered at the elevator buttons. The door would not budge. I tried to get a bead on Heilong Li, but Rachida would not stand still. They ran as a group for the stairs. I went after them. The doors of the elevators hissed open and they turned, again as a screaming bunch, and made back for the elevators. It was almost comical in a grotesque way. I bellowed at Rachida, "*Drop to the floor! Move!*"

They bundled inside and the doors started to close. And then behind me, for the second time, all hell broke loose. But this time it was not an explosion. This time it was the storming of boots, the rattle of automatic fire and the screaming of military voices.

I turned and saw the double doors flung open, four men in uniform holding assault rifles at their shoulders, trained on me, and behind and beyond them, at least two dozen men also in uniform and all armed with automatic rifles. Thirty men. Double what that son of a bitch had told me. All armed to the teeth and all after me.

In that moment I knew with cold certitude that I was going to die. And if I was going to die, I knew with equal certitude that I was going to take each and every one of those sons of bitches with me.

I roared, a horrible, unnatural sound, and sprayed the door and the plate-glass walls with fire. I saw their guns spit maybe five or six times. Around me I was aware of plaster and concrete erupting as the hot lead smashed into the walls and spun whining past me. And at the same instant I was aware of the vast spider web of cracks racing through the huge sheets of glass that stood poised above the soldiers.

Their faces were no longer looking at me. They were upturned into the cruel, lethal shower of glass that was exploding from the walls and plunging down on them. I took two seconds to let off three short bursts of fire into their midst, and then I was sprinting up the stairs after the elevator, leaving the screams of pain and terror behind me.

I came to a landing that made a dogleg to the right ahead of me and realized absently that I was on a staircase that spiraled up around the elevator shaft. Before I could give it any thought I heard enraged shouting and fifty or sixty furious boots storming across the lobby after me. I ran, crashed around two corners, passed the elevator doors and heard the elevator clunk past on its way up.

A plate-glass door ahead of me gave onto offices. To the right the stairs climbed higher. I took them three at a time. Behind me I could hear the soldiers tramping after me. The rucksack was growing heavy on my back. I dragged at the banisters with my hands as I pounded the steps with my feet.

Another landing and I knew I was one floor from the top. I scrambled around to the elevator doors. Above me I heard the elevator stop and the doors hiss and rattle open. A shout behind me told me the soldiers were gaining on me. I had feared getting trapped, and now I was at the top of a four-story building with thirty fully armed soldiers closing in on me from below and no way out above.

A final burst of energy, fueled by the close proximity of death, drove me up the last flight with the 416 at my shoulder. My heart was pounding hard high up in my chest and I was fighting to ignore the voice in my head that was telling me I had screwed up bad.

Real bad.

By the time I got to the top Heilong Li, Yang Dizhou and Rachida had gone and the elevator doors were standing open. Without thinking I stepped in, pressed the button for the ground floor and stepped out again as the doors began to close. There were boots already tramping up the final flight of stairs. I hurled myself at the plate-glass door and barreled through into a maze of corridors and offices. The lights were dim, barely enough to see, but straight ahead I could see an illuminated room, like a boardroom, with three tangled, black silhouettes scrambling through the door.

I sprinted, but as I did so I heard the doors behind me burst open and a voice bellow. There was a passage on my left and another on my right. I didn't think. Ten or fifteen assault rifles opened up and tore the walls to shreds; I hurled myself to the floor and rolled into the passage.

I lay on the floor. Screaming men were storming

down the corridor toward me, no more than ten paces away. There was a door on my right, maybe an office. I blew out the lock and crashed through it. It had been a forlorn hope, but it had paid off. There was a second door in the far wall. I gave it the same treatment and barged through to the passage where I had seen Heilong Li and Yang Dizhou moments before. And six or seven paces from where I stood, there was the door, still illuminated, through which they had pushed. Either side of it the walls were plate glass, but concertina blinds had been drawn across them. Behind them, light glowed.

I didn't hesitate. I let off a burst of fire at the wall. The slugs ricocheted dangerously down the hall. Bulletproof glass. Only a couple of seconds had passed, but now soldiers swarmed into the passage ahead of me. Five men across, four deep. More of them were crowded into the corridor from which they had emerged, blocking off my exit to the stairs and the elevator.

They took aim and I threw myself back against the open door of the office. A hail of bullets tore through plaster and wood and I scrambled back to take cover behind the steel desk. For a moment I thought I was hallucinating as the wall through the door seemed to dance and wobble. Then I realized the concertina blinds were being drawn back. Heilong Li wanted to be in on the kill, behind three inches of bulletproof glass.

I worked feverishly and wrenched open the rucksack. I heard orders being shouted in French. Men dispatched to come and kill me, drag me out. The fingers of my left hand found a pack of EPX 1 and fumbled it from the sack while my right kept the 416 trained on the door. My breathing was harsh and shallow. I pulled another four packs out as three uniforms charged through the door. But I had already started firing when I'd seen the toe of the first guy's boot. A shower of hot lead tore through the wooden jamb, plaster and brick, flesh organs and bone.

I wrenched the magazine free and slammed in another. Voices were shouting. They were preparing to come through the other door. I jammed the detonator into the cake of plastic, stuffed the cake back in the rucksack and scrambled on my hands and knees to the devastated door. Boots scrabbled outside the other door, the one I had come in through. I riddled it with automatic fire, heard screams of pain. I knew I could not hold out. Once they decided to storm both doors I would die.

I stood, leaned out the door and lobbed the rucksack as hard as I could. Twenty-one pounds of high explosive sailed through the air in a deadly arc. I ducked back in the room as a hail of fire shattered the wall, whined and pinged around me. But my right hand was already pressing nine on my cell phone.

One pound of C4 will tear a bus to pieces. What twenty-one pounds did to almost thirty men in a confined corridor was ugly. It was nightmarish. But I didn't hang about to meditate on the existential aspects of what I had done. I charged out the far door with the 416 at my shoulder.

There was no one there to meet me. At the intersection of the corridor there were five men. One was sitting down holding his head, one was on his knees, a third was on all fours. The fourth guy was lying facedown with his arms over his head and the fifth was struggling to get to his feet, leaning against the wall. These five had been protected from the main blast, as I had suspected. But they were not protected from me. I moved through them systematically, triple taps. The guy who was standing first, the three rounds exploded into his chest. Then the guy on his knees, his head erupted in an ugly mess across the wall. Then the guy who was sitting, the guy on all fours, and finally the guy who was lying down and had started to weep.

I turned the corner and saw the horrific carnage. It was impossible to tell how many men there had been. It was just an indescribable mess, a charnel house of blood from floor to ceiling, mixed with tangled camouflage and dismembered bodies.

At the far end the bulletproof door and walls had been shattered by the blast, and on the floor I could see three bodies; one of them was Rachida's. I walked back through the office, stepped through the shattered wall and over to Yang Dizhou's prone body. He was groaning and looked up at me with dull, dilated eyes. I took my knife from my boot and drove it into the side of his neck. He shuddered and jerked, and his eyes dulled.

Across the floor Heilong Li was groaning too, struggling to lift himself off the floor. Beyond him Rachida was still motionless. I stood and walked over to Heilong Li. I stood over him and stamped hard with my heel on the small of his back. His eyes went wide and he gasped. His arms collapsed under him and his face hit the floor. I knelt on his back and grabbed a fistful of his hair, then leaned down to snarl in his face.

"You think it's OK to experiment on people? You think it's OK to wipe out entire towns and murder children? You think that's OK because you get rich and become powerful as a result? Is that what you think? Or is it that you believe you are somehow special, above the common mass, Li?"

His eyes were wild, staring at me sidelong. He was shaking his head. He burbled, "No, no, you're making a mistake..."

"I'm not making a mistake, Doctor. You made the mistake. It's not OK to do what you do."

"Wait! Wait, I can tell you..."

"Tell me what?"

"You are CIA? Take me with you. I can tell you everything. *Everything!* Just, don't kill me. Please don't kill me! I can tell you."

"Tell me *what?*"

"It's not what you think." He reached for me with claw-like hands. "It's not a vaccine. *It's not a vaccine!* It is an attack! An attack on the Western economy..."

Death came too fast for him. Faster than he deserved. It spilled from his neck, thick and red, pulsing onto the filthy floor, littered with shattered glass. I wasn't there to listen to bullshit. I was there to execute a bastard who had massacred tens of thousands of people for the simple reason that they were vulnerable. I didn't want to hear his bullshit.

Not then.

Finally I went over to Rachida. I moved her hair and felt the pulse in her neck. It was strong and steady. I lifted her up in my arms and carried her from that place of carnage and destruction.

FIFTEEN

I carried her in my arms, back through the shattered office, down the long corridor, back down the stairs to the lobby. I was aware that I was being watched by men and women in white coats. I didn't care. I knew that everyone who could have hurt me was now dead. Destroyed.

But I was not done. I had more to do.

I found Heilong Li's driver lying beside his SUV. The doors of the car were still open. I laid Rachida on the back seat, then crossed the parking lot to the large, barn-like construction that lay at right angles to the main building. There was a simple padlock on it. I blew it off and dragged open the sliding door. There were strange noises which were at first hard to identify, like moaning animals, whimpering, grunting...

I used my cell as a flashlight and found a lever-switch beside the door, pushed it to the down position and heard a loud "clack" high in the raftered ceiling. A string of arc lights came on and flooded the vast space with soulless, ochre light. And in that gloom I saw cages, row upon row of cages, each seven or eight feet square, six feet high, six or seven feet apart. There were a hundred or two hundred of them, in ranks across the floor. At the end, at the back of the barn, stairs led up to walkways that ran around the walls, and on these walkways there were more cages. And each cage contained five or six people, men and women, emaciated, drawn, sick. Some were standing, reaching out to me through the bars of the cages; others were seated, keening, rocking back and forth where they sat; others lay dying.

I took a few steps in and a terrible howl went up and echoed in the high ceiling. My skin went cold as I looked from one tortured face to another, from one hellish prison to another, where a thousand voices cried out in a cacophony of pain and grief, begging for human compassion. My hand went to my Sig, to blow out the nearest lock and release the wretched bastards from their hell. But as my finger touched the trigger I heard another, different howling wail. One that came straight from the gates of Hades. And as it reached my ears, it brought with it a deeper, darker realization. I backed away from the cages, stumbling back, out into the night.

They came screaming out of the night, five Royal Moroccan Air Force F-16 Fighting Falcons. I sprinted like all the hounds of hell were on my heels. The air was full of the Doppler screech of missiles. Two struck the main building, sending up a swirling black and orange mushroom of fire into the black sky. Two more roared over my head. I hurled myself to the ground and rolled as they smashed through the wall of the barn. The air smacked hard. My head rang like a bell. I scrambled to my feet again, stumbling backwards as the barn walls seemed to expand, the roof danced and a fireball erupted through the doors. I fell back, dizzy and nauseated, sprawling in the dirt. The air was scorching. I struggled to my hands and feet, running like a chimpanzee, trying to get my balance in an inferno that seemed to rock back and forth as I moved.

Six more missiles streaked past on my left, exploding into the tanks of liquid, sending huge clouds of boiling steam into the air. I scrambled around the hood of the SUV. Kicked the rear door closed, ripped the driver's keys from his pocket and slid behind the wheel as the F-16s circled around for another strike.

I slammed in reverse and floored the pedal, spinning the wheel as I went. Then I rammed in first and hit the gas, skidding around the building among towering flames, ramming the stick shift through second, third and into fourth, bounding over small dunes, jarring through dips and potholes, while the jets screamed overhead again and the fire from their rockets lit up the night. Behind me I could hear Rachida yelling at the top of her voice.

Another series of explosions tore the night in half. I knew that we had been seen and I knew that within seconds they'd be coming after us. I slammed my foot on the brake and kicked open the door. I swung out, ripped open the back door and dragged Rachida out by the scruff of her neck, screaming at her, "*Run! Run! Run!*"

I dragged her after me, pushing through the sand, and hurled her over a small dune. I bellowed at her, "*Lie flat!*" and peppered the gas tank with molten lead from the 416. Through the darkness I heard the diabolical, mournful howl of the fighters circling above us.

The detonation shook the air. The car jumped as the fireball engulfed it. I grabbed Rachida and hissed in her ear, "*Move and I'll cut your throat!*"

The jets circled a little longer, and after a minute the high whine of their turbines became dim and they vanished into the black, headed back toward their base.

Rachida said nothing. She just lay staring at me

with huge eyes, panting. Finally, quietly, she whispered, "Who the hell *are* you?"

I stood, grabbed her by her collar and dragged her to her feet. I thrust my face close up to hers and growled, "Who am *I?* Who the hell are *you?*"

I shoved her ahead of me, north, away from the vast flames that were lighting up the night, into the engulfing darkness. She walked in silence for a minute, maybe two, then turned to look at me. Her face was twisted with anger, all her beauty turned sour with rage.

"I *knew* you were a goddamn soldier! I *knew it!* Why didn't I trust my *fucking* intuition?"

"Keep walking, sister."

She staggered back a few steps to draw level with me. "You played me, you son of a bitch! You *played me!*"

We stood staring at each other, with the dancing orange light of the distant fire playing across her dark skin.

"What is that…?" I asked, but she interrupted me and half screamed, "You *played me! You son of a bitch!*"

"Keep screaming and I'll knock you cold and carry you. What's that accent? Yesterday you'd learned your English in London under the tuition of Professor Higgins, with an exotic hint of French Moroccan thrown in. You don't sound so exotic now, Rachida."

"Fuck you!"

She turned and started walking away from me, with the shadows of the night playing around her. I went after her, insisting, pushing. "I asked you a question. Where is that accent from? I'll tell you what. To me it sounds like California. Where are you from, Rachida? Is that your name?"

"Fuck you!" She turned and screamed at me as she

walked, "*Fuck you!*"

"That won't get you very far. You have a choice: me or the desert. Choose the desert and I'll shoot you and leave you for the jackals. Cooperate with me and you stand some kind of chance..."

She stopped and turned again, snarling at me. "Of *what?* What the hell do *you* think you can do to me? I'm a high-class hooker who had a client who was doing shady deals. Show me one high-class hooker who hasn't got a client involved in shady deals! I gave you everything I had and you *screwed me! You son of a bitch!*"

She started walking again and again I went after her. "It's a good act, Rachida, and an even better recovery. But you don't stand a chance and you know it. Once the interrogation starts they will strip you naked and the truth will come out."

"Fuck you!" This time she muttered it.

"And you will be a damned sight better off if you have cooperated from the start. Be smart. I don't want to hurt you."

The plane had come into sight and she was making directly for it. She didn't speak and I knew she was thinking. That was fine by me because I knew she was smart, and I was pretty sure that once she'd thought it through she'd cooperate. I had done my job. My work was finished. But I felt sick and hollow inside.

The whole issue of the vaccine stunk in my nostrils. It was plain to see this had been no vaccine factory. What they were breeding here, in the tanks and in the cages, was not vaccines. It was also plain to see that Rachida knew more than she was prepared to admit. But getting her to cooperate and talk was not going to be as easy as it was with May Ling.

Ten minutes later we arrived at the Cessna. She stood, breathing hard, with the cold desert breeze moving her hair and making her shudder. She turned to face me, her jaw clamped shut and her fists clenched. I thought for a moment she was going to stamp her foot.

"What do you plan to do with me?"

"That depends on you."

"Let me go."

"Don't be stupid."

Now she did stamp her foot. "I am just a *whore,* for crying out loud! I am no *use* to you!"

"That's bullshit and you know it." I pointed at her. "With your kind of clients there's no such thing as 'just a whore,' and there are too many unexplained issues around you, sweetheart. Get in the plane, and the sooner you start answering my questions, the easier it is going to be for you."

She thought about running. You could see it in her eyes. She glanced around. She took in the barbed wire, the distant glimmer of the burning lab, the gun in my hand. She narrowed her eyes, shaking her head, and asked again, "Who the fuck *are* you?"

I didn't answer and she walked around the plane to climb in the passenger side, slamming the door shut with a force that said she wished she was slamming it on my head.

I got in beside her. She was staring at me like she was having trouble getting to grips with how stupid I was. She shook her head and looked away. I said:

"They knew I was coming." I shook my head. "No, they knew somebody was coming, but they didn't know who, or what to expect. So they concealed their men and waited to see what happened. Did you tell them?"

"Fuck you."

"Did they call you, and ask you about the gift your driver had sent?" She didn't answer. I went on, "You told them I was a soldier playing at investigative journalism. An amateur. You thought I wasn't slick enough to be a pro. So the last thing they expected was one man to turn up alone and do this much damage." I paused. "The last thing they expected, and the last thing you expected."

"You're full of shit. You don't know what you're talking about. I'm just a damned escort trying to do my job."

I didn't answer until we had jerked, bounced and jolted over the rough desert ground. I had lifted her nose up toward the stars and we were curling away, north, back toward Casablanca. I kept her low, just a few hundred feet above ground level, high enough to clear high buildings and trees, but low enough, I hoped, to avoid radar.

As we climbed slowly into the highlands, toward *Barrage al Massira*, the ground was swallowed by blackness and only the altimeter gave me any idea of how far above the desert we were. Through the windshield there was only stygian space, the cold sparkle of the stars above us and the odd, distant wink of a light: a tiny village, a house or a car in the night. We were isolated in the fragile cabin. The darkness robbed the plane of any sense of motion, and the absence of motion robbed us of any sense of time. The only sound was the drone of the single engine, relentless and unchanging, which somehow increased that sense of timelessness. Finally I asked her:

"How did you know I had a Mercedes?"

She frowned hard, turned to look at me, the dim light from the control panel on the planes of her face.

"*What?*"

"After dinner, at Rick's Café, you were drinking cognac and discussing what league you thought I was in. You were trying to make me understand I was not in your league, or Stuart Chen's..." I paused and looked at her a moment. She was still frowning, but her eyes were no longer narrowed. I went on. "You said I had, and I quote, a '...nice suit, well cut, but off the peg, not bespoke.' My shoes were, '...two hundred dollars, two fifty tops.' I was staying at the Hyatt, a nice hotel, but not the Casa Diamond Suites. And then you said, 'You drive a Mercedes. Nice car, but it's not a Ferrari, a Bentley or an Aston Martin.' Now I am asking you how you knew I drove a Mercedes."

She looked away, out of the side window. She didn't say anything.

"Don't think too long, Rachida, or your explanation won't be worth a damn. And right now, believe me, you need credibility."

"Amin told me."

"What for? What purpose could Detective Amin have for telling you what car I drove?"

She still wouldn't look at me. "I wanted a profile of you."

"Yeah? What else did he tell you?"

She sighed noisily, raised her hands and let them drop heavy in her lap. "Jesus! I don't know! He said you looked like you had money but you weren't rich, you had an air of authority about you like you might have been in the Army, you were tough, a hard man..."

"Bullshit."

Now she snapped round and stared at me, hard. "Why?"

"Because everything you say is bullshit. Because everything you have told me since I first phoned you has been bullshit."

"All right!" she screamed. *"Fine!* I have a very delicate relationship with Amin. He stays off my back and allows me to cultivate my clients. In exchange I give him information I pick up! And sometimes I keep an eye out for him on people he suspects or wants to keep tabs on. He wanted to keep tabs on you and asked me to help. I have friends at the Hyatt and I asked them for a heads up! *Satisfied?"*

"Bullshit."

"Why?" Now she sounded exasperated. *"For crying out loud! Why is that bullshit?!"*

"Because Amin knew exactly who I was, and he did not need a high-class whore to tell him. There is more. It does not explain why you only show up in Moroccan official records five years ago, and it does not explain why you have interchangeable English and American accents, or why your French and Arabic are grammatically correct in a way no native speaker ever is. You speak Moroccan French the way Blofeld speaks English."

She shook her head, incredulous. "Again, *what?"*

"However smart you are, Rachida, I do not buy your story that you were raised in a Casablanca ghetto and were magically transformed, like Elisa Doolittle, after seven years in London with Professor Higgins. You have Ivy League written all over you, and I want to know the true story."

She scowled at me and curled her lip. "You're full of shit." She turned away and looked out of the side window again. I glanced at her and saw her ghost looking back in from the black world outside.

"You can talk to me or you can talk to the Agency at Langley."

I studied her face with care as I said it. There was no response. I had been wondering if she was with the Firm from the time Amin had first mentioned her to me. Her lack of response confirmed my feeling that she was not. But if not the Firm, who?

"Is that who you work for?" she asked, finally. "The CIA? You're about their level."

"Who I work for is not the issue here, Rachida. The question is who do you work for? If you're not CIA, who are you? And why are you interested in me?"

She closed her eyes and sagged back in her chair. She sounded suddenly weary. "I don't work for anybody, Guy. I work for me: Rachida Whoring Enterprises Incorporated. I manipulate billionaire clients and I buy and sell information. I work for myself."

She turned her head to stare at me. Her expression was one of exhaustion and her left hand found my thigh and stroked it. Unexpectedly she smiled.

"You're a hell of a lover, you know that? We wouldn't be bad together, you and me..."

"Cut it out."

"Come on..." She squeezed my leg and leaned toward me, grinning. "Don't pretend it hasn't crossed your mind. You and me, we could clean up. And the fun we'd have..."

Her hand crept up my thigh toward my hip. I snapped, "Cut it out!"

"Why, don't you like it? You sure seemed to enjoy it in bed. Come on, what couldn't we do together. It would be wild..."

I saw it too late. It was just a glimmer in her right

hand as her left hand gripped my crotch. Then I felt the piercing bite of a sharp blade stabbing hard into my thigh. The pain was an intense, maddening thing. I screamed through gritted teeth, only half aware that she was turning the knob to thin the mixture in the fuel with her right hand, while she twisted the knife with her left. I clawed at her hand and she wrenched the blade from my thigh, then pulled hard on the yoke and the plane began to climb. I screamed at her, "*What the fuck are you doing?*"

She snarled back, "Hit the gas or we'll stall!"

I tried to force the yoke forward, but the knife stabbed twice at my thigh again, biting deep. I could feel the warm blood oozing down my leg, saturating my jeans. I screamed at her to stop. She leaned in and screamed in my face, "*Climb! You motherfucker! Climb!*"

I hit the gas, biting back the pain. "*What the fuck are you doing?*"

"*Climb!*" She rammed the blade down to my inner thigh and drove the point through my jeans until I could feel it tearing the skin. "*Just give me a fucking excuse and I'll cut your arteries and leave you to bleed out in this flying, fucking coffin!*"

I watched the needle climb to two thousand five hundred feet while she reached under her seat and pulled out the parachute. With the knife still pressed into my inside thigh, she slipped her right arm through the strap. Then, with no warning, she rammed the knife hard up and back into my chest. I felt the blade crunch through my second and third intercostal. The pain was like nothing I had ever felt in my life and for a second I thought I might black out. I stared down and saw the bright red handle of a Swiss Army knife poking out of my chest. I heard myself say, "Jesus…!" and looked at Rachida.

She had slipped her other arm into the parachute and snapped the buckle. I saw her right hand open the door and freezing air battered my face. With her left hand she snatched the knife from my chest. Warm blood flooded out, down my belly, saturating my shirt.

"Bye, Guy. I'll never know who you were, but if you're dead, it doesn't matter a whole lot, does it? Bleed out, motherfucker!"

And then she was gone.

The air slammed the door shut again. The engine droned. I could feel my consciousness ebbing away, out of my chest and my savaged leg. With fumbling fingers I pulled my cell from my pocket, easing down the yoke, blinking at the control panel, trying to blink unconsciousness from my eyes. My hand was shaking, I struggled to focus on the screen. Pain throbbed in my chest. My heart raced. The phone slipped in my fingers and fell to the floor with a clatter. The light was slipping from my brain and I bellowed at myself to stay awake. I shouted, "*Hey, Siri!*", fighting to raise my voice above the drone of the engine.

"Hi, I'm listening."

"*Call the brigadier!*"

"I'm sorry, I'm having trouble understanding. Tell me again..."

"*Call the fucking brigadier!*"

"I'm sorry, I don't have bucking brigadier as a contact..."

"*Call—the—brigadier!*"

Silence, then...

"OK, calling the brigadier..."

The cockpit was filled with the sound of ringing. My eyes were tired, heavy, closing. A voice in my head kept telling me I needed to sleep.

Then the brigadier was talking, saying, "Harry, where are you?"

I shouted, *"I'm in a Cessna, somewhere above* Barrage al Massira, *badly injured and coming down. Get off the fucking line and I'll send you my location…"* The line went dead. Suddenly I didn't know if I had got through to him or not. I could feel I was losing the plane. The nose was going down and I could not control it. I shouted again, *"Hey! Siri!"*

"Hi, what can I do for you?"

"For fuck's sake send my location to the brigadier!"

"Would you like to repeat that? I am not sure I understood."

"Send - my - location - to - the - brigadier! Send my location to the brigadier!"

Now I could see the luminous water of the vast lake rising up to meet me. Siri said, "Would you like me to send your location to the brigadier?"

"Yes! Yes! Yes!"

Then there was an almighty smash and the world was full of wild, exploding foam. My body was rammed violently against the yoke and yanked back equally violently by the safety belt. Black water washed over the cockpit and I was engulfed by deep, black, wet unconsciousness. My last thought as I sank beneath the surface was, *So this is how I end.*

SIXTEEN

For a long time there was only blackness. The blackness was liquid, and it enveloped me on every side. At first there was panic. It thrashed in my belly and my chest like a spiked lizard. But finally it grew still, and I knew it was OK to breathe, to take the vast ocean of darkness into my lungs, and there would be peace. Death and peace must come eventually to the warrior in equal measure. Because the warrior's moment of peace, is his moment of death.

I thought these thoughts, and then darkness came and brought with it peace.

But the peace was only temporary. Slowly, by degrees, pain returned, seeped in through blades of light in oblivion. I wasn't aware yet of my body, of my limbs, so the pain was a generalized ache that permeated all of my being. It may have taken minutes, or it may have taken days or weeks, but gradually I became aware that the pain was in my ankle, it was tearing at the sinews of my thigh, it was in my chest, stabbing at my heart, and like three cancerous tumors these centers of pain sent tendrils throughout my body.

Finally, I opened my eyes, and there was light.

For a moment I had a sinking sensation of grief on realizing I was not dead. The fight, for me, was not over yet. There was more pain, more struggle yet to come.

I was in a room, the kind of anonymous, cream and white room they have in hospitals. Slowly I took in the details. The foot of my bed was steel tubing, chromed. A clipboard hung from it. There was a sage, vinyl chair beside my bed. To the left of that was a door, and on the back of the door there was another clipboard.

To my left, across a beige carpet, a double set of windows offered a view of the tops of palm trees, a strip of ocean and sky. A cloud moved silently across the glass, while the treetops tossed gently.

A hospital.

Then I slid into dark sleep for a while, interrupted by brief moments of consciousness: dusk through the window glass, a moon casting yellow light tinged with green in a translucent turquoise sky. For a while it seemed that the moon whispered telepathically to me through a holograph of reality, but that was a dream. Then, after deeper sleep, there was the gray pink of a new dawn, the dawn chorus of a million birds and cool air on my skin. Because the window was open, and the curtains were wafting on the morning breeze.

Voices.

The door opened and Colonel Jane Harris was there. Her hair was in a loose bun behind her neck. She wore a cream suit that did nice things to her legs, a blue blouse open at the neck and a string of pearls that made her neck look nice. She stood looking at me through expressionless blue eyes for a while, until I managed to smile at her. Then she said, "Good morning."

"I must be real bad," I said, "I'm actually pleased to see you."

She raised an eyebrow and one corner of her mouth, then came and sat in the sage vinyl chair beside me.

"How are you feeling?"

"They must have me pumped full of painkillers. I was in a lot of pain, but I don't feel anything at the moment. Except sleepy."

"You were lucky."

"That's nice to know. I didn't see it that way till just now when you explained it."

"Always the contrary bastard. The knife wounds in your leg were ugly, but they missed all the major veins and arteries. And the wound in your chest was a full inch from your heart."

I gave a couple of slow nods. "I guess that is lucky."

"Who did it?"

"Help me sit up, will you?"

She stood and took my arm, and we struggled and fumbled in an awkward kind of intimacy for a moment, until I was sitting up with the cushions stacked behind me. Then I asked her, "Can you see my cell around anywhere?"

She found it in a drawer in my bedside table, handed it to me and sat down again. "You going to tell me who did this to you?"

I nodded as I went into Google on my phone. "I just want to make sure. Where are we? Casablanca?"

"No, we're in Spain. It's a private clinic in Marbella."

I found what I wanted on the screen and smiled without much humor.

"You figure we're done in Morocco, huh?"

She gave her head a little twitch to the side. "We don't know. You destroyed the lab. There were a lot of dead bodies there. A *lot*! Heilong Li's car was there… I'm hoping you'll tell me they are dead and the job is done."

She gestured at my chest. "And who did this to you?"

I ran through everything that happened, omitting no detail, up to the point where Rachida stabbed me and jumped from the plane. The colonel sat in silence for a while after I'd finished, and then gave a sly smile without malice.

"That must have hurt," she said, "on many levels."

I returned the smile and shook my head. "I am not that naïve. I know what a woman can do to a man."

"I'm glad to hear it." She took a deep breath. "So, the job is done."

"I don't think so. You see, I don't think the man I killed was Heilong Li."

She frowned. "What are you talking about?"

"He said something to me just before I killed him. At the time I didn't pay much attention, but what happened after made me review it. I was mad and I asked him if he thought it was OK for him to massacre innocent people to make himself rich, and he answered, 'No, no, you're making a mistake...' I told him I wasn't making a mistake, and he said he could tell me something. Then he asked me if I was CIA, begged me to take him with me and insisted he had something to tell me. I asked him what it was he wanted to tell me and he said, verbatim, 'It's not what you think. It's not a vaccine.' He emphasized that: '*It's not a vaccine!* It is an attack. An attack on the Western economy...'"

She frowned. "He was bullshitting you to save his life?"

"That's what I thought to begin with. That's why I killed him. But then I got to thinking."

"About what?"

"About Rachida. I'd noticed early on, when I was

having dinner with her at Rick's Café, that there were things about her that just didn't make sense. For a start she knew I drove a Mercedes, when she'd never seen my car. That suggested to me that she'd had someone check up on me. Why would she do that? When I challenged her she said that Amin, the brigadier's tame cop, had told her about me and she had wanted my 'profile.' What the hell would she want my profile for?"

She grunted. "Odd, but hardly compelling. Anything else?"

"Yeah, then she tried to tell me that she had a mutual back-scratching relationship with Amin, and he had asked her to keep an eye on me. That was obviously bullshit because Amin already knew I was working for the brigadier. So that was two questions: one, why was she keeping tabs on me; two, why was she lying and trying to tell me it was Amin who was keeping tabs on me?"

"OK..."

"Also, she only appears in official Moroccan records five years ago. Buddy says that's not unusual, and that may be so, but when you add to that the fact that her English is flawless, just tinged with a French-Moroccan accent, until she gets mad, and then she breaks into educated West Coast American, it starts to look decidedly odd. And besides..." I shook my head. "I just can't buy her story that she was raised in a slum in Morocco. She has Ivy League written all over her. And if not Ivy League, a damn good university." I paused, thinking, and added: "When I pressured her in the plane to give me an explanation, that was when she drove her damned Swiss Army knife into my leg and jumped. You don't learn that kind of stuff at whore school in the back streets of Casablanca."

She closed her eyes a moment and sighed. "You

sure have a way with words sometimes, Harry."

"Sure, but I'm not wrong, am I?"

"No, you're not wrong. But what is your point?"

"She is one of three things, Colonel." I held up three fingers. "She is CIA," I closed one finger, "which I do not believe because I threatened to hand her over to Langley and she didn't flinch. She is MI6," I closed a second finger, "which I don't believe because the Brits don't operate that way and besides, when she gets mad she reverts to American English. Or, number three," I dropped my hand in my lap, "she is the Black Dragon."

She laughed. "The *what?*"

I held out my phone for her. She took it and frowned at the screen, then at me. "Heilong means black dragon?"

"That's what it looks like. It's a hunch, but it's a strong hunch. I think Rachida Ait is probably Sally Brown, Mary Sue Smith, whatever, Jane Doe, from Orange County, a chemistry graduate from UCLA, recruited long ago by some subsidiary of United Chinese Petrochemicals. Rachida Ait, the high-class hooker, was just a cover."

"That is one hell of a leap, Harry."

"I'm not saying it's true. I'm saying that's my hunch. It is very hard to explain her behavior otherwise. There is also the question I never got around to asking her."

"What's that?"

"What the hell she was doing there that night. In ancient China it was not unusual for a very powerful man, a mandarin or an emperor to have a double or a stand-in. My hunch is that what Heilong Li wanted to tell me was that he was not in fact Heilong Li at all, but a stand-in. It would have been a perfect cover for her. When

I showed up, if Amin was her source in the *Police National Judiciaire*, he must have told her that I was interested in the Trans Arabian Transportation Company, and she must have wanted to know why. Obviously Amin could tell her only so much, because that was all he knew."

She thought about it a while then shook her head. "I don't know how we would even go about testing this theory, Harry."

I shrugged. "You could start by running her through facial recognition databases in the USA. Meanwhile, how old is she? Thirty? She showed up in Casablanca five years ago, which would make her twenty-five at the time, recently graduated; allow a two-year margin of error either side. Start with leading Californian universities, but include East Coast Ivy League universities too. You're looking for outstanding, first-class chemistry students. You're looking for the highest-performing, award-winning graduates of their year. She is a girl and she's black, she will stand out. If she is there, any decent investigator will find her."

"OK, I still think you're jumping the gun. I think what you had there was a crazy, brilliant hooker who panicked, but we'll check your angle."

"Good. How long do I have to stay here?"

"I told you, you were lucky. You'll be limping for a few days and you should try not to sneeze or cough too often, but the doctors here are satisfied you are out of danger. They want you in for another day, but tomorrow you can go home."

"Go home?"

"Yes, go home. As it stands, you completed the mission."

I shook my head. "No. Heilong Li is still alive. I'll

tell you something else. That lab was a research plant where they were experimenting on human subjects with something very, very bad. Somewhere else, probably in the Far East, there is a production plant where they are producing a vaccine. But that plant in Morocco was producing the infection the vaccine is designed to stop. We need to have a meeting, you, me and the brigadier, today."

She raised an eyebrow at me again. "Are you sure you wouldn't rather it was just you and the brigadier?"

"No, I want you on board. And, Colonel? We need to find out yesterday where Rachida has gone."

She stood. "I'll alert our friends. And see if we can find out who she is."

"She won't be in China, but maybe Indochina, Vietnam, Cambodia, Thailand, maybe Indonesia..."

"Based on...?"

I took a deep breath, asking myself the same question. "Conveniently close to China, corrupt, easily bribed authorities, geographical locations that are hard to police, gut feeling..."

She shrugged. "Fine. I'll send a car for you tomorrow after breakfast."

"Where am I staying?"

"Buddy has a villa here in *Nueva Andalucia.* You'll stay with him."

"Give me his address."

"Do you know you're a pushy son of a bitch?"

"Yeah, my mother told me every time I asked for more porridge. What's his address?"

"*Calle del Naranjo, 23, Nueva Andalucia.* Happy?"

I smiled at her. "Yes, thank you, Jane. I owe you a candlelit dinner."

"Go take a hike—*soldier!*"

She stepped out the door and left. I sat a while staring at the wall, trying to think of ways in which I might be wrong. In the end I couldn't think of any, so I gave up and called the nurse. She was an Andalusian, five-foot-two babe with black eyes and black hair who told me, "*No, no, no!*" and wagged her finger at me when I told her I was going home. I told her, "*Si, si, si,*" and she went to get the doctor.

The doctor was another Andalusian, five-foot-two babe with black eyes and black hair who also told me, "*No, no, no!*" and wagged her finger at me. "You are injure," she said, frowning with oddly attractive severity. "You muss estay in de be'! O' you no get better!"

I smiled and shrugged and made a "watchagonnado?" face.

"It's been nice, but I have to go. Please, my clothes, *mi ropa, por favor.*"

They looked at each other, shook their heads and muttered something that sounded rude and involved my ancestors. Then the nurse brought me my clothes and the doctor brought me a document to sign in triplicate, absolving the hospital of any responsibility if I dropped dead from an injured thigh and a very nearly injured heart. I signed, dressed and hobbled painfully down to the lobby where I had the Andalusian girl on reception, who was five-foot-two and had beautiful black eyes and hair, call me a taxi.

I limped out onto the seafront. It was like Los Angeles, only with even less soul. I watched a nine-hundred-year-old woman in a pink tracksuit, with peroxide hair and vibrant red Botox lips, totter by with the world's smallest, ugliest dog on the end of a pink leather lead. Her path crossed with that of Mr. Universe on a bicycle.

He was dressed in nothing but Bermuda shorts and green and red Havaianas that flapped on soft, pink feet as he pedaled his bike. His face, under his flowing blond hair, evoked a song in my half-doped mind: "I Only Have Eyes for Me."

Sitting on the low wall that separated the *Paseo Maritimo* from the beach was a fat guy in a straw hat and shorts, reading a local newspaper.

I limped and hobbled to the corner, where my cab turned in from the *Avenida Severo Ochoa*, and pulled to a halt. I leaned in the window and the driver said, "'Arry Bauer?"

I said, "Yeah," and did some more limping, this time linguistically: "*Por favor, Avenida del Naranjo,* number, um...*veinte y tres, Nueva Andalucia. Gracias.*"

He gave me the thumbs-up and said, "OK, *Macay*!"

I climbed in the back of the cab with difficulty and, as we pulled out onto the main avenue and headed north and west toward the A7, *Autovia del Mediterraneo*, and *Nueva Andalucia*, I noticed absently that the fat guy with the straw hat and the shorts was behind us on a moped.

SEVENTEEN

Brigadier Alexander "Buddy" Byrd had a large villa at the end of the Avenida del Naranjo, just off Pleiades Street, not a stone's throw from Oxford Street. Nueva Andalucia was nothing if not universal in its naming of streets.

The house was a large, sprawling, three-story affair on several levels, with a variety of orange, corrugated tiled roofs. It had whitewashed walls and arched doors and windows. It also had colonnades, fountains, palm trees and poplars. It was remarkable that, being an actual, real, authentic Spanish villa, it managed to look fake. This, I reflected as I looked at it, was the genius of Marbella. And it was another way in which it echoed Los Angeles. It gave everything a veneer of shallow impermanence. Even the luminous green lawn, the luminous turquoise pool and the luminous burgundy tennis court.

A guy with a French accent, a white jacket and white gloves let me in and called the brigadier. The brigadier appeared, frowning, and told the guy with the French accent, whose name was Jacques, to take me up to the large guest room and then make some chicken stew. Both sounded like excellent ideas and I followed him upstairs. Behind me I could hear Colonel Jane Harris making small hissing noises, presumably in the brigadier's ear.

The redoubtable Jacques introduced me to a large,

double-poster bed, opened the windows onto the lawn and the pool, showed me where the en suite was and left, wishing me a good rest. I dragged off my clothes, climbed into the bed and sank quickly into sleep, with the gentle twitter of birds in the background.

I slept for eighteen hours straight. At one point, it may have been a dream, I opened my eyes and saw the moon hanging over the pool, and thought about Rachida, falling from two thousand feet into the blackness of the night, over the *Barrage al Massira* lake. I imagined her, with her mass of black tight curls, and her long arms and legs, crashing into the crystal turquoise of the pool. That made me smile and I drifted off to sleep again.

I awoke with the sun streaming through the open window and the lace curtains moving gently on the morning air. The birds were still singing and there was the sound of water not quite splashing, but sploshing, as someone moved about in the swimming pool.

I pulled myself out of bed and winced a few times as I limped to the bathroom, where I showered and shaved; and finally I dressed in clothes I found unexpectedly, folded on my chair.

After that I winced my way downstairs to the patio, where the brigadier was eating breakfast and watching the colonel doing lengths in the water. He saw me approaching and rang a small brass bell. Jacques emerged from the house as I sat and I told him I wanted lots of black coffee, bacon, eggs, toast and mushrooms. He nodded with a sideways twist of his head and went away.

"How did you sleep?"

"Better than I would have in hospital." I waved at the colonel but she ignored me. "Thanks for the clothes."

"That was Jane's idea. It would never have crossed

my mind, I'm afraid. She tells me you have a theory."

He said it as though having a theory was one of the more lamentable aspects of my existence.

"Yeah, and the more I think about it the more convinced I am it's not a theory. I can't find any way around it."

He sipped his tea and regarded me over the bone china cup. "Oh dear. Heilong Li was not Heilong Li but merely a shield for the real Heilong Li, who is your Rachida, Lady of the Night."

"If I adopted that tone of voice I could make Newton's three laws of motion sound ridiculous. I could make your breakfast sound ridiculous." I mimicked his cut-glass English accent. "Oh dear. Eggs and bacon, toast and marmalade, and no doubt a cup of Ceylon tea."

"Very good, but my breakfast, and Newton's laws of motion, actually exist in reality. Our intelligence was first class and there is absolutely no reason to believe that Heilong Li was not Heilong Li. And as for Rachida—"

"Lady of the Night—"

"Quite so, nobody has ever heard of her except Amin, who swears that she is nothing more than a high-class hooker."

"A high-class hooker who was at Heilong Li's lab when she had no conceivable reason to be there, a high-class hooker who almost killed an eight-year veteran of the Special Air Service."

He sighed. "Growing up on the mean streets of Casablanca can teach you that kind of skills."

"A high-class hooker raised in the ghettos of Casablanca, who speaks English with a Valley accent, and Moroccan French like she learned it at university. That is some hooker. And since when does a bent Moroccan cop become a reliable witness?"

He didn't answer and I sighed and rubbed my face. "I grew up on the mean streets of the Bronx, sir. I know all about what the streets can teach you. That girl did not learn her skills on the streets, because that girl is upper middle class and well educated."

"Recruited by United Chinese Petrochemicals."

"Yes."

"Far-fetched."

"More far-fetched than the Russians planting honey traps for British and American officers?"

"Yes."

"More far-fetched than the Russians building entire towns identical to American and British ones in order to train sleepers?"

He hesitated. "No, granted."

"More far-fetched than having two hundred cages full of infected people? More far-fetched that Auschwitz and Bergen-Belsen? Nothing is far-fetched when you throw power-hungry bastards with lots of money into the equation. Besides, once again, what the hell was she doing at the lab?"

We sat in silence for a while. Jacques emerged from the house with a tray and silently set out my breakfast in front of me. He poured my coffee and withdrew. As I started eating the brigadier said:

"I can think of a number of reasons why she was there, but I must admit none of them are very convincing."

I answered with my mouth full.

"If we are supposed to believe that she is a high-class hooker, I can think of a number of reasons why she would be in his suite at his hotel. But I can't think of a single reason he would take her to the lab, eighty miles from Casablanca, where he was developing a biological weapon that involved keeping human beings in cages. There is no logical, feasible reason for him to do that that does not involve her being somehow involved."

After a while he nodded. "I have to agree."

He leaned back in his chair and we both watched the colonel climb out of the pool in her dark blue bikini. She didn't look much like a colonel doing it, and it was a nice thing to watch.

She picked up a towel from a brightly striped deck chair and stood drying her hair, then walked toward us wrapping it around her waist.

"Good morning. Feeling better?"

"Lots. Thanks for the clothes."

"Clearly you couldn't continue wearing what you had on. It was a public health risk." She sat and helped herself to coffee. "Are you discussing Rachida as a target?"

"Yes."

The brigadier grunted. She said:

"We are waiting on results from your suggested lines of inquiry. But there is another, arguably more pressing question."

I glanced at the brigadier because he had glanced away quickly, at the trees, like he was embarrassed.

I said, "What?"

Who should carry out the execution."

I felt a hot pellet of anger flare up in my belly. "What the hell are you talking about?"

She gestured at me with her open hand and there was amusement and triumph alive in her eyes.

"Look at you! You can hardly walk! Your thigh is torn to pieces. Do you know how many stitches they had to put in there? It was like a needlework workshop in that theater! And as for your chest, you're lucky you're alive!"

"I'm fine! I just need a couple of days to recuperate. Hell, by the time you find somebody capable of carrying out the hit I'll be fully operational!"

She sipped her coffee, watching me. "What makes you think we haven't already found someone? You're not *that* good, Harry. You're good, but there are people equally as good as you and better."

I looked at the brigadier. He was busy examining the cypress trees that bordered the property. I got no joy there so I looked back at the colonel.

"Fine. You've got my nuts in a vice and now you are going to enjoy castrating me. I'm sure your daddy would be very proud of you. But leaving egos and dick measuring aside, this is a very difficult, dangerous hit and however good or mediocre I may be, I know the target and I have some experience of how she thinks and behaves!"

"I am quite sure you do—assuming she *is* a target at all. I'll discuss it with the brigadier. Meantime, you try to recover."

She stood and went inside. I stared across the table at the brigadier, who gave me an inscrutable look and said, "I shall be glad when you two stop sparring. It is not helpful."

"What am I supposed to say? She started it?"

"Please don't."

"This hit is mine, sir."

He nodded. "But you have to stop hobbling, and very soon. There is also the fact that the target knows you, which is a drawback."

I spent the rest of the morning resting and doing relaxation and visualization exercises to help heal my wounds. A lot of people believe the techniques are BS, but I've used them for years and in my experience—and there is a lot of it—a focused mind can have a direct impact on how fast and how well you heal.

I had lunch alone because both the brigadier and the colonel had gone out after breakfast, and at six PM they returned in the brigadier's Range Rover. They must have called Jacques from the car because two minutes after they had joined me on the lawn he came out with a tray of drinks: gin and tonic for the colonel, martini dry for the brigadier and me.

It was the colonel who spoke first.

"It seems I owe you an apology, Harry." I watched her, waiting, but didn't say anything. So she went on: "Our team in San Francisco ran Rachida to ground. That is..." She held up both hands like she was trying to stop me from doing something. "They found *her records*. They didn't find *her*. She graduated *summa cum laude* in molecular biology from the University of Michigan Ann Arbor, nine years ago, aged twenty-two. From there they were able to trace her back to Fountain Valley in LA. It seems she was a gifted child, and very beautiful, and things came easy to her. She left home at sixteen to go and live with an aunt in Detroit. There she gained admission to the University of Michigan and came to the attention of her tutors early on. One in particular, Oswald Chen, her molecular biology tutor, mentored her and put her in touch with Bio-Tech International, a research and development company which, you will not be surprised to learn, is wholly owned by UCP."

"United Chinese Petrochemicals." She nodded. I asked, "What's her name?"

"Mary Jones."

I smiled. "What's in a name, huh?"

The brigadier sighed. "A rose by any other name… Her teachers at primary school and at high school noticed that she was gifted. Apparently she had emotional problems and saw the school psychologist on and off for several years. Dr. Shariff, at her high school, expressed concerns that Mary had a, and I quote, '…startling lack of empathy…' which she would normally associate with a sociopath. Though Mary exhibited no other serious behavioral pathologies."

I shook my head. "Shrinks insist on thinking that evil is a pathology. It's not. It's a trait we need as a species in order to survive. The trouble with people like Rach… Mary Jones, is that they have nothing to balance it with. So where is she now?"

The colonel answered. "She's still in Morocco. She was seen entering the Trans Arabian Transport Company early this morning in a white 1970s Mercedes. She has stayed there all day. We will be notified as soon as she leaves."

I picked the olive out of my martini and examined it, like it was Mary Jones, aka Rachida, and it could tell me what her plans were, and what her destination was.

"She'll go east," I said. Then I looked at the brigadier. "Who owned the twentieth century?"

He looked surprised. "I beg your pardon?"

I explained: "The British owned the nineteenth century. The twentieth century belonged to the Soviet Union and the United States. Who is going to own the twenty-first?"

The colonel answered. "The USA and China."

"Correct, and the Chinese know that better than anybody. Now, I don't know how, but they are going to try to destabilize and bring down the Western economy in order to establish themselves as top dogs. That is what this is all about." I sat forward and leaned my elbows on the table. "You have to let me go after her. I understand her. You've seen that. She almost killed me. She *will* kill anybody else. She is mine, and I take her down."

The colonel's face contracted into a scowl and she opened her mouth to answer. Before she could the brigadier snapped, "Agreed. But be aware, you have about forty-eight hours to get in shape. Then, ready or not, you go after her. And there is no room for failure here. You take her down and you take down whatever operation she is involved in."

The colonel's cheeks flushed and her eyes were bright as she stared at the brigadier. She went to speak a couple of times but bit back the words. Finally she said, "We need to consider very seriously handing this over to the Agency—at least that part of it that relates to the operation. This goes well beyond our standard brief."

He shook his head. "I'm afraid I don't share your faith in the Agency, Jane. There are too many conflicting interests involved. We need Mary Jones taken out, and we need her project closed down, quickly, and as quietly as possible."

"Quietly? Really? The way the lab was closed down in Morocco?"

I leaned toward her. "I didn't do that and you know it. That was the Royal Moroccan Air Force. Somebody alerted the Moroccan authorities of what was going down. Chances are they had an informant at the plant. When I killed Yang Dizhou and the Heilong Li stand-in, they probably decided it was time to remove any evidence of their cooperation with Beijing."

She scowled at me a moment and turned back to the brigadier.

"Alex, we have not got the resources to take on an operation of this size..."

He pulled down the corners of his mouth. "I disagree, Jane. We are not planning to invade China. This is a surgical strike, and Harry is more than capable..."

I interrupted. "Two gets you twenty the Agency are going to be there. I can take out Mary, and if I see that dealing with her project, whatever it is, is beyond our resources, I'll call in the cavalry."

She made a big, elaborate sigh. "But, please, Harry. Let's not make this about your manhood, your testosterone or your balls. This is about neutralizing a very dangerous woman and her work."

I regarded her a while with dead eyes, trying to keep my mouth shut. Finally I decided what the hell and said, "It's a shame you didn't explain that to me before—I wouldn't have wasted everybody's time by stealing Heilong Li's diary, notebook and hard drive. And I wouldn't have sent you on that wild goose chase to Michigan and LA...or taken out Yang Dizhou..."

"Fine! You made your point, Harry. Let's just try to keep it low-key."

I was going to answer her, but Jacques stepped out into the gathering dusk and said, "Dinner is ready, *monsieur*, will you eat out here? Or will you dine inside?"

We decided to eat outside, under an early moon, with the pool lapping softly in the background. And while Jacques and a pretty maid set the table and brought out the food and the wine, the brigadier gave me a look that advised me to lay off Colonel Jane Harris, for the sake of continued peace. I gave him a look that said I would, for now.

EIGHTEEN

Rachida, aka Mary Jones, did nothing for three days. At four in the afternoon on the third day, four bombs went off at different locations around Casablanca, one of them outside the building on Boulevard Mohamed Zerktouni that housed the Sureté Nationale and the Police Prefecture of Casablanca. They all exploded within two minutes of each other and cast the entire city into chaos. Every available officer was called in and, five minutes after the alarm was raised, an old, 1970s cream Mercedes-Benz, exactly like thousands of other old, 1970s cream Mercedes-Benz all over Morocco, rolled out of the offices of the Trans Arabian Transport Co. SL, and headed, sedately and completely unnoticed, out of the city along the N11 and then the A7.

Unnoticed by anyone, that is, except the private eye that the brigadier had had sitting on the site for the past week. He followed the Mercedes at a discreet distance all the way to the airport. There he noted that Mary Jones, aka Rachida Ait, checked in on a flight to London, and he stayed with her until she went through security to make sure she didn't change her flight at the last minute. The guy was a pro.

He kept the brigadier appraised of developments as they happened, and the brigadier contacted Detective Amin ben Abdullah to have him check the passengers on the plane and find out their final destinations. Amin wasn't there, so he spoke to his partner, Mustafa ibn Suleimani, who called back half an hour later saying that Rachida had boarded the flight with a United States passport in the name of Carol Santos of New York, destined for London and then Phnom Penh, in Cambodia.

When she arrived, an operative in Phnom Penh was there to see her emerge from arrivals. He saw her pick up a hire car and followed her across the border to Thailand at Krong Paoy Paet, and from there on to Bangkok, where she drove to an apartment on Ton Son Alley. By this time, two and a half days had passed since the bombs had been detonated and she had fled Casablanca, and, on calling Detective Amin again to see if there was any information of interest to us, the brigadier was informed that both Detective Amin ben Abdullah and Mustafa ibn Suleimani had been gunned down in a drive-by shooting. They were both dead. The gunmen in the car had both been pursued and killed by the police. They were both Chinese and nobody had the vaguest idea why they had killed the detectives.

Nobody, that was, in the Prefecture of Police. To us it was, as the brigadier had put it, a case of *res ipsa loquitor:* The thing spoke for itself. Rachida had fled and was tying up her loose ends.

By that time my new papers had arrived. For my journey there, and at the hotel, I was Clive Anders, a property speculator from Texas. For the journey back I was William Fitzgerald. My leg and chest wounds were on their way to recovery, but I was still far from being anything you could describe as fighting fit.

After extensive and at times intense discussion the brigadier and the colonel had reached an agreement. The overriding imperative was to eliminate Mary Jones, the true Heilong Li. So the plan, such as it was, had been slimmed down and was now simplicity itself: Go to Bangkok, contact a friendly weapons dealer on Burapha Road, in Bangkok, kill Mary Jones, return to New York.

The members of the European Union's External Action Service, O'Hanlon, Hans Grinder, Ruud van Dreiver and Michelle des Jardins, and the American negotiators, Gutermann, Goldbloom and Browne, were all still under review. They might, or might not, become targets at a later date.

So finally, as the summer approached its end, the brigadier drove me to Malaga International Airport and put me aboard a flight for Bangkok, with the simple instructions: eliminate Heilong Li and come home.

The journey was long and, with my various injuries, exhausting. By the time we finally touched down at Suvarnabhumi Airport, early in the morning on the last Monday in August, my ankle, thigh, chest and head were all in bitter competition to see which one could cause me the most pain.

I hobbled through baggage reclaim, reclaimed my baggage, and did some more hobbling through into arrivals where I hailed the driver who was there to meet me. He smiled a lot and did a lot of bowing, but when I asked him if he spoke English he just smiled more broadly and made ambiguous noises of amusement.

He took my trolley and led the way through the seething crowds toward the exit, where he had his Toyota SUV parked with his hazards flashing. He slung my cases in the trunk and we drove at terrifying speed along the freeway, weaving in and out of traffic from lane to lane until we came to the center of town. Here we slowed, but not much, and moved, hooting and honking, among cars and motorized rickshaws, in a city that looked like it was built in the twenty-fifth century to be inhabited by people from the fifth century.

We dodged and weaved, accelerated and braked, along Ratchaprarop Road and finally turned left into Rama I. There we slid into the drive of the Intercontinental and my smiling, nodding driver carried my bags as far as reception, where I tipped him handsomely and he left, walking backwards, saluting and bowing.

Reception, like the rest of the hotel, was large, cavernous, shiny and amber, and looked very much like a set from *Star Trek*. There I checked in, was given a key and a bellboy and dropped my stuff in my room.

Once the bellboy had gone, I put on a hat and some heavy sunglasses, and stepped out into the tropical heat for a walk in the late August morning.

I walked east for half a mile along Rama I through the swarming Bangkok crowds as far as Ton Son Alley, where Mary Jones apparently had her apartment. There I pulled out my cell and strolled for a couple of hundred yards staring at the screen and taking in everything else through my peripheral vision.

It was a quiet, leafy street with tasteful apartment blocks set back from the road behind gardens and security gates. The roadside parking was not restricted and I counted six cars parked at various random points along the road.

The alley was long, over half a mile from north to south, but I only followed it as far as Lang Suan Alleys One, Two, Three, Four and Five and then returned. I saw no sign of Mary Jones and made my way back to the Intercontinental.

There I booked a small, green Toyota Sienna with

tinted windows, told the receptionist I would collect it later that afternoon, and went to my room to sleep for four hours.

At two thirty I rose, showered and dressed, and came down for a martini and a hamburger in the bar. I then had the valet bring my nauseating small car round, managed somehow to cram myself behind the wheel and headed off on a roundabout route, dodging rickshaws and a swarming population that spilled dangerously from the sidewalks, back to Ton Son Alley. There I found a shaded spot under what looked like a huge, shaggy pine tree, fifty paces from Mary Jones's apartment block, and parked.

It was a long, slow wait. She didn't show till gone six PM, when a BMW X5 rolled up and parked just outside her security gate. Nobody got out and a couple of minutes later she emerged from the building at a quick walk. I almost didn't recognize her. She was not the same woman I had met in Casablanca. She even looked a little shorter. That was probably because instead of three-inch heels she was wearing old-fashioned blue canvas sneakers.

The sneakers were not the only thing that had changed about her appearance. She was dressed in straight-cut jeans, a sweatshirt and a leather bomber jacket. Her abundant hair was pulled back behind her neck, and she had on a baseball cap and a pair of Wayfarer sunglasses. If I had not been waiting for her, expecting her, I would probably not have recognized her.

She climbed in the back of the X5 and the car took off at a brisk pace, not fast enough to be reckless, but definitely at a speed that did not want to hang around.

I let them get a hundred yards ahead and then pulled out to follow. They turned onto Rama I and after winding north and west through a maze of streets, came out onto the A7, headed east out of the city.

At the Sri Nagarindra interchange they began to pick up speed toward Lat Krabang and it was hard for me to keep up with them. They hit a hundred and twenty moving south past Don Huaro and Bang Phra, Laem Chebang and Ban Chang, until we finally came to Rayong. By now dusk was turning to night and all about, warm headlamps and streetlights were coming on.

They turned off onto the 3392 toward the port. I followed, but slowed and kept my distance. Pretty soon we crossed over the railway lines and we were into a heavily industrialized area illuminated by tall, thin steel lamps that rained a dead, orange light onto a concrete wasteland that was occupied by factories, plants and warehouses. They turned left at a small roundabout and followed Pha Deng as far east as it would go, then turned right, down into the port.

They came finally to a factory opposite a strip of wasteland and turned in through large, red gates. The legend over the gates read simply, Consolidated Research and Development Inc.

I kept going, without slowing, turned left when I couldn't go any further and eventually found my way back to the 3392 and, outside Huai Pong, I pulled into a gas station where there was a 7-Eleven and stepped into the café for a beer. I sat at a table in the corner by the window, sipped my drink and called the brigadier.

"Yes."

"The apartment is occupied as expected. I picked her up and followed her to the port town of Rayong. She was being driven in a BMW X5." I gave him the license plate and went on. "The factory is on the east side of the port, by the jetties, opposite some wasteland. It has red gates and it's called Consolidated Research and Development Inc. She's there now."

"OK, good. I'll see what we have and what we can gather from our friends. Have you a plan?"

"First I need to go and see your pal on Burapha Road and collect some hardware. Then, I haven't made up my mind yet, but I'll either take her out as she's picked up or as she enters the factory."

"Factory..."

He said it absently, like the word was new to him and he thought it was interesting. I picked up the tone and said, "Yeah. If you have any pull with the Regiment, sir, you need to send in four of the guys to clean this up. I don't know yet what they're doing, but if it needs a vaccine, it needs to be shut down."

"I know, but the powers that be are reluctant to act. There is precious little intelligence to go on, and it would be very easy to make a serious mistake."

"Mistake? Like what?"

"Like destroy the vaccine instead of that which it is intended to protect us from."

I sighed. "Yeah, OK, I see that. Look, sir, let me see what I can gather. I am not going to hang around. I have a bad feeling. I think we are running out of time fast and we could be looking at a very ugly situation."

"I agree. Will you go in tomorrow night?"

"I think so."

"Good. Give Scotty a call now. I've told him to expect you. Go and see him tonight. He's a good man. He'll have whatever it is you need. Act tomorrow, but keep me in the loop. I'm as uncomfortable about this as you are."

"Ten-four. I'll call you tomorrow."

I hung up, took another pull of beer and called the

number the brigadier had given me. It rang twice and a Scottish voice that sounded like it had been marinated in nicotine and whisky for the last ten years growled at me.

"How do yiz have this fuckin' number?"

"My fairy godmother gave it to me."

That was the exchange they had agreed on.

"Who's yer fuckin' fairy godmother?"

"Mind your own fuckin' business. Are we done?"

I heard a hoarse chuckle. "What can I do fer yiz, sir?"

"I need some hardware. It's pretty urgent. I need it tonight."

"Nay a problem, pal. Where are you?"

"Central Bangkok."

"Come to the shop, then. You know where it is?"

"Thirty-Four, Burapha Road?"

"Tha's the one, pal. When can you be here?"

"I'll be there in a couple of hours. Anything I can bring with me?"

I already knew what he would say—Buddy had told me.

"Aye, a wee bottle of Scotch would no' go amiss."

"I have a bottle of The Macallan in my luggage. I'll bring it along."

I heard the rasping chuckle again. "Good man, I'll see yiz in a while, then."

Burapha Road is one of the main streets in the center of Bangkok. It runs from the south near the river to Siri Phong Alley, Romaneenart Park, the Wat Suthart Thepwararam Buddhist temple and City Hall. It is also the road where most of the gun shops in Bangkok are located. In a country with a gun culture that makes the States look like a nation of pacifists, that is no mean claim.

Scotty Gordon, a veteran of the Regiment and an old friend of the brigadier's, had apparently felt an affinity with the Thai culture, had managed to get himself a resident's permit and a license to open a gun shop on Burapha Road, and settled here. There were rumors that there were people in high places that owed him some pretty big favors. That may or may not have been true, but the only comment the brigadier would make on the subject was an abstracted smile.

People who didn't know drew their own conclusions from the huge trade Scotty carried out selling guns on the black market without ever getting investigated. People who did know observed a judicious silence.

By the time I got there it was almost nine PM, and I rang the bell. He left the lights off, raised the electric, steel roller blind and pulled open the bulletproof, plate-glass door.

I stepped inside, the door closed behind me and I heard the roller blind rattle down. I wasn't surprised then to feel the hard pressure of a gun barrel in the middle of my back.

"No offence, pal, but you'll understand I haven't the first fuckin' idea who y'are. So, start talkin'. Who are you?"

The brigadier had warned me this would probably happen and advised me to play it straight. I smiled.

"I'm Harry Bauer, and the brigadier warned me you'd do this. Otherwise you'd have your own Sig stuck between your teeth right now and three 9mm rounds keeping company with your haggis dinner."

There was a grunt that sounded vaguely amused. "The brigadier?"

"Yeah, Alex 'Buddy' Byrd. I met him in the Regiment and now I work with him sometimes."

"You was in the Regiment?"

"You know damn well I was because the brigadier told you. All right, so tell me this then, on which forearm has he got 'Who Dares Wins' tattooed?"

"You need a better line in questions, Scotty. The guys in the Regiment don't wear a regimental tattoo. We're the invisible men in gray. Now, do you want this Macallan or do I take it home and drink it myself?"

"OK, through the curtain at the end and down the stairs."

I pushed through a heavy drape and found myself on a small landing with a door in front of me and another on my right. On my left there was a flight of stairs going down to a steel door. I descended and as I approached it I heard it click.

"It's open," he said from behind me. "Just push."

I pushed and went through. The light came on automatically and I found myself in a concrete room about twenty foot square. The walls were lined with cabinets beneath which were heavy wooden benches, and beneath these were stacks of wooden crates. Immediately on my left there was another door, also steel.

Scotty stepped in behind me and I heard the loud click of the lock. He patted me down and said, "OK, turn around and let's have a look at ye."

I turned and as well as a P226 in his right hand, he had his cell in his left. It flashed and he kept one eye on me and another on the screen.

"Don't be offended. It's not you. I do this t'anyone I don't know. You just can't be too careful. I'm running you through facial recognition, pal." He had a long, thick moustache that went all the way down to his chin, like a giant "M." After a moment he used it to grin. "Oh, aye, seems yer who you say y'are." He stabbed at the screen a couple of times. "See, I'm eliminating your pic, look."

He showed me his cell and deleted the photograph he'd taken. I raised an eyebrow at him. "Thanks."

He laid his Sig on the bench and put his cell in his pocket, holding out his right hand to shake. "Scotty, I'm glad to meet you, Harry. I had another American pal in the Regiment. Walker. He spoke highly of you."

"Captain Walker? Our paths crossed a couple of times. He wasn't exactly subtle. He wasn't happy unless he was blowing stuff up."

He laughed as I set the bottle of The Macallan on the bench beside his gun. "We all just put that down to his being an American, pal, know what I mean? You Yanks are always blowin' stuff up."

"Yeah, right. Well, I have to tell you, all my skill in blowing things up I learnt from the Brits. You got some glasses?"

He chuckled and produced a couple of shot glasses and two wooden stools.

"So what d'you need?"

I grinned. "Well, besides a Fairbairn and Sykes and a Sig Sauer P226 TacOps, I'm going to need a lot of either C4 or EPX 1."

He screwed up his face and wheezed a smoky laugh. "See?" he said, "What'd I tell you? Yer always fuckin' blowing things up!"

NINETEEN

I would not normally share details of an operation with anyone outside the operational group. But Scott was a Regimental vet who understood how we operated, and the brigadier had already told me he had total confidence in him. I didn't tell him who the target was, or why we were after her, and he didn't ask; but I did tell him where and when and how many. I told him we'd had zero time to prepare and gather intel and that it was Code Red urgency. It had to be done now and it had to be a success.

"So, if I understand you, your options are four: one, hit her at home; two, hit the car before it goes in through the factory gates; three, hit the car once it's inside as she is getting out; or four, forget the car and hit her once she is inside the building."

I nodded and sipped my whisky, leaning with my elbow on the wooden bench.

"Correct. If we had more time to gather intelligence, her home or inside the factory would probably be the best options. But I have zero information about where she lives aside from which apartment block she is in. And as for the factory, the same applies. I know where the target gets picked up and where they get dropped off. She is vulnerable at both locations."

"But you don't want to hit the target on pickup because you want to hit the factory at the same time. So that narrows it down to outside or inside the factory gate." He shrugged and spread his hands. "No brainer, pal. It has to be inside. The kill is easier outside, but then you have the problem of getting in to hit the factory."

"Unless..."

"Unless what?" He had made an accurate sketch map of the port and the factory. He stabbed the gate now with his finger. "Once you hit that car the factory will go into lockdown. The gates will close. Private security will be all over the place like a rash on a missionary, and before long you'll have the police swarming all over the port like ants—but not before private security has given you a good seeing to. You'll never get inside, and you'll never leave the port, not in a million years."

I smiled. "Unless..."

"OK," he said and refilled our glasses. "Unless wha'?"

"Unless I am already inside."

"Say what now?"

"The car gets hit before coming in to the factory. It looks like an attack from the outside and the factory goes into lockdown. Private security and the cops are looking out for the attacker, but the attacker is already inside, and that gives me relatively easy movement around the plant to lay my charges."

"OK, that's nice. But two questions: one, how do you take her out if you're on the inside? And two, how do you get in in the first place?"

I pointed at the area of wasteland opposite the factory. "I need a UV laser hidden among the trash in this area of wasteland. The laser acts as a trigger either for a laser-guided RPG or a couple of pounds of C4 concealed at the gate."

He pulled down the corners of his mouth and gave his head a small sideways twitch.

"If you take that route, I'd say you're better safe than sorry. You don't know if the car's blast-proof. You want at least four pound a' C4 for a job like that. And then you've got the worry about where you put the package. If we start digging holes outside the gate now, we're going to attract attention."

"We?"

"Manner a'speech, pal. I think you want UV laser targeting with an integrated trigger attached to an RPG launcher. We can set that up tonight and put it in place in the wee hours."

"Two rockets, with a two-second delay."

"Ay, no problem. And how are you going to get in?"

"Is an EMP too much to hope for?"

He puffed out his cheeks and blew. "No." He shook his head. "To be honest it's no'. But if it's going to have any range at all you'll need a fuckin' truck, and it'll take two months to get that bastard here."

"We only need to blow out the closest streetlamps and the cameras over the gate."

"Ay, and then what? You go over the wall?"

"Sure."

"What're you going to find on the other side?"

"I don't know, but so far security doesn't seem too tight."

"Tha's no an approach you learned at the Regiment, pal."

"No," I shrugged, "but we haven't got the luxury of a proper recon. We just haven't got the time. This has to go down tomorrow morning and I have to be in there tonight."

He narrowed his eyes at me for a while, then sat back and crossed two arms over his chest that could have crushed a boa constrictor.

"D'you mind telling me why it's so important you do it tonight?"

I drained my glass and sat examining it for a while, sucking my teeth. I handed him my glass to refill, and as he pulled the cork from the bottle I said:

"To be perfectly honest, I don't know. And that is part of what makes it urgent. The target works for UCP, United Chinese Petrochemicals, as a molecular biologist. But for the last five years she has been working undercover in Morocco, posing as a high-class hooker, while a Chinese guy has acted as her public face. Testing of whatever it is she's been developing was carried out, with the collusion of corrupt government officials, on remote villages along the coast of western Africa."

"And you was sent to close her down."

"Yeah, but when I got there we discovered that the research she was engaged in was all about vaccines, and the facility they had in the desert in Morocco was some kind of experimental research facility where they were testing..." I spread my hands and shook my head, "... viruses? Bacteria? I don't know, but two gets you twenty they were making something that would require a vaccine."

"They were creating a demand for their product."

"Exactly. Only, the place was destroyed before I could find out what, exactly. They had people in cages in a hangar, and those people were dying, in a lot of pain."

"So she got away."

"She got away and the Moroccan Royal Air Force took out the site. Now she's shown up here, at that factory," I jerked my chin at the drawing, "and my gut is telling me that the bacteria or the virus, whatever it is, is done, and what they are doing now is to finish up the vaccine. Beyond that I don't know what to tell you. I don't know what they are planning or when they aim to execute that plan. What I do know is that I need to stop it before she has a chance to see it through. And I also..."

"You also need to know exactly what her plan is. Biological warfare is nay fuckin' joke. Millions could die."

I sighed. "That's not my mission."

"Says who?"

I was surprised by the question and my face told him so. He gave a short, dry, nicotine laugh. "Anyone can give you a mission, Harry. Only you can accept it. Likewise, there is nothing to stop you from takin' on a mission of your own." He put his hand on his chest. "Tha' was always my reading of the Regiment. None of us was ever recruited because we were obedient. We were recruited because we worked from our own fuckin' initiative. Am I wrong?"

"No."

"And if you are thinking, as I am thinking, that these bastards are aiming to create some kind of fuckin' pandemic so they can clean up on the vaccine, then I think you need to set yourself the personal mission of finding out what the fuck they are up to. Tha's just my fuckin' interpretation of the situation. Know what I'm sayin'?"

I nodded for a while. "I agree. I think I had pretty much come to that conclusion anyway, but it's nice to have somebody confirm it."

"Ay, pal. I know. I've been there. Now, there's only one problem left."

I knew what he was going to say. I suppressed a smile and downed my shot, then refilled the glasses. "What's that?"

"You can't fuckin' do this on your own. It's the craziest fuckin' plan I ever heard. Buddy told me you're good, but however fuckin' good y'are, you won't last ten minutes on your own."

"You volunteering?"

"Well, it looks like we'll be fighting the fuckin' zombie apocalypse if I don't. So whether I like it or not, looks like I haven't much choice. Let's go up to the kitchen, fix some coffee and scrambled eggs, go over the plan in detail, and make a list of the hardware we're going to need. We also need some kind of extraction plan. You don't seem to have thought about that."

"I haven't exactly had time."

"Ay, I know. How d'yiz like your eggs?"

We spent the next four hours going over the plan, such as it was, in minute detail, examining all the potential eventualities and discussing how we would deal with each one.

I told him about the lab in Morocco, and how it had looked poorly guarded from the outside, but how there had been over thirty soldiers there, guarding the place and waiting for me to show up. When it comes to the art of war, the Chinese are subtle, and it had struck me at the time that Mary Jones and her pals had half expected me, and wanted to lure me into an apparently undefended lab, only to trap me and kill me once inside.

He made a face and sipped strong black coffee, leaning back in his chair against his vast American fridge.

"Maybe. But I tell you what, you can do that in a desert like the Sahara. It's not so easy to do it in a city, especially at a busy port. You might find there are heavily armed guards in there. I don't doubt it. But I doubt there'll be more than ten or max fifteen guys, and the heaviest weapon you're going to come up against is an AK47."

"OK, I buy that. So what do you suggest?"

"We set up the hit like you said, with the UV laser targeting and trigger. We disguise it with a couple of cartons and a pallet or two. Again, like you said, we take out the cameras and the streetlamps with a small EMP in the car boot. Then we go up on the wall, you at the south end, me at the north. That way we cover the yard in a crossfire. We'll need night-vision goggles. If we meet hostiles..."

"Maxim 9 for close quarters, crossbows for longer distances. Question, what range has the EMP got? Will it knock out any radios in the yard?"

"'Bout two hundred yards. Ay, it will."

"OK, so if we encounter hostiles in the yard we take them out with crossbows or Maxim 9s. Now here we have to make a choice. If we encounter no resistance we simply lay low until morning, and when all hell breaks out at the gate we go in and let all hell loose inside. But if we do encounter resistance in the yard, it's not so easy. We need to decide whether we lay low and risk the bodies being found..."

"Which they will be."

"Or go in immediately, destroy whatever this facility is, and risk the alarm being raised and Mary Jones doing a runner."

We sat in silence for a while, he staring at the crumbs on the Formica tabletop, I staring at the blackness of predawn in the kitchen window. Finally I said, "There is no realistic option. If we encounter hostiles in the yard we take them down, and then we go in all the way and finish the job—or at least lay the charges to finish the job in the morning."

"Agreed. So how do we stop them alerting your target?"

My mind went back to a certain night at Salton Sea. "Can you recharge the EMP?"

He shrugged. "Ay, I could…"

"Then we rethink the whole thing. Listen: I go up on the wall, you stay in the car and recharge the EMP. I'll take out any hostiles using the crossbow. Then I drop and open the gate. You drive in, right up to the building, release another blast and we take out all the electronics in the building. Then we go in and kill everybody, collect all available intel, set the charges and wait for the target in the morning. Take her out and destroy the facility. No need for the UV laser. We let her and her driver in, and we take them out quietly."

He nodded slow and steady for a long while. Then said, "Ay, tha's the way to go. Silenced TARs."

I nodded. "Agreed."

He gave me a Sig Sauer P226 TacOps with extended magazine which I tucked under my arm in a shoulder holster, and a Fairbairn and Sykes which I slipped into my boot. It's the best fighting knife ever made, and the fact is I feel naked when I'm not wearing it.

As well as that we packed a kitbag with two small but powerful crossbows with six quarrels each. Frankly, I prefer a longbow, but a small crossbow is easier to carry. Scotty selected two Israeli TAR-21s. I have a personal preference for the HK416 because I am used to it, but if there's one assault rifle on Earth that tops the Heckler and Koch, it's the Tavor. It's tough and reliable, you can fit a grenade launcher and a night-vision sight, as well as a silencer;

plus, with an extended magazine it can load a hundred rounds and deliver nine hundred rounds a minute. It is a serious piece of hardware.

Scotty fitted the extras, then packed night-vision goggles, ten pounds of C4 and remote detonators.

All of that bar the rifles went into a rucksack in the trunk of my car. In the trunk of his car, down in his garage, we placed a crate four foot by three, and three feet deep, that weighed a good fifty kilos. It was the EMP machine.

"How reliable is this thing?"

"To be honest, I haven't used it a lot, but so far it's pretty good. They're still kind of experimental. Buddy's lads are trying to develop a more efficient version, but at the moment they're big and awkward and pretty limited."

I nodded. "I know. I've used one, bolted to the back of a truck."

"Oh, aye? I look forward to tha' story. We'll need to get right up close to the building to be sure of taking out all the communication."

I slammed the trunk closed. He dropped a tablet on his front passenger seat and pointed at it.

"I control it from that baby. I'll go in first and park outside the site. When you see the lights go out, you approach, go over the wall, do what ye have to do and open the gates. And pal, you had better be fuckin' greased lightning. Then we'll take in both cars. That OK?"

"Sounds about right."

I watched him pull out of his garage and the automatic door closed, shutting him out of view. I turned and climbed the steps at a run, stepped out into the muggy, small hours of the city and slipped behind the wheel of my hire car, then set off, for the second time that day toward Rayong. If we pulled it off, if we could make it work, it should be a simple, efficient operation. But if it went wrong…

If it went wrong I had no idea what might happen, but I knew it would be bad. Real bad.

TWENTY

I left a good fifty to eighty yards between us. The port area was desolate: a vast area of darkness relieved by pools of limpid light that hung like gossamer over dead factories and silent cargo ships. I stopped at the corner and watched the yellow halo of Scotty's headlamps, and the two red daemon-eyes of his taillights recede along the road and come to a halt outside the factory where Mary Jones had driven in the day before. The glow of the headlamps died, and a fraction of a second later so did the red spots of his taillights. I counted five seconds and the two streetlamps outside the factory died too.

I fired up the hire car, left the lights off and accelerated along the road to pull in just behind Scotty. I already had the crossbow on my back and the night goggles on my head as I jumped out of the car and made for the wall. Scotty was already there, making a stirrup of his hands. I placed my left foot on his linked palms. He heaved and I reached for the wall, got a firm grip and pulled myself up, swarming onto the thin ledge.

I remained motionless. I could hear bodies moving and quiet voices. I slipped down the goggles over my eyes. The world became a familiar yet eerie black and green place of imminent death.

There was a yard, maybe thirty paces across, fifteen or twenty deep. On the far side there was a large, concrete nave with a gabled roof. At either side of the building the yard fed into a passage that seemed to lead to the back. It was simple and functional.

Beside the door there were two guys with rifles. They were not in uniform. They were looking about them, like they thought the explanation for the loss of light might suddenly appear in the air.

I sat up, took the crossbow from my back and fitted a quarrel with a broad tip. I took careful aim at the guy on the right and loosed the shaft. It whispered and thudded home right through his heart. Death must have been almost instant.

He didn't move. He just stood there and died, and as his legs died he started to keel over. By that time I had loaded again and lined up his pal, who was now looking up at the air. It struck me as ironic that he was looking for light in the darkness. I get deep like that sometimes.

His pal hit the dirt with a heavy thud. He turned his head to see what the noise was and the second shaft thudded home with the information he was looking for. He gave a little shudder and joined his pal in the Land of Eternal Nod.

I took fifteen seconds to scan the area, listening for movement in the darkness. There was none, so I slipped off the wall and lowered myself down. Then sprinted on silent feet to the gate and opened it, dragging it back on its rollers.

I didn't wait for Scotty to come in. I ran for my own car, slipped behind the wheel and drove in fast. When I got there I saw that Scotty had reversed right up to the wall, beside the door, maximizing every foot of range of the EMP. And while he discharged it for a second time, I rolled the gate closed again.

I dumped the crossbow in the trunk of my hire car and pulled out the rucksack. I slung it on my back and grabbed the two TAR-21s. Scotty grabbed one and took up his position beside the door. I blew out the lock, yanked open the door and Scotty stepped in with his weapon at his shoulder. He stepped to the right and I went in after him, moving to the left.

In this black and green world there was a broad staircase that rose directly ahead of us, with a passage to either side. The floors were luminous, surrounded by darkness. An indistinct voice echoed along the tiles and was answered. They came from along the corridors that flanked the stairs.

I signaled to Scotty to go right and I went left. As we circled around the stairs it became clear that the two passages met in a single corridor behind the staircase. That passage ran the length of the building to the back wall. Approaching we saw two black figures dancing and weaving as they walked toward us, playing a couple of brilliant green flashlights ahead of them. I looked for Scotty and found him fifteen paces away, beyond the stairs, on one knee with his rifle at his shoulder. There was no need for verbal communication. We both knew what had to be done.

I lined up the guy on the left. I knew he'd take the one on the right. Our rifles spat, triple tapped, and the two men went down, and the flashlights did a crazy green dance on the floor.

We moved forward at a silent run, the TARs still at our shoulders. We confirmed the kills and took in what we had ahead of us. It was a long corridor with doors to right and left, evenly spaced every twenty feet or so.

I signaled Scotty to cover the stairs and I moved

down the passage from door to door, opening them one after another. Each one of them was empty. Marks on the walls showed shelves and benches had been attached and then removed, but aside from that the rooms had nothing to show, nothing to tell. And at the end of the passage there was just a blank wall.

I returned at a run and found Scotty on one knee at the foot of the stairs with his weapon trained on the empty space at the top. He put his finger to his lips and tapped his ear. He had heard something. I pointed to the far side of the stairs, and then up. He gave me the thumbs-up and we started to climb in silence. I had the left side, covering the right. He had the right side, covering the left.

At the top we found a passage. It was similar to the one we had seen below, but this one had just four doors: two opposite each other at the beginning, and two opposite each other at the end. That meant bigger rooms, maybe labs.

We were three steps from the top. We lay down, paused and waited in total silence.

Nothing happened. We heard no sound. But some part of my mind was back in Sulfur Springs, lying in the shade of the pines, watching the shadows in the woodland. I had known the bull elk was there, just like I knew now that there were men here. They were there, still, silent, listening for us in the dark, waiting for us to move in closer. Waiting to kill us.

I looked over at Scotty. He was looking at me and he didn't need to tell me he was thinking the same. He pointed at the nearest doors and I agreed. That would be the obvious place for an ambush. Had they known we were coming? Had they been told by somebody? Or had they simply reacted to the blackout?

I made a crouching, silent run to the nearest door, hunkered down beside it and reached for the handle. I counted out three with my fingers, so Scotty could see it, yanked hard and pulled the door open. Then I rolled away and lay flat with my hands over my ears because I knew what was coming next. He didn't wait. His grenade launcher coughed twice, and twice there was the clatter of metal on tiles. Then there was screaming and shouting, and the tramping of feet, but too late. The blasts were violent and shook the walls, and next thing Scotty's Tavor was spitting fire through the open door in controlled bursts of five and six rounds. Rounds that ricocheted off the walls inside the room, killing anyone who might still be alive. Nobody came out.

I put the rifle to my shoulder and covered the second door. It suddenly exploded violently outward and a stream of men burst out the dark portal, screaming and showering the passage with reckless, blind gunfire. Burning lead spattered the walls, tore at the open door opposite, gauged showers of plaster from the concrete, and suddenly the landing was swarming with men.

In the black and green madness of the night-vision goggles it was hard to estimate how many there were. It might have been six or it might have been ten or even fifteen. They were all running, jostling, screaming and pushing against each other in a frantic panic.

I was on my belly and I knew that Scotty was lying on the stairs with his weapon laid flat on the landing. In the hail of molten lead it was just a matter of time before we were hit by a ricochet. So I opened up, and Scotty opened up too, and we caught them in a deadly crossfire from which there was no salvation. It lasted no more than five or six seconds during which the wretched bastards jerked and twisted in a grotesque, morbid dance. The last man slipped on the bloody floor and went down. And silence washed in like a black tide.

I waited a few seconds, then got to my feet and ran to the door from which they had emerged. I went in, with Scotty covering the entrance. It was empty, like the rooms downstairs.

I stepped out and snarled, "There isn't a goddamned thing in here!"

We ran down the passage. Scotty took the door on the far side and shouted, *"Clear!"*

I opened the door on the near side and froze. In the weird, green light it was easy to see what it was; what it had been. Scotty came up by my side and said, "Shit..."

"A lab."

I reached for the switch and flipped it. After a couple of seconds dull neon light flickered, hummed and held the room in its depressing glow. I said, "It's simple, basic. This is not a research lab. This is a simple lab designed to produce something."

Scotty snarled, "Ay, but there are no fuckin' chemicals here. There are no wee colored fuckin' bottles. There are no fuckin' petri dishes. There's nothin' here but fuckin' equipment! And no' much of that!"

"Which means we're too damned late. This whole damned place has been cleaned out and these guys were left here as a reception committee for anyone who came looking." I stepped out into the passage and flipped the switches there. A limpid yellow light rained down from the lamps overhead, revealing twelve dead men sprawled, twisted and torn, saturated in their own blood. They wore sandals, Bermuda shorts and flowered, short-sleeved shirts. They were amateurs, street punks hired for what they thought would be easy money, to take out some foreign pain in the ass.

I glanced in the first room, the one Scotty had hit: another eight men in there, dismembered, sleeping in their own gore.

"She knew you were here, Harry, and she closed down the operation."

I shook my head. "No, she hasn't closed down the operation. She has taken it into its final phase. She closed it down from Morocco, when she thought I was dead. And she came here to wrap it up. This is what happens when you build an operation on too little intel. God *damn* it! She has moved to execution! I need to go to her apartment. I need to go there now."

I ran. Scotty was right behind me. I barked her address over my shoulder, wrenched open the rear door and threw in the rucksack.

"I'm going into the apartment block. Cover the exit. She's about six foot, slim, black, Afro hair. Hard to miss. If she leaves, snatch her!"

I floored the pedal all the way back to Bangkok. By the time I got there dawn was barely an hour away. Once in the city I stuck to the speed limit, with Scotty right behind me. The last damned thing I needed right then was to be pulled over by the cops, with an arsenal in my car and an EMP in Scott's.

I turned into Ton Son Alley as the sky was starting to turn gray in the east. I parked opposite the exit and Scotty pulled in slightly ahead of me. I didn't pause. I climbed out of the car and crossed the road at a run. I went past the barrier and through plate-glass doors into a brightly lit lobby. There was a porter in uniform behind a desk who saw me and frowned. I guess I looked a bit like a man who had just massacred two dozen men. He stood and, without pause, I vaulted the desk, rammed my right fist into his solar plexus, dragged him wheezing and gasping to the floor and rammed the muzzle of the P226 into his mouth.

"Sorry, pal. I have no time to explain. Mary Jones, tall, black, gorgeous, big hair. Which apartment?"

His eyes were watering and his mouth was trying to work around the gun. I removed it and repeated, "Where?"

"Six fifteen, please, not hurt me."

"I'm not going to hurt you." I dragged him to his feet and knocked him back over his desk with a moderate smack on the tip of his jaw that put his lights out. Then I was running up the stairs, keeping an eye on the elevator in case she left while I was on my way up. I reached the sixth floor. Two minutes later I had found apartment fifteen and blown out the lock with the Maxim 9.

There was a short passage. The lights were off but the gray light of dawn seeped in. Immediately on my right there was a door open onto a small kitchen. Ahead the passage opened out into a comfortable living room with sliding glass doors onto a large terrace. The door was open and a gentle breeze was coming in off the gardens beyond the balustrade. The sky was paling and there was a cacophony of birds.

She was sitting in a bamboo chair on the terrace, watching me like Black Emmanuelle. I checked the room, then peered into the small bathroom and the bedroom. We were alone. I stepped out onto the terrace. She said, "You're too late."

"For what?"

"To stop it."

"Stop what?"

A slow smile dimpled her cheeks. I was struck forcefully again by how beautiful she was.

"I could tell you you'll have to wait and see."

"Then I'd have to blow your kneecap off."

She shook her head. "I am not good at tolerating pain."

"You're pretty good at inflicting it."

She shrugged. "I do what I have to do to survive. Just like you."

"I know who you are, Mary."

Her eyes widened and her eyebrows arched. "Really? You're smarter than you look."

"I'm here to kill you. But I am willing to give you a chance. I know what you're doing involves a virus and a vaccine..."

"How do you know that?"

"That doesn't matter. Agree to work with us and I'll spare your life. Otherwise I will kill you, right here and right now."

She sat chewing her lip, looking out across the gardens. Eventually she said, "What do you want to know?"

"The diary and notebook I recovered from your stand-in's room in New York. Are they yours? I know you're the Black Dragon."

She gave a small laugh. "My, you are a clever boy, aren't you. Yes, they were mine. I suppose you have experts analyzing them now. They won't get far. The shorthand is my own. Only I can decipher it."

"So what have you done? You've bred a strain of bacteria, or a virus..."

"A virus."

"And you have created a vaccine for that virus..."

"That much must have been obvious."

"So where is the vaccine? Why wasn't it at the facility at the port?"

She stared at me for a long moment, then said unexpectedly:

"You ditched in the lake, *Barrage al Massira*. But when you were rescued by your friends—by the way, I still have no idea who you work for."

"Finish, and I'll tell you."

She sighed. "When you were rescued, you were seen and I was informed. Our project was pretty much finished by then anyway. Those poor men you killed in the lab in Morocco, they were just glorified salesmen, closing the deal. Anyway, we were pretty much done, so I had them wrap things up here.

"One of my men followed you to Spain and then to the airport. I knew by then that you were coming here. And, Guy, or whatever your name is, you were very careless when you sat outside my apartment block. I did see you, you know."

"Where is the vaccine?"

"On a container ship which has already left port, headed for China."

"And you have become fabulously rich selling licenses to Padraig O'Hanlon, Hans Grinder, Ruud van Dreiver and Michelle des Jardins, Gutermann, Goldbloom and Browne."

"Oh my dear Guy." She smiled, then threw back her head and laughed. "You are so delightfully small-minded and naïve. The United States government was falling over itself to buy concessions to manufacture and distribute the vaccine. They have known we were working on it for the last three years. And so has the European Union. The concessions have been agreed and sold, and you are quite right, I have become obscenely rich. But that was never the purpose of the game, Guy."

"What was the purpose of the game? Enlighten me."

"This is the dawn of the twenty-first century. You know each century begins fifteen to twenty years in, don't you? The twentieth began with the Russian Revolution and the First World War, the fall of Germany and the rise of Russia. The nineteenth with the end of the Napoleonic Wars, the fall of France and the rise of Britain..."

"Cut the crap, what are you talking about?"

"The beginning of the twenty-first will be marked by the great plague, a virus that will sweep across the world, claiming millions of lives..."

She was smiling, but there was something in her eyes, an amusement that went beyond what she was saying, an amusement that said she knew something more than what she was telling me. I shook my head.

"No, that's not enough to define a century..."

"Really? It only takes a few thousand deaths, Guy. It only takes a few thousand deaths to spark a panic."

"We saw that with the AIDS epidemic..."

"But AIDS was spread by intimate sexual contact, Guy. What if the virus was spread on the air, or as simply as touching the same surfaces as somebody else? What if the virus was spread by standing close to somebody in a supermarket line? What if all you need to do is pick up a book in a bookstore that somebody else had been holding five minutes before? What if the virus spreads by touch and by breathing?"

I frowned. "You can't be serious. Then you would be talking about hundreds of millions of deaths world-wide. You would lose control of it. It would be a pandemic that nobody could stop..."

She laughed a little more. "What measures would we have to take, do you think?" I shook my head and she went on. "The whole of the Western world would have to go into quarantine, Guy. It would spread like wildfire and the whole of Europe and the USA would have to go into quarantine until a vaccine was found." She sat forward, with her elbows on her knees, a smile of triumph on her face. "Can you *imagine* the impact on the Western economies? Every place of business where people came into close contact with each other would have to close: shops, bars, restaurants, libraries, schools, offices, factories..."

"They would be crippled. Entire industries could collapse."

"The entire industrial economy of the nineteenth and twentieth centuries is built on manufacturing and distribution. And both of those will grind to a shuddering halt. The entire Western economic system will implode."

"But surely, so will China. How could you stop it..."

She cut across what I was saying. "Not if it starts there, in one city, and is rapidly contained and that city is quarantined. Not if China has a vaccine. And besides, China does not *want* the West *totally* annihilated. Only severely weakened. It will be discovered, too late, that it is not as virulent as it at first seemed, that many people develop natural defenses to it. But by then it will be too late. The damage will be done."

She sat back. There was gloating in her beautiful eyes. "The West will recover, but it will never quite be what it was. This will be a new age, dominated not by America's imperial Anglo-Saxon culture, but by China. Prepare for change, Guy. It is coming."

I felt sick, and for a moment the world seemed to rock under my feet. There was an unreality to the situation. I remembered my own words to the brigadier.

"So the twenty-first century will be defined..."

"By China's rise to become the world's number-one, undisputed industrial, military and economic superpower. *That* was the game, all along."

"Jesus, this has been years in the planning..."

"Oh yes, Guy. It has. And it is too late. The virus is on its way, and the vaccines are too." She must have seen the look in my eyes because she laughed again. "I should mention that you are infected, Guy. The factory was full of it, and my door handle was smothered with it. You have about two weeks."

"Why? Why would you do that?"

"It's called insurance. You were supposed to be killed in Morocco, twice, and you were supposed to be killed at the factory here. But you seem to be hard to kill, like a cockroach. I will be picked up here by a car in about twenty minutes. It seemed prudent to me to have an insurance policy in case you showed up again."

"How is my being infected an insurance? What's to stop me killing you right now?"

"The cure, Guy. Only I have the cure and the vaccine."

I nodded. "Stop calling me Guy, will you. My name is Harry, Harry Bauer, and I work for Cobra."

The smile slipped from her face. For a second there was something tragic about it. She knew what it meant. She knew what my telling her my name and who I worked for meant. It could only mean only one thing. She frowned.

"Harry? But the virus..."

I shot her between the eyes and she leaned back in her chair, staring up at the top of the sliding-glass doors. I don't kill women or children, but Mary Jones was not a woman in any meaningful sense of that word. She wasn't even human. I went over and looked down at her.

"I died a long time ago, Mary. Your cure can't save me. I'm living on borrowed time. You? You have to go now."

I watched her a moment longer. She didn't look quite so beautiful now. I guess beauty really is just skin deep.

TWENTY-ONE

I found what I was looking for in the bathroom. I wiped my prints off anything I might have touched and ran down the stairs calling the brigadier as I went.

"Mary Jones is dead."

"Where are you?"

"Leaving her apartment block now."

The porter was still out for the count as I walked past the reception desk and out into the gray morning light. I jerked my head at Scotty and mouthed "Go!" as I walked past him toward my car. All the while I was speaking into my cell.

"You need to listen. There is a container ship that left the harbor at Rayong in the last few hours. It's carrying large amounts of a vaccine. You need to stop that ship as soon as it is in international waters and take possession of the vaccine."

"What the hell are you talking about, Harry?"

I filled him in as I climbed into the car. Ahead I could see Scotty pulling onto Rama I. The brigadier was quiet for a long while as I pulled away and headed back toward the hotel. Finally he said, "So, are you infected?"

"No."

"How can you be sure?"

"For a start her story was bullshit. They want the

epidemic to start in China, where they can control it and confine it in one place before it spreads across the country. It has to start in China so they can legitimately claim they got a head start on creating the vaccine. Obviously it can't get out that the vaccine was created before the epidemic. If she started recklessly spreading the virus in Thailand instead of China, it would make a mess of their plan."

"I hope you're right."

"I am. I'm pretty sure I was spotted in Marbella, leaving the hospital, so two gets you twenty she knew I was here. The operation was finished and the factory was cleaned out, so she led me there to walk into an ambush. She was sure I would not survive, and if Scotty hadn't been there maybe I wouldn't have. So when she saw me turn up, she panicked and made up the first story that came into her head. She was cool and convincing, but the story didn't hold water."

"I hope to Christ you're right," he repeated. "Either way you should go into quarantine right away."

"Yeah, unfortunately that's not possible, sir. I need to clean this car, clean my room and get the hell out of Dodge. And you, with all due respect, need to make arrangements to intercept that ship before the Chinese get hold of it. If we have the vaccine instead of them, they won't trigger the epidemic."

He grunted. "I wish I shared your confidence."

"Yeah, I wish I did, too."

I hung up and took the car to a car wash. By the time I was done there wasn't a particle in the car. I dropped it at a public parking lot and took a taxi back to my hotel. There I gave my room the same treatment as the hire car and called Scotty.

"What?"

"All good?"

"Ay, why not?"

"Where were you last night? I missed you?"

"I was at my favorite whorehouse, and I have six babes who remember it vividly. You remember when you've been with a Scotsman, y'know."

"I believe you. If you're ever in my part of the world, drop in and say hello."

"I'll do that, pal. Hang loose."

"You too."

I took a taxi to the airport and bought a first-class ticket to New York as William Fitzgerald. I had an anxious two-hour wait in the VIP lounge, but by three PM we were in the air and rising high over the southern Pacific Ocean. Somewhere down there, I thought, as the afternoon sun cast vast sheets of silver over the black water, somewhere down there was the cargo ship, headed for China, loaded with vaccines which, if they reached their destination, would trigger the deaths of hundreds of thousands of people. Probably millions.

I had my lunch, popped a sleeping pill with a large Scotch and allowed myself to slip into oblivion.

***

It was two AM by the time I opened the door to my small, blue clapboard house on Shore Drive at Eastchester Bay. I dropped my bag beside the sofa, dumped my coat on top and made my way to the kitchen. There I brewed some strong black coffee and laced it generously with Scotch. I had slept too long on the plane and my mind was buzzing. I made a ham and cheese sandwich and carried it and the coffee to the sofa. There I switched on the TV and turned to CNN.

The first scene to appear on the screen was a large cargo ship on the high seas. Alongside it was a US Navy ship. A man's voice was speaking over the image.

"It is not clear yet precisely what's happening, John, but it seems that just a couple of hours ago, the USS *Buccaneer* intercepted and boarded the Chinese vessel, *Chénxīng*, which, according to unofficial and unconfirmed sources, was transporting stolen cargo. It is quite extraordinary, John. I don't think there is anything like this in recent history that we can compare it to, unless we turn to Cold War fiction, but that is the story so far..."

A second, female voice interrupted and the shot cut back to the studio where the anchors were sitting behind their desk. The woman was saying:

"In fact we are right now receiving a statement from AMBI, the American bio-chemicals giant, who tell us they will be holding a press conference later today. For now, Ms. Angela Goldbloom, director of research and development at AMBI, has issued a statement to the effect that an unspecified amount of a highly sensitive vaccine had gone missing from one of their warehouses at Rayong, in Thailand, and that intelligence received a suggestion that the vaccine had been loaded aboard the Chinese cargo ship, *Chénxīng*. It seems AMBI contacted the US authorities and, once the ship was in international waters, the USS *Buccaneer* was instructed to take action..."

I sighed and switched off the TV. Angela Goldbloom. Was that any better than Heilong Li? I didn't know, but it depressed me all the same.

Fifteen minutes later the phone rang. I picked it up.

"Yeah?"

"Harry, it's Buddy."

"So in the end the bastards won anyhow, huh?"

"In this game the bastards always win, Harry. If they didn't, there would be no need for Cobra."

I gave a listless snort that didn't quite make it to a laugh. "I guess."

"How are you?"

"Fine."

"You should see one of our friendly doctors."

"I'm fine. I just need a few days off."

"OK, but the first sign of anything…"

"I'll go and see the doc. Don't worry."

"All right, get some rest. And, Harry?"

"Yeah, what?"

"Thank you."

"Yeah, sure. Take care, sir."

EPILOGUE

Three days and two thousand miles later I was at Sulfur Springs again. I left my Jeep in the Roast Buck Eatery parking lot and scanned the other trucks there. It didn't take me long to find what I was looking for. Rex Trent's white Ford was parked not far from my truck. So I figured Rex Trent was inside. I hoped he was with his pal, Jacob.

I crossed the lot and pushed through the door. It didn't take me long to spot him. He was sitting up at the bar with his lackey, and each of them had a beer on the bar in front of him. I crossed the floor until I was standing behind Trent. He heard me and he could feel me, but he didn't look around.

"Good morning, Mr. Trent."

Now he turned to look at me, slow, taking his time. "Do I know you, son?"

"I explained to you last time we met, that I am not your son. We have met, yes, but I don't believe you know me. If you did, you would not have stolen my elk."

Now he turned fully around on his stool and leaned his elbows on the bar. Jacob turned with him, grinning, anticipating fun.

"Now, let me see if I understand you...son, are you callin' me a thief?"

"You owe me a bull elk. I am happy to take the

going price. But you should know that I do not plan to leave Sulfur Springs without either my elk or due payment in cash."

They looked at each other and laughed. I said:

"And there is another thing: when we last met you threatened to kill me. I am going to need either an apology, or for you to make good on that threat." The smile faded from his face and his eyes became dangerous. I pressed him a little more. "So that will be three hundred dollars and an apology."

He telegraphed the right cross well in advance. I stepped to the left and drove my right fist deep into Jacob's gut while Trent stumbled off his stool, drawn by the weight of his punch. I grabbed Jacob's hair with my left hand and smashed my right fist into his jaw. His legs turned to jelly, I let him drop to the floor and turned.

Trent was charging me, his arms wide for a crushing bear hug. I could have given him a straight right to the jaw, but I didn't want him unconscious. I wanted him hurting. So I drove that straight right into his nose instead. I felt the cartilage crunch under my knuckles, and the warm gush of blood. He staggered back. His eyes were wide with pain and his hands cupped over nose and mouth. I stepped in close and drove my fists, right, left, right, hard into his floating ribs.

He dropped to his knees, vomiting profusely onto the floor. I took a handful of his permed gray hair and dragged him stumbling to his feet again. Holding him there, I turned to look around me. There were maybe a dozen people, seated at tables and at the bar, all staring, expressionless. A couple might have been tourists, but I figured most were locals.

I spoke loud, looking at them all: "You going to kill

me, Rex?"

He was wheezing badly, his hands flailing. "Please don't hit me anymore, please..."

"I asked you a question, Rex. You threatened to kill me. Are you going to make good on that threat and kill me, Rex?"

"No, no, of course not!"

"Then I am going to need an apology."

"I'm sorry, please don't hit me again. I am sorry. I apologize."

"And now I am going to need three hundred bucks for the elk you stole from me."

His bottom lip was quivering and he started to cry as he fumbled in his jacket and pulled out his wallet. I watched him pull out three hundred bucks and hand them to me. I took them from his fingers and stuffed them in my back pocket. Then I let go of his hair and grabbed a fistful of his collar, dragged him close up to my face and snarled.

"Now, I am going to be here next season, and I had better not hear any stories about Rex Trent terrorizing hunters and townsfolk, or I am going to come looking for you, and next time, asshole, I will not be so gentle. Do we have an understanding?"

"Yes..."

"Mr. Bauer."

"Yes, Mr. Bauer."

I dumped him in a chair and stepped outside into the early September sun. I crossed the parking lot to my Jeep and stood looking up into the mountains. I am no philosopher, but the mountains have a way of making a man ask himself questions, the kind of questions that have no easy answers; or maybe no answer at all. Right then I was thinking about the elk, and the coyote and all the animals that live in the wilds. And I wondered, what kind of god creates a world where the only way to survive is by eating other living creatures? What kind of god creates a world where the only way to live is by killing?

I didn't know the answer. Maybe there was no answer. But one thing I did know was that my destiny on this Earth was to fight and to kill, like the wild animals in the forest. That would be the way, until I took my final, dying breath.

WHAT'D YOU THINK?

Nothing is more annoying than someone asking for a review, but unfortunately they "matter" or something. I don't know why, but the vast majority of readers won't buy something unless they see that other's already have and had a good experience.

Therefore, if *you* happened to have a good experience at any point during this read, then I would be exceptionally grateful if you would consider taking a moment to leave behind a quick review. Honestly, it can be super short (or super long...if that's your thing), but even a couple words and a good star rating can go *miles* for a self-published author like myself.

Without you all, I wouldn't be able to do this. I'd have to go out and work in the real world...and that's simply not as fun. I much prefer killing people, err—I mean *writing* about killing people...

Anyways, if leaving a review is something you'd be willing to do, that'd be incredible. But even if you don't, I want you to know just how thankful I am that you even gave my work a chance and made it this far. Seriously, you are the bomb!

EXCERPT OF BOOK 3

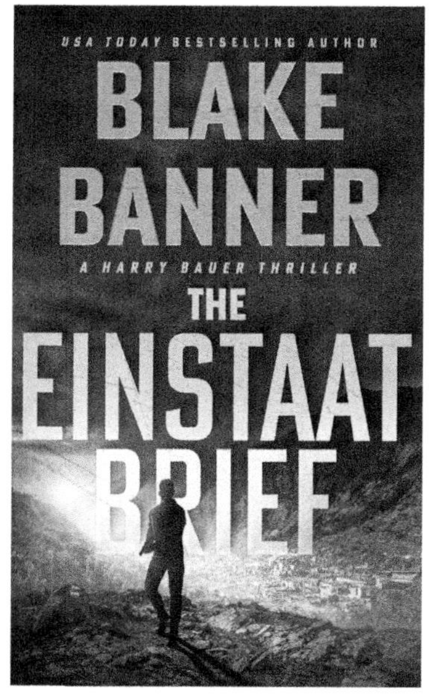

One thing Harry Bauer knew for certain: He was not a man who could ever fall in love and make a home.

Until it happened. And then he knew something else. He had to give up his job as an assassin for Cobra. He could not lie to that woman, he could not bring danger into her life.

But then a hit squad came after him, and Cobra made him an offer he could not refuse. One last job, the Einstaat Brief, and they would keep her safe.

One last job:

A job that would take him to Andorra, high in the Pyrenees, to a secret conference of 130 of the world's most powerful men and women, cloistered in a luxury hotel to discuss the future of the world. Among them, Stephen Plant, Andrew Ashkenazi and William Hughes; IT billionaires, believers in 'strong Ai'. Each one of them must die. Because their plans for humanity cannot be allowed to succeed.

There was just one problem. It had to be done then, right then, with no planning and no intel.

And only Harry Bauer could do that...

ONE

They came from all over Europe, and from North America. They called themselves the Einstaat Group, because the small village of Einstaat, on the border of Germany and Luxembourg, was where they had their first meeting, way back in 1950, in the wake of the Second World War, ostensibly for the purpose of cementing Anglo-American relations. Since then their purpose had evolved; into what, nobody but them knew.

The name was not official, because the Einstaat Group was not any kind of official body. It was just an informal name—a useful handle—that had stuck. They had a steering committee who arranged the annual Einstaat Meetings, and that was co-chaired by the eminent Belgian economist Marcus Hoffmeister, and billionaire entrepreneur Anne-Marie Karrión. Who the members of the steering committee were, aside from the chairman and chairwoman, was a better-kept secret than what the Freemasons did with their balloons and aprons. What happened to anyone who spilled the beans was an equally well-kept secret.

Another, even better-kept secret was what they talked about at those meetings. The theory was that they talked about how to maintain world peace, freedom and democracy—those cornerstones of Anglo-American society. Back in 1950 everybody was worried that the United States and Russia would slide helplessly into a third world war, and the Europeans were especially worried that they would provide the battleground. So a small group of what was left of Continental Europe's aristocracy got together and had a quiet chat with General Walter B. Smith, the director of the CIA, who in turn had a quiet chat with General Marshal and advised him to advise Truman to hold private talks with Peter Zeeland, an exiled Polish politician, and Prince Joseph Alexander of Belgium. Some said that Prince Philip of the United Kingdom was also there. Others said he came in later. But the gist of that very private conversation was that it would be helpful to create a British-American axis of power to protect Western interests in the world, and to that end it would be a good idea to hold a weeklong, informal meeting once a year, at a different, undisclosed venue on each occasion, and invite the most eminent and influential heads of state, politicians, business leaders, academics and scientists of the day to attend. The meetings themselves would not be secret, but whatever went on at them, and whatever was discussed, would be. That way the attendees could enjoy total freedom of expression, and have fully frank and open discussions.

And so it happened that the Einstaat Group was born, and with it the conspiracy theory that this small, elite gang used it as a kind of AGM to run the world. According to that theory, they got together and planned wars, economic recessions, the price of oil, pandemics —you name it, they conspired to make it happen, and all for the benefit of that small elite. Naturally it was a crazy idea. Who the hell would believe that if you got the Western world's richest, most powerful men and women together in a luxury hotel for a week, with no reporters and a no-holds-barred policy, that they would plot and conspire to exploit world events in their own interest?

Naturally, since the '90s, guests invited to attend had increasingly included dot-com billionaires and, above all, software developers. And since the new millennium, those software developers had increasingly included experts in the fields of social media and what had come to be known as "Strong AI": that branch of artificial intelligence that holds that consciousness is nothing but a set of really complicated algorithms, and all we need in order for computers and robots to develop sentience is a software that is complex and sophisticated enough to contain such algorithms.

So they came, one hundred and thirty guests from twenty-three countries: heads of state, captains of industry, economists and financiers, academics and scientists, from all over Europe and North America, to the tiny Principality of Andorra in the Pyrenees, nestled between Spain to the south and France to the north. Among the subjects for discussion that year, at the sixty-eighth meeting, were: a Stable Strategic Order, the Future of Europe, Brexit and Morality and Artificial Intelligence,

Given the topics for discussion it was no surprise that William Hughes, the software giant, was on the guest list, along with Andrew Ashkenazi, the social media mogul, rated by *Forbes* at the age of thirty-two as one of the ten most powerful men in the world, and Steve Plant, creator of the SearchEngine, a veritable software empire that had effectively shaped the late twentieth and early twenty-first centuries.

They had taken over the Grand Continental, a super-luxury five-star hotel, for the week. It was situated on the edge of the Grandvalira Golf Course, near the tiny ski town of Soldeu. The hotel was closed to the public and the press, and a cordon of local cops, Europol, CIA and French and Spanish secret service had put the place on total lockdown three days before the guests had started to arrive

Andrew Ashkenazi, the creator of MyPal, was among the first to arrive, driving himself in a bright red, customized Aston Martin DBS Superleggera. He pulled up on the gravel drive outside the hotel lobby: a vast, sweeping gable in dark wood, faced with enormous sheets of bronzed plate-glass that reflected the green, snow-tipped peaks as though they were a dimly seen parallel universe.

He threw his keys to the waiting valet and strode toward the doors, creating a small, oddly menacing black silhouette against the vastness of the reflected mountains. He moved like a man who owned the world. He almost did.

A small group of hotel staff were waiting to greet him: Eugenio Costas, the hotel manager, and five pretty women in hotel uniforms. Men like Ashkenazi are not required to check in, show documentation or sign anything less momentous than a billion-dollar deal. They have people to do all that for them. All men like Ashkenazi have to do is demand. So Costas, a man with a shiny bald head and a blue blazer with brass buttons, bowed.

"Mr. Ashkenazi, may I say what an honor..."

Ashkenazi, a man in 501s and a Harvard sweatshirt, with nearly a hundred billion dollars in the bank, cut him short.

"Sure, it's nice to be here. Did my things arrive this

morning?"

"They did, and your PA, Ms. Fenninger, has taken care of them. May we offer you…?"

"What about William Hughes? Has he arrived yet?"

"He is in the Emperor Suite, Mr. Ashkenazi. He has asked whether you would join him when you arrive, after you have rested…"

"Get me a Coke. You…" He pointed to one of the pretty girls in uniform. "Take me to his suite." She led the way across the marble floor toward an arch that gave onto a cobbled path, a wooden bridge and abundant, green gardens. She smiled at the thirty-two-year-old billionaire, while Costas issued orders for the urgent dispatch of a can of Coke to William Hughes's suite on the upper slope.

The girl and Ashkenazi followed a wending, cobbled path past weeping willows, over rustic bridges and among more gardens until they eventually came to the Emperor Suite. As she knocked and opened the door, Andrew Ashkenazi smiled at her.

"Make yourself available. What's your name? I'm going to ask for you personally if I need help with my bath, or pulling down the sheets."

The pretty girl giggled and said her name was Begonia and she would be happy to help with anything he needed. With which she left and closed the door behind her.

The Emperor Suite had a broad, galleried entrance occupied only by a sixteenth-century French credenza and a large mirror. Beyond the wooden balustrade, down three shallow steps, there opened out a spacious room with polished hardwood floors, minimalist white leather and suede armchairs and sofas and a square, copper fireplace that occupied the center of the floor. Randomly scattered bearskins littered the floor. The far wall, like the entrance to the building, was composed of vast sheets of plate-glass, and overlooked a deep, green valley, half-smothered in dense pine forests.

William Hughes had been sitting on one of those suede sofas, and now he stood and smiled in spite of himself. To him Ashkenazi looked like a child and privately, to him, his success seemed in some way obscene. But to Ashkenazi, Hughes looked old and tired. With his thin hair and liver spots on his temples and hands, to Andy Ashkenazi he was a relic and belonged in a museum, along with Windows 1.1 and Word Perfect. His smile looked weak. But he spread his arms, laughed and shook his head.

"What?" he said, "What is it with you? You own the One Ring of Power or something? You never grow any older?" Hughes laughed and Ashkenazi trotted down the steps. They embraced. "I used to read articles about you when I was fourteen. You look exactly the same now."

"Yeah?" Hughes laughed some more. "That's because you were fourteen last week." He pointed to a chair. "Sit down. Shall I tell you my secret? My secret is to eat less red meat, meditate regularly and only meet with very short-sighted people."

Ashkenazi didn't laugh. He smiled and grunted. "You had this place swept by your people?"

"And so have you. We can talk freely, Andrew."

There was a knock at the door and the pretty girl in uniform, named Begonia, entered with a silver tray, a glass of ice and lemon and a can of Coke. Both men watched her in silence as she opened the can, poured the drink and left. When she had gone, Ashkenazi said, "OK, tell me, no bullshit, no stories, no runarounds. When will it be ready?"

Hughes smiled. "It's ready now, but what we need is a system of delivery." He gestured at Ashkenazi with an open hand. "Have *you* got that? Last I heard you were ready to provide us with a delivery system."

"Delivery is not a problem..."

Hughes made a face like an indulgent parent and shook his head.

"No, see? This is why I find it so hard to trust you. You're a slippery snake, Andrew."

"Ha! Feel free to insult me! I'm just a jumped up little Jewish kid."

"I don't care if you're a Japanese geisha. You're a slippery bastard, Andrew. You know what 'Delivery is not a problem' tells me?"

"I know *you're* going to tell *me*."

"It tells me you have not arranged delivery of the product, and you are trying to manipulate the launch in a way that benefits you."

"Don't be so damned suspicious, Will!"

William Hughes grunted. "It seems to me you have a long track record of screwing over partners who should have been a little more suspicious of you. I'm not going to make a moral judgment, Andrew, but you should know that I am not about to make the same mistake as all those other people you screwed. You don't get sight, sound or smell of the product until I see that delivery is firmly in place."

Ashkenazi leaned forward and stared at William Hughes for a moment before reaching for his glass.

"Delivery is one hundred percent in place."

Hughes shook his head. "I don't want a fucking

virus, Andrew."

"You're not going to get one. You're going to get what you asked for."

"It has to recycle itself..."

"It will do more than that, Will. It will integrate itself into the very fabric of the virtual world. It will become the DNA of the entire global network."

Hughes did not look satisfied. He gave a small sigh. "Delivery is everything, Andrew."

Andrew Ashkenazi shrugged and spread his hands. "What's wrong with you? What more do you want? What better than the world's largest social media platform? There is hardly a person, physical or fiscal, on the whole planet who isn't a member, and there sure as hell isn't a business. Not in the West. And you know as well as I do that we can creep in the back doors of the Eastern networks."

"That's theory, Andrew. Have you got an actual, operational delivery system?"

"Yes."

"Good." He didn't beam. His face just said he was satisfied. "Then we only have to fix a date. We can discuss it with our partners this evening. What was the other thing you wanted to discuss with me?"

Andrew Ashkenazi picked up his glass and drained half of it. He smacked his lips as he set it down and said, as though he was talking to the glass, "A few of our friends got killed."

Hughes didn't say anything. He just gave a small nod. Ashkenazi went on:

"Mary Jones..."

"That's it. Just Mary Jones."

Ashkenazi made a face like he was being patient.

"OK," he said. "She's the only *real* friend..."

Hughes interrupted him again. "And she might well have been killed by the Chinese. She went bad."

"They say not."

"Of course they do. When have you ever known the Chinese to tell the truth? I don't like this paranoia, Andrew. It is not healthy. I'm getting reports that you are talking like this to other people."

"Yeah, Will, because something has to be done."

"Something, like what?"

"Like at the very least we need to look into it."

Will Hughes shrugged and spread his hands. "Look into what, for Pete's sake? Mary was playing a very dangerous game, double-crossing everybody. She was going to get killed sooner or later. And besides, it played out for us in the end. We got the vaccine."

"Forgive me for being blunt, Will, but you're being really shortsighted. It's not just her death. It's the very fact that we *did* get the vaccine. How the hell did the Navy know the vaccine was on the *Chénxīng?* How did they know it was on that *particular* ship? Where did they get that information from, Will?"

"I don't know."

Ashkenazi stood and walked to the vast glass wall overlooking the deep green valley. "There is something else," he said, without looking back. "I have sources that say her operation in Morocco was destroyed."

"Yeah, by the Moroccan government."

Now he turned to face Hughes. "Why would they do that? They stood to make a killing if they backed her. I'm telling you, Will, somebody is interfering. I want to know who, and why."

Hughes was quiet for a long while, then he pulled a

cell phone from his jacket pocket and dialed a number. It rang a couple of times before he smiled and spoke.

"Gina, how are you, sweetheart...? Sure, sure... Well, you know, I'm trying to look after myself, less red meat, cutting down on the alcohol, trying to enjoy life more, the small, good things, you know what I'm talking about..."

He waited a moment, listening, nodding, smiling.

"Well, that's right, Gina. That exactly it. There's gotta be more than work, right? Listen, I'm here at Soldeu..." He laughed. "Einstaat Week, that's right. Yeah, you'll get the report. And anyway, we were just talking about Mary Jones. You remember her? That's the one, black, beautiful, all the way up legs..." He laughed at something Gina said, then went on. "Thing is, Gina, I'm hearing that there are rumors..."

He went quiet again, listening. After a bit he glanced at Ashkenazi and said into the phone, "Their room at the Mandarin Oriental? Really? And, here's the sixty-million-dollar question: do you know how the Navy got to know it was the *Chénxīng* carrying the vaccine?"

He listened some more and started frowning.

"Mohamed Ben-Amini? But he was not a friend... Oh he was? You'd turned him? Shit... You got any ideas who it might be?"

He leaned back in the sofa, crossed one long leg over the other and listened for a good three or four minutes without speaking. Then he said, "OK, Gina, thanks. Listen, you should come over, spend the weekend. I'll call you when I get back. Yeah, you take care."

He hung up and Ashkenazi said, "So?"

"The Firm are aware that there may be somebody interfering."

"Who?"

"They don't know. They think it may be an internal agency. She thinks we could cooperate."

"Shit."

"Shit's right, and we have to make sure it doesn't hit the fan. They have an individual they are looking at. They have tabs on him and they're hoping he'll lead them to whoever he works for."

"Who?"

"A guy called Harry Bauer, ex British SAS. Resigned under peculiar circumstances. Returned to New York, has no obvious source of income but lives well. Travels abroad sometimes."

He pressed a buzzer on the table and after a moment a door opened in the far right wall. A man in black pants and a white jacket came in and bowed.

"Whiskey. Get a bottle of Black Label, ice..." He made an inquiring face at Ashkenazi and on receiving a nod said, "Two glasses."

When the flunky had gone Ashkenazi said, "We need to know who he is, or who they are. We need to know who the fuck is doing this and what they want. And why the fuck the Agency isn't protecting us!"

"Don't panic, Andrew. I'll put some people on it. We'll get to the bottom of this, and snuff it out."

Ashkenazi studied Hughes's face a while, then nodded.

"You'd better, old man. You'd better."

That was the way I heard it, much later.

TWO

She had red hair and freckles. Not many women can pull that off, but she could. She also had dark blue eyes that seemed to smile on their own. But when her mouth joined in, she had dimples too. Her name was Kate, and she was from Texas.

We were sitting on the warm, stone steps at the Central Park Reservoir. She was eating an ice-cream cone and kept glancing at me. The sun was bright among dappled shadows on her pale skin.

"How many dates is this now, Harry?"

"I don't know. I lost track. The last few all just kind of blended in to one because you refuse to go home."

She stopped eating and looked at me, her eyes flitting over my face to see if I was serious. I smiled to show I wasn't.

"You want me to go?"

I was kind of surprised to realize I didn't. "No," I said. "I've grown accustomed to your face."

"Is that supposed to be a compliment?"

"It's an easy face to get accustomed to, so I guess it is."

She went back to her ice cream.

"Don't get too accustomed. You don't want to take me for granted. Texas farm girls don't take too kindly to that."

It was eleven in the morning and the crowds of visitors and tourists were growing thicker. A guy on a skateboard rattled past me, inches away, and I watched him jump on the rail and slide down. I said:

"You want to walk?"

"Sure." She stood and took my hand. "You're kind of tense. You OK?"

We started walking, flanking the reservoir, keeping the water on our left, moving north. After a moment I smiled at her again.

"I'm OK. I'm not tense. What's on your mind? Why'd you ask about how many dates?"

She didn't answer for a while. Instead she gazed out at the small glinting waves: a glare of light on one side, black on the other. She squeezed my hand and leaned gently against me as we walked. Eventually she said, without looking at me, "You know, I don't want to stereotype, but at heart I am just a plain, old-fashioned Texas country girl." She paused and looked up at me. Her eyes were uncertain, searching. "I've been in New York for two years, but I have not really become a New Yorker. Do you know what I mean, Harry?"

"I know what you mean. I don't know what you're driving at."

She screwed up her face and sighed, then looked away again at the water. After that it was at her feet as she walked.

"I guess, you guys..."

"Y'all?"

She laughed. "Yeah, y'all, are kind of free and easy,

you hook up, hang out and move on. You go on a date, like each other and hit the sack. I'm not saying that's wrong..."

"You don't do that in Texas?"

"Don't tease me, Harry. Sure, in Dallas and Houston and Austin. In the cities I guess people are more liberal. Half of 'em ain't Texan anyhow. But mostly we have our feet pretty firmly on the ground."

I stopped walking and turned to face her under the shade of the trees. A couple of people jostled past and I moved her over to the rails overlooking the water.

"Are you asking me what my intentions are? Shouldn't your dad be asking me that, while he polishes his Colt revolvers?"

"Don't make it sound stupid, Harry."

"That's not my intention. I like that you're asking me."

"It's been a month now, since we started seeing each other, and half that time we've been pretty much living together. I guess we know each other pretty well by now."

I nodded. "We do, I guess."

"Am I scaring you? Have I screwed things up?"

"No. No, not at all."

"What is it, then?"

"It is very difficult for me to explain..."

"Is there another woman?"

I laughed. "No, no, there is no other woman. If only it were that simple."

Her forehead clenched like a fist. "Well, what is it then, Harry?"

I turned away, feeling suddenly ashamed and humiliated. How do you explain to a kind, humane woman that you kill people for a living? That that's the only thing you know how to do well? I leaned my elbows on the iron rail and looked down at the small, lapping waves, silver and black. She came up close beside me and put one hand on my arm.

"It's my work," I said, and heard how lame it sounded.

"Your *work?* Well, now, that sounds like a real poor excuse!"

"No." I shook my head. "It's not an excuse, Kate. I have to travel quite a bit, at short notice..."

"Well, shoot! I don't mind that." Her face lit up. "Especially if I can come along sometimes!"

The thought of it made me smile. "My work is quite dangerous, sometimes."

"Dangerous? How dangerous?"

I took a deep breath and held it for a moment. "It's very specialized..."

"Like working on an oil rig?"

"Something like that. Sometimes the locations can be...uncomfortable."

She was frowning hard now. "I don't know why you're being so cagey. Let me ask you something, Harry."

I looked at her and waited. She held my eye.

"What were you planning to do? What did you think was going to happen with us? You thought one day you'd go off to your work and when you got back you simply wouldn't call? And that would be the end of Kate?"

"No!" I shook my head with feeling. "No, not at all!"

"Well, what then?"

"I hadn't thought that far ahead. I had avoided thinking about it. Sometimes I just take things one day at a time..."

"Well, this girl ain't a one day at a time kind of girl."

"I know that."

"So...?"

I put my arm around her and started to walk again.

"I've been thinking for a while now that I should leave my job."

"*Leave* your *job?* You can do that? My word, Harry! I don't want you to leave your job on account of me! What would you live on?"

"I've been thinking about it for a while, Kate. Before we met."

"Don't you like your work? What would you do instead?"

"It's..." I smiled grimly at the leaves overhead, at the people passing by in their infinite variety. "Sometimes it is very satisfying. But it's draining too. I am very tired."

She pulled away slightly, still holding my arm, and frown-smiled at me.

"You are being *awful* mysterious! You don't work for the CIA, do you? Or the FBI, or the NSA?"

"No, Kate. I am not a spy and I am not a federal agent. It's nothing like that. I just have a dangerous job that keeps me away from home sometimes. But I'll tell you what I'm going to do."

I stopped and took a hold of her shoulders in my hands. She felt small and fragile, and I suddenly desired her intensely. Her face lit up as she looked up into mine, and her eyes were incredibly blue.

"What?" She gave a small, childlike laugh.

"I'm going to talk to my boss today. I'm going to give him notice. I'm going to quit my job."

She frowned, cocked her head on one side.

"Harry? Are you serious? You're going to quit your job so we can be together? Isn't that a bit weird? I have to tell you, you got me a bit worried. I can't afford to keep us both..."

I laughed. "I know that. And it's not weird."

"What are we going to live on?"

"Oh," I shrugged and shook my head, "I'm OK financially. I guess I don't really need to work."

She was still frowning. "Seriously? You don't need to work?"

"Yeah, come on." I took her arm and we started walking again. But she was resistant and kept hanging back. I said, "I made a lot of money in my time. I can take early retirement."

She stopped and I stopped to turn to face her. I frowned.

"I thought you'd be pleased, Kate."

"I guess I might be if you weren't so mysterious. Harry, are you involved in some kind of crime? Are you a gangster or something?"

"No."

"Then why can't you tell me what you do?"

I sighed, looked out over the reservoir for a moment, sucking my teeth, then made up my mind.

"Kate, you know what a confidentiality agreement is, right?"

"Of course."

"Well, I work for a company that deals in huge sums of money, millions, tens of millions, and sometimes they need a tough guy like me to troubleshoot for them. Now, if you're troubleshooting a problem in LA, or Washington, it's no big deal. You just talk tough and look mean. But if you have a problem on a pipeline in Baghdad or

Thailand, then it's not enough to talk tough. Things can get pretty dangerous. And believe me, these people take their confidentiality agreements very seriously. So I can't tell you the details."

She made a big round O with her mouth and nodded a few times. Then she took my arm and we started to walk again.

"So how come you're such a tough guy?"

"Well, I can tell you that. That's not a secret. I was in a special ops regiment in the UK."

"You were a soldier? Like the SEALs?"

"Yeah, for eight years. We were in Iraq and I did a lot of work in Afghanistan."

"So you've shot and killed people."

I didn't answer for a while. Eventually I said, "Yes, Kate. I have killed men. Is that a problem?"

She gave a nervous laugh and there were colored spots on her cheeks. "Hey! I'm from Texas, remember? I like my boys tough. And I guess that's why they paid you so well."

"There are perks to the job, yeah."

"I bet. You sure you're ready to give it up? A man can get addicted to that kind of life."

I looked into her big blue eyes for a long time before answering. I was remembering Iraq, the dismembered bodies in the dust by the roadside, the torture and murder in the jungles of Colombia and Mexico, the massacre at Al-Landy in Afghanistan. And above all, the rampage of murder I had embarked upon since I'd left the Regiment.

"I'm sure," I said. "It's time for a change." I smiled. "You want to buy a ranch in cowboy country? We could raise horses, cattle and kids."

She put her arms around me and held me real tight. And I held her back. After a moment I held her face in my hands and tilted it up to mine.

"Listen, let's do something. Instead of lunch, let's buy some pizzas. We'll go to your place, collect your stuff and arrange a removal company to come and get the rest..."

Her cheeks flushed and she went on tiptoes.

"Really? Oh man! But my furniture. It won't all fit in your house..."

"We'll put it in storage till we find a bigger place."

"In New York?"

"You want to move? You want to go back to Texas? California? Wyoming?"

"Wyoming? Oh my god! I *love* Wyoming!"

"You want to look for a ranch in Wyoming?"

She leapt and hung on my neck and I laughed and held her while she squealed like a kid and kicked her feet.

We drove back to her place. She had a small, detached house on Hollywood Avenue, near Locust Point, which she'd rented from a friend of her parents while she got settled, teaching at the Villa Maria Academy. We spent the afternoon loading up my Jeep and ferrying over the stuff she wanted to take with her, while she telephoned removal companies and storage companies and got the bulkier furniture ready for collection the next day.

By eight PM we were pretty much done and Kate put a cold beer in my hand, dropped on the sofa and grinned at me.

"You mind if we stay the night here?"

"You don't like my house?"

"Your house is cute, but what can I tell you? I'm sentimental. I've been here a whole month and..." She shrugged. "I'd just like to say goodbye. We can cook something nice, get some wine..."

"All your pots and pans are at my place..."

"So we'll get takeout. Better still, it's a twenty-minute stroll to Paddy's, down on Pennyfield Avenue. They do draught beer and burgers. We'll chill there, then stroll back here for dessert."

She winked and I smiled. "What the hell are we waiting for?"

"I'm going to shower. And you..." She stood and gave me a lingering kiss. "...you have a think about packing in your job. I want you to be sure about what you're doing, mister. And, remember this: as long as I *know* what you're doing, you don't need to stop doing it if you don't want to. Stand by your man, and all that."

She kissed me again and went up to the shower.

We spent the evening relaxing by the river, drinking beer and eating burgers with hot chili sauce, and talking about possible things we could do with our future lives. It was an odd and novel feeling for me, but it was something I felt I could get used to pretty quickly.

By the time we left it was gone twelve and the streets were very quiet. It had been a short walk coming, but now it seemed like a long, dark walk back. The trees were abundant and obscured a lot of the houses on the left side of the road. The streetlamps, bolted to wooden poles, cast a dim, limpid yellow light, and the only sound aside from a desultory foghorn on the river was the crunch of our feet.

Behind us I heard the low hum of an engine. I turned and looked, vaguely aware that I hadn't heard the slam of a car door. Headlamps approached and I eased Kate onto the sidewalk. A dark Audi cruised past and was swallowed by the diminishing glow of its own lights.

I felt a tug on my arm and her hand on my chest.

"You *are* tense. You sure you're OK?"

"Sure. Old habits." I smiled.

We arrived at her place fifteen minutes later. The streets were still and quiet, and the sound of her key in the lock was surprisingly loud. While she opened the door into the dark house I scanned the street. The light was poor, all the drapes in all the windows were closed, and the yellow lamplight reflected dully on the black windshields of the Fords, Buicks and Hondas, and on one dark Audi. It was hard to tell, with the lamplight reflected bronze on the windshield, whether there was anybody in it or not.

A snap behind me told me Kate had put on the hall light. I turned and climbed the stairs, went inside and closed the door behind me. She smiled at me and placed both her palms on my chest.

"You go up and get ready for bed. I have a little surprise for you."

I raised an eyebrow. "I'm not used to pleasant surprises. What is it?"

"Just something I got while you were delivering my books and my bedding. Don't be so uptight. I'll be up in a second."

She disappeared toward the bathroom and I climbed the stairs to the bedroom. As I stripped for the shower I peered out of the window. The Audi was still there, and the copper reflection of the streetlamp still made it impossible to see inside. I figured maybe Kate was right and I was being paranoid, but like I'd told Kate, old habits die hard, and the careless die young.

I stood under the shower for five minutes. While I

was toweling myself dry I heard the bedroom door open and close, a soft clunk as of something heavy being laid down. I pulled on my pants and opened the door.

She was sitting on the bed in a transparent negligee. On the bedside table there was an ice bucket and in it there was a bottle of Moet Chandon French champagne, and two champagne flutes chilling in the ice.

She smiled and her cheeks colored.

"You gonna make it pop, tough guy?"

That was when I heard the door open downstairs.

THREE

I pointed at Kate and mouthed, "Stay there." Then I killed the lights and closed the drapes.
One step took me to my bedside table. The drawer was polished and oiled and slid open noiselessly. I took out my Fairbairn & Sykes fighting knife, and my Sig Sauer P226. I knew it was loaded because I always keep it loaded. Just like I keep all the hinges in my house oiled, except the front and back doors. I want to hear anybody coming in. I don't want them to hear me coming down to get them.

I cocked the Sig and knelt beside the door, trained the weapon at where the intruder's belly would be if he had climbed the stairs, and eased it open. I knew, because I had run the simulation a dozen times in my mind over the last month, that there would be enough filtered light from the bathroom window, and from the living room window downstairs, for me to see a body on the stairs or on the landing. But the bedroom would be nothing but a black hole.

There was nothing to see. But there was a soft creak from the third stair from the bottom. I stood and took one long, silent step to the banisters and looked over. There was one guy in black with a balaclava over his head.

He had a semiautomatic in his hand and he was standing immobile, waiting, listening. I waited and listened with him. I was aware of just one guy, but that didn't mean there weren't more down there.

He glanced back over his shoulder, made a gesture with his left hand and took another step. I smiled. There was at least one more, but I doubted there were more than three.

I vaulted the banister, twisting my body so I was facing down the stairs, and landed slamming my heels into the top of balaclava's head. I felt the crunch of his skull cracking under my bare feet, and the snap of his neck. His body yielded and toppled under my weight and I fell, crouching, toward the bottom of the stairs.

As I fell and rolled I caught a glimpse of a silhouette against the streetlight coming in through the living-room window. I saw the unmistakable flash of fire, then heard the spit and *phut!* of a suppressed weapon as two slugs thudded home into the wall behind me. That was followed by a muffled curse.

The thought flashed through my mind of returning fire, but the last thing I needed, if I could avoid it, was my neighbors calling the cops. So I grunted and stifled a cry, like I'd been hit, as I put the Sig in my waistband and slipped the hard, steel blade from my boot. Then I crouched and stormed across the dark room at the blackness where the shots had come from. Again two more flashes of hot light. Again the double, lethal spit of flame and the hot pop of air by my ear as the slugs flashed past.

Then there was the heavy, intimate contact of a large, hard body as we collided. I grabbed for his right wrist, intensely aware of the semiautomatic he was holding, expecting at every fraction of a second the fierce explosion and the scorch of the bullet. I felt the hot barrel in my hand and levered down savagely. And then a ton of bricks smashed into my face.

The pain was excruciating and for a moment a wave of nausea swept over me as my legs went to jelly. But I felt the pistol come away in my hand and whipped it hard across his face. He cursed. I stumbled forward another step and backhanded him with the butt of the semiautomatic. He roared in the darkness and I knew what was coming. So I ducked and stepped in close and to the side, willing my legs to respond, as two massive hooks tore the air above my head. Then he lashed out blindly with his right foot and his boot scraped my thigh. But it didn't hurt. The blood was pounding around my body again and I was ready to move in for the kill.

The great thing about the Fairbairn & Sykes fighting knife is not the razor-sharp double-edged, carbon steel blade, or the rutted, steel grip of the handle. It's the needle-sharp, tapered point. You don't need to exert any pressure, you don't need to stab. You just need to get up close and let him come at you.

And that was exactly what he did.

I whispered, "I'm here, asshole," and he came at me; and walked right onto the needle-sharp blade. It slid in effortlessly and for a moment he didn't even know he'd been stabbed, until I wrapped my left arm around his neck and levered the blade up, cutting through his liver and into his diaphragm. Then I eased him down to the floor.

I should have cut his thigh instead, or his underarm. I should have kept him alive and made him talk, made him tell me who the hell he was and who he worked for; why he had come to kill me. But in the dark, with

Kate's life at risk, I could not afford that luxury.

I left the lights off and checked the ground floor quickly. I peered out though the window. Everything was still and quiet. The Audi was still there, dark and motionless. I went to the kitchen and peered out into the backyard. There was nothing, nobody. So I sprinted up the stairs to the bedroom.

At the door I paused.

"Kate, it's me. It's all clear. I'm coming in. You OK?"

She didn't answer. I moved into the room. She wasn't in the bed. I froze, listening. I could just make out the stifled breath in the darker shadows beyond the bed.

"Kate, it's me, Harry. Everything's OK. I'm going to put on the light so you can see me."

I had the Sig in my hand, trained on the darkness where I could hear the stifled, shaky breath. I snapped on the light.

She was sitting on the floor, pressed into the corner clutching her knees. Her eyes were squeezed tight and her teeth were clamped onto her lower lip. I stepped over to the window, flattened myself against the wall and moved the drape an inch. There was still no movement in the street. The Audi was still there, with the amber light reflected on its windshield. Nothing had changed. Everything was still and quiet.

I turned back to Kate. She had opened her eyes and was staring at me, at my body, trembling. I went and hunkered down in front of her.

"It was a break-in. It's over. There is nothing for you to worry about. There is no danger. OK?"

She gave a small, terrified nod. I gave her my hand and pulled her gently to her feet, then sat her on the bed.

"I'm going to make a call. Are you OK?"

"Police?"

I hesitated for a fraction of a second. "Yeah, the police."

I went out on the landing and called Cobra. It rang once and a woman's voice said, "Please identify yourself."

"It's Dirty Harry. I need the cleaning service."

I knew I was being fed through voice recognition. There was a pause. Then, "Where was the spillage?"

I gave her the address and added, "I have two suits that have been stained with tomato ketchup. The carpet's been ruined."

"Has anybody else been notified?"

"No."

"Are you alone?"

"I'm with my girlfriend."

There was a sigh. "I'll have to notify Buddy."

"Yeah, I know."

I hung up and turned toward the bedroom again. She was standing in the doorway with her hands clenched in front of her belly. She was still trembling and her face was confused and scared.

"Harry, what's going on?"

"Nothing. You should stay in the bedroom until…"

"Who were you talking to? The police will want a statement from me."

I didn't answer. I couldn't answer.

"Why did you call yourself Dirty Harry? What is a cleaning service? Who are you, Harry?"

"I told you."

"No, you lied."

"I didn't…" I had to stop. The lie stuck in my throat. "I can't tell you. Don't ask me, Kate. I told you I was going to resign."

She looked past me at the stairwell.

"What did you do?"

"I did what I had to do to protect you."

"You killed them."

"What should I have done? Should I have let them kill me? Should I have let them climb the stairs and rape and kill you?"

She stared at me for a long moment. Her eyes were wide, uncomprehending. "I don't know who you are," she said.

I gripped her shoulders, feeling a hot pellet of anger and frustration burning in my belly. I snarled, "I am exactly who you thought I was this morning, goddammit!"

"You're scaring me."

I closed my eyes, took a deep breath.

"You don't need to be scared of me, Kate. I just put my life on the line to protect you."

She backed away a step. "If they had been burglars, if it had been a home invasion..."

"Maybe that's what it was..."

"But the phone call, who did you call, Harry? You said, 'I have two suits that have been stained with tomato ketchup. The carpet's been ruined.' What the hell, Harry...?"

I spoke savagely, my fingers biting into her shoulders:

"You can't know any of this! You can't be a part of this!"

"*But I am a part of it!*" Her eyes welled with tears and she bit her lip hard. "What you just did made me a part of it..."

I shook my head. "No, you have to go. Take the car.

Go to…"

"Harry, stop it! Just tell me what the *hell* is going on and who the *hell* you are!"

I closed my eyes and pulled her to me, holding her tight. "No, no, you mustn't know. It's over. I am ending it tonight. Just forget this…."

"Forget it?" she shouted and pushed away from me, staring into my eyes like I was crazy. *"Forget it? How the hell am I supposed to forget it?"*

Outside I heard the hum of a car turning into the street. It stopped and after a moment the door slammed.

"Stay here. Don't leave this room. Try and sleep."

I closed the door and went down the stairs to open the door. Captain Russ White was there in a Fedora hat and a trench coat. A cigarette poking out of his mouth said he still didn't care too much for what was socially acceptable in the twenty-first century. With him were two guys with dark eyes and olive skin, dressed in blue overalls and baseball caps. I said:

"Hello, Russ," and stood back to let them in.

He stepped over the threshold and stood in the gloom of the living room looking around, then turned to the boys standing in the doorway.

"It's a three," he said, and the boys turned and went back to the car. Russ went to the stairs and stared at the crumpled, broken body there.

"It's true what they say about you. You did this in the dark?"

"There was some light from the window."

He jerked his chin at the semi-disemboweled body on the floor, then pointed at my belly as he spoke.

"But you made an unholy mess with this guy."

"I couldn't see him. I had to take the breaks as they

came."

"You said there's a girl?"

"Upstairs."

"She seen the state you're in?" I didn't answer, remembering her terrified eyes as she stared at me. "Is the NGO compromised?"

I scowled. "NGO?"

He arched an eyebrow. "Non-Governmental Organization, Harry. Cobra. Are we compromised? Did you tell your friend upstairs anything?"

"No, of course not."

I heard a trunk slam outside and turned to watch the two boys struggling down the path with two cases of equipment. Russ watched me watching them and as they humped the stuff through the door he said:

"You know we don't hurt innocent people, Harry. But if she knows something—anything—we need to manage it and limit the damage."

"She knows nothing. She knows I have skills and she knows I was in the British Army. That's it."

He moved across the room and into the open-plan kitchen as the guys dumped their equipment and went to work on the gutted body with a plastic sheet.

"Let's get ourselves out of the way and let them work. You have any whisky in this place? I seem to remember you kept a fine Macallan…"

"Yeah." I reached in the kitchen cabinet and pulled out a bottle of Johnny Walker. "This isn't my house."

I paused and we stared at each other a moment. Then I took two glasses and spilled some whisky into each. He said:

"So this isn't your house. She knows you were in the SAS and you have the skills that go with that. That's it, but…"

He took a sip and smacked his lips.

"But what? But nothing."

"But there is something else. I have a sixth sense about this. I read people, Harry. That's my superpower. There is something else. What is it?"

I sipped my whisky, and as I rolled it around my mouth I stared into the glass and tipped it this way and that. It was as good as telling him he was right. I asked:

"You talk to the brigadier?"

"I live in his pocket. I take care of business, Harry. We talk every day. He doesn't sneeze without running it by me first. What's on your mind?"

"I'm going to quit, Russ. I want to get married, settle down, have a normal life."

He snorted. "A normal life? I hear people talk about that sometimes. I think I saw it in a movie once too. Something out of Hollywood."

"I didn't say a perfect life, Russ. Just a normal one, where I don't have to kill people for a living. Where I don't wind up at two in the morning drinking whisky in the kitchen, while two guys I never met remove dead bodies from my living room, and my girlfriend trembles in terror upstairs."

He set down his glass and reached in his breast pocket. "She's probably in shock. Give her one of these."

He handed me a small sheet with six tablets in it. I took it. "Thanks." Then I looked at him. "You think this is normal?"

He shrugged. "They told me there was a girl here. It'll help her get over the shock."

I took a glass and filled it with water. He watched me and added: "If you give it to her with a glass of whisky it will work faster. But make sure you cover her well. And wipe all that damned blood off of you before you go and see her again."

He grabbed a kitchen towel, screwed it up and threw it at me. I soaked it in water and poured washing-up liquid over it, then washed myself clean. When I was done he held out his hand for the towel. I gave it to him and climbed the stairs with the water and the tranquilizer.

– END OF EXCERPT –

ALSO BY BLAKE BANNER

I have a huge catalog of eBooks online, but am slowly turning them all into paperbacks. If you'd like to see what I have in paperback at this very moment, then please visit the following site.

www.blakerbanner.com/books

Thank you once again for reading my work!

Printed in Great Britain
by Amazon